I0687562

PUSS IN D.C.

AND OTHER STORIES

ALSO BY PAMELA SARGENT

NOVELS

Cloned Lives
The Sudden Star
The Golden Space
The Alien Upstairs
The Shore of Women
Alien Child
Ruler of the Sky: A Novel of Genghis Khan
Climb the Wind: A Novel of Another America

THE WATCHSTAR TRILOGY:

Watchstar
Eye of the Comet
Homesmind

THE VENUS TRILOGY:

Venus of Dreams
Venus of Shadows
Child of Venus

THE SEED TRILOGY:

Earthseed
Farseed
Seed Seeker

SHORT FICTION COLLECTIONS

Starshadows
The Best of Pamela Sargent
Behind the Eyes of Dreamers
The Mountain Cage and Other Stories
Eye of Flame and Other Fantasies
Thumbprints
Dream of Venus and Other Stories

NONFICTION

Firebrands: The Heroines of Science Fiction and Fantasy (with Ron Miller)

STAR TREK NOVELS (WITH GEORGE ZEBROWSKI)

A Fury Scorned (The Next Generation)
Heart of the Sun (The Original Series)
Across the Universe ((The Original Series)
Garth of Izar (The Original Series)

PUSS IN D.C.
AND OTHER STORIES

PAMELA SARGENT

Introduction by Eleanor Arnason

WILDSIDE PRESS

Copyright © 2015 by Pamela Sargent
Published by Wildside Press LLC.
www.wildsidebooks.com

"Introduction" is published here for the first time. Copyright © 2015 by Eleanor Arnason.

The Afterwords to each story are published here for the first time. Copyright © 2015 by Pamela Sargent.

"Puss in D.C." was first published in *Little Red Riding Hood in the Big Bad City,* edited by Martin H. Greenberg and John Helfers, DAW Books, 2004. Copyright © 2004, 2015 by Pamela Sargent.

"Strawberry Birdies" was first published in *Asimov's Science Fiction*, December 2011. Copyright © 2011, 2015 by Pamela Sargent.

"After I Stopped Screaming" was first published in *Asimov's Science Fiction*, October/November, 2006. Copyright © 2006, 2015 by Pamela Sargent.

"The Rotator" was first published in *Future Americas*, edited by John Helfers and Martin H. Greenberg, DAW Books, 2008. Copyright © 2008, 2015 by Pamela Sargent.

"The Falling" was first published in *Isaac Asimov's Science Fiction Magazine*, March 1983. Copyright © 1983, 2015 by Pamela Sargent and George Zebrowski.

"Strip-Runner" was first published in *Foundation's Friends*, edited by Martin H. Greenberg, Tor Books, 1990. Copyright 1990, 2015 by Pamela Sargent.

"A Smaller Government" was first published in *Fast Forward 1: Science Fiction from the Cutting Edge*, edited by Lou Anders, Pyr Books, 2007. Copyright © 2007, 2015 by Pamela Sargent.

"Not Alone" was first published in *Cosmos*, August/September 2006. Copyright © 2006, 2015 by Pamela Sargent.

"The Drowned Father" was first published in *Polyphony 6*, edited by Deborah Layne and Jay Lake, Wheatland Press, 2006. Copyright © 2006, 2015 by Pamela Sargent.

"The True Darkness" was first published in *World Literature Today*, May/June 2010, http://www.ou.edu/worldlit/onlinemagazine/2010may/sargent.html. Copyright © 2010 World Literature Today and Board of Regents, University of Oklahoma; copyright reverted to the author in 2012. Copyright © 2012, 2015 by Pamela Sargent.

The above stories are reprinted here by permission of the author and her agents, Richard Curtis Associates, Inc., 200 East 72nd St., New York, NY 10021.

Contents

INTRODUCTION, by Eleanor Arnason. 7

PUSS IN D.C. 10

STRAWBERRY BIRDIES 36

AFTER I STOPPED SCREAMING. 61

THE ROTATOR 67

THE FALLING 78

STRIP-RUNNER 87

A SMALLER GOVERNMENT 117

NOT ALONE 133

THE DROWNED FATHER 138

THE TRUE DARKNESS 158

ABOUT PAMELA SARGENT 175

ABOUT ELEANOR ARNASON 176

To the memory of Magda Cordell McHale,
artist, mentor, and friend

INTRODUCTION, by
Eleanor Arnason

I first encountered Pamela Sargent in 1975, when she published *Women of Wonder*, an anthology of science fiction by women As far as I know, it was the first such anthology. The book was hugely important to me, at the time a fairly young, barely published woman writer, trying to make my way in a field that was utterly dominated by men. Two more anthologies followed: *More Women of Wonder* (1976) and *New Women of Wonder* (1978). One of my stories was in the last.

I became aware of her fiction later. I can't remember the first stories I read. The novels that have stayed with me are her Venus trilogy, about the terraforming of Venus, a far more difficult planet to change than Mars. (*Venus of Dreams* [1986], *Venus of Shadows* [1988] and *Child of Venus* [2001]). The novels give us a slow, thorough portrait of an almost impossible project. I pair it in my mind with Kim Stanley Robinson's famous Mars trilogy, though—because Venus is so very hard to terraform—it's more amazing. Science fiction does not always have to think big, but I really enjoy SF when it does. I also like *Ruler of the Sky*, a historical novel about Genghis Khan (1993), which begins with a traditional tribal bride stealing and ends with the horrific conquest of much of Asia. The arc is smooth. We can see one act of violence leading to another, until cities and countries are destroyed. And I like *Climb the Wind* (1998), an alternative history that imagines a leader like Genghis uniting the plains Indians during the mid nineteenth century and stopping the westward expansion of white America.

I have to mention "Danny Goes to Mars," a 1992 story that won the Nebula Award. It's about Dan Quayle, who may have been the most ignorant American vice-president ever. He is famous for saying that Mars—as it is now—is habitable. So Sargent wrote a funny, sweet, sad story about Quayle going to Mars, which is—of course—uninhabitable.

You can see some of Sargent's range: classic hard SF, political SF, social SF, satire, fiction about history and alternative history. This is a wide range and not at all usual. Most good writers of hard SF don't write well about social issues, and most good writers of social and political SF are weak on the hard sciences.

(In case you are wondering, the hard sciences are physics, chemistry, engineering and maybe biology, though biology is considered to be a bit soft and squishy. Sociology, anthropology, political science and history are not hard sciences, and fiction about them is not hard SF. Don't blame me for these definitions. I didn't make them up.)

Sargent has a quality usually associated with hard SF: a certain kind of intellectual rigor. With her, it carries through all of her work. She thinks things through.

Notice, when you read this collection, how many different kinds of stories are here and notice the range of moods: the stories go from really funny to really dark, with a lot in between.

I also want to mention Sargent's persistence. Writing is a hard life. Many good woman writers I admired in the 1970s, '80s and '90s have vanished. They stopped writing or stopped trying to sell their fiction or changed their names and moved to writing romance, gay romance, generic fantasy—whatever they could sell. In one way or another, they were silenced. Sargent has kept doing thoughtful, serious fiction, dealing with the issues that interested her.

The longer I am around, the more I value persistence. It is an essential trait for writers.

This brings me to the current collection. Reading the stories, I've been trying to define what I like about Sargent.

I like her focus on ordinary people and ordinary life, as it is changed by something extraordinary. "Strawberry Birdies" starts with a graduate student family in the 1950s, stressed by small children and too little money, and then introduces time travelers, who are trying to change history and prevent an awful future. The viewpoint character is the family's young daughter, trying to deal with her family and the paranoid '50s. While the other kids on the block imagine Communist spies, she actually meets secret agents from the future.

"The True Darkness" is made doubly disturbing by the ordinary people it describes. As far as I'm concerned, being a convinced urbanite, darkness is a fine metaphor for life in the suburbs, at least as I imagine it to be. Think of the poor woman in the story, who is dragged by her husband out into the suburbs, and then *the light—all the light—goes out.*

A lot of the stories here are political, which I love: "Puss in D.C.," "The Rotator" and "A Smaller Government."

Science and technology are fine, and they are a main topic of science fiction, but it's politics that decides how science and technology are used. "The Rotator," for example, uses new technology to move a couple of high-profile American politicians in trouble into an alternate world, where things do not work out as planned. A better use for the technology could have been found, and the device should have been tested longer, as any engineer will tell you.

In "A Smaller Government," people simply accept the shrunken White House and Capitol—and diminish themselves by this acceptance, as the Homeless Philosopher points out. (I love the Homeless Philosopher and the Homeless Lobbyist.)

I like her feminism, which shows up strongly in "After I Stopped Screaming." Of course King Kong is looking for his real mate: a large, self-actualizing, female ape. Why on Earth would he be interested in tiny and vulnerable human women?

"The Strip Runner" is a feminist homage to Asimov's *The Caves of Steel*. As wonderful as Asimov could be, he imagined that women would live in the future the way they lived in 1950s sitcoms, trapped in the kitchen and their family. Sargent has written a fun, old-fashioned SF story, and she gives her young heroine a way out of a dreary life.

A couple of the stories here give us a look at the utter strangeness of contemporary physics: "The Falling" and "The True Darkness." There actually is a theory that our universe has an unstable ground state and could collapse into another reality. That's the way I read "The Falling." Reality has collapsed into something else that does not look friendly.

Something equally disturbing is happening in "The True Darkness," though I don't know what. I suppose one way to understand these stories is to remember J.B.S. Haldane's famous comment: "The universe is not only stranger than we imagine. It is stranger than we can imagine." And it is not a safe place.

"The Drowned Father" is the only story in the collection that is not science fiction or fantasy, and I like it a lot, though I am not a fan of contemporary realistic fiction. The story does have a slight SF flavor, because we know the viewpoint character is a liar and we aren't sure that the other character—the woman—is telling the truth. So reality has been undercut.

It's a classic story of coming to terms with a parent—or, in this case, not coming to terms with a parent, made more interesting because the difficult parent in a fine, possibly great writer.

I won't say more for fear of spoiling the story.

That's about all I have to say. Enjoy the collection. The stories are enjoyable and easy to read. But there is also a lot in them. Notice Sargent's range and thoughtfulness and what I have to call moral seriousness. We tend to undervalue moral seriousness nowadays. But caring about people and human decency—and the big questions of life—always has value.

PUSS IN D.C.

I was trained to be discreet, to keep my extraordinary abilities to myself, but still retain my dreams of public glory, of being openly acknowledged for my accomplishments. Perhaps one day, I muse to myself while grooming my fur or lying about on my favorite pillow, I'll be able to dictate my memoirs and see them set down on paper.

Given the stories I have to tell, there's no question that my book could fetch a large advance from a major publishing house. I can hardly watch television lately without imagining myself matching wits with Charlie Rose, or responding to Larry King's amiable goofball questions with answers that would shame him with my eloquence. Surely Oprah would be interested in a guest who would most likely be the first ever to sit on her lap during the interview, and if Bill O'Reilly got excessively argumentative, a snarl and a display of my front claws should be enough to calm him down. As for book signings, my pawprint on the title page ought to serve as well as an autograph.

I would of course insist on certain amenities during the rigors of any book tour: a personal assistant to help with grooming and running errands; a comfortable carrying case with ample cushioning; shrimp and crabmeat at least once a day; bottled spring water and the occasional bowl of cream; first class seating instead of consignment to the luggage and cargo hold; and a good workout chasing mice at least two or three times a week. I dream of it all—being number one on the *New York Times* and Amazon lists, being offered a fat chunk of cash for the movie rights to my story and, most important, finally receiving the credit that I deserve for all I've done.

Not that my life is so bad as it is, and there are certain impediments to full disclosure. There's my knowledge of certain Agency operations, for one thing, although I would happily make an agreement not to give away any classified information. And Maury, in spite of his gratitude for everything I've helped him accomplish so far, probably wouldn't want the world to know exactly how much he owes to me, especially now, with more victories assuredly lying ahead of him. There's also the matter of my legal rights, since as a cat, I currently lack the status to sign contracts and make any binding agreements, and wouldn't care to spend the rest of my life in court being a test case for animal rights.

So perhaps these musings of mine should be regarded as mental notes for a memoir I'll probably never be able to write.

* * * *

The Agency was where my life truly began, with Maury's father, Charles Carabas, as my caretaker and mentor. I have no memory of my life before Mr. Carabas found me, an abandoned kitten, outside his house in Georgetown. Moved by my piteous meows and my plight, he took me in and gave me a home. As a widower who lived alone, he was grateful for my presence, since his son Maury was in law school at the time and came home only for holidays.

Not long after Mr. Carabas had given me shelter, he discovered that I had the ability to speak when I, tiring of my usual fare, politely requested a can of tuna for supper. A lesser person might have been convinced that he had gone mad, and run to a psychiatrist; a more fearful one might have regarded me as a freak of nature and disposed of me somehow. It was my good fortune that Mr. Carabas not only welcomed a feline companion with whom he could carry on a conversation, but also enabled me, with his example, to acquire a verbal facility I might otherwise never have attained. He was an erudite man, a graduate of Harvard and Oxford and occasional lecturer in political philosophy and foreign affairs at Georgetown University. He read voraciously and spoke several languages, which is how I managed to pick up French, Spanish, German, some Japanese, and even a decent command of Arabic. Because he had been employed by the Agency for almost forty years, he had also been well schooled in secrecy and discretion, and taught me to follow his example. I concealed my conversational abilities from other human beings, even from Maury when he was home between semesters.

Often Mr. Carabas brought me to his office at the Agency's headquarters in Langley, Virginia; his fellow intelligence officers tolerated this eccentricity out of their esteem for the old man. I knew how to conduct myself, was soon roaming freely from the seventh-floor offices of the chiefs down to the cubbyholes on the floors below, and quickly became a kind of mascot. Analysts, operatives, and directors welcomed me into their offices, offered me toys stuffed with catnip, fed me treats fetched from the building's dining room, allowed me to nap on their desks or in chairs, and marveled at my ability to perch on toilet seats in the rest rooms in order to relieve myself, thus sparing anyone from having to maintain and clean a litter box for me.

Mr. Carabas had named me Angleton, after James Jesus Angleton, the legendary chief of counterintelligence during the Agency's glory days, and it was a more suitable moniker for me than any of his colleagues realized. As I prowled the hallways and perched on desks, I overheard a good many tidbits, and passed the tastiest of them along to my human companion. Learning how to read, which presented fewer impediments than mastering speech, also enabled me to surreptitiously peruse many a highly classified document; as a result, Mr. Carabas cemented his reputation as someone who knew all, could never be deceived, and was to be feared and respected.

My mentor and caretaker often thought of retiring. For well over a decade and a half, the Agency had endured scandals, humiliating Congressional hearings, ruined careers, and rules that had made nearly everyone overly cautious and suspicious. Operatives who might be required to support covert operations took out liability insurance, foreseeing the day when they might have to face committees of angry politicians demanding answers, along with heavy legal bills. Analysts who reported to the chief of counterterrorism sifted through their data to the point of obsessiveness, fearing that they might miss important clues and thus have to live with being responsible for the deaths of fellow citizens, deaths they might have prevented. All of them were deeply suspicious of a government that promised them support one day, yet might leave them all hanging out to dry the next.

The atmosphere in Langley was not a healthy one, and Mr. Carabas had been warned by his doctors that stress was taking its toll on his heart. But he was a patriot, and devoted to his craft. He would do what he could for his country for as long as possible.

I often think of the last operation he dreamed up but was never able to carry out, the one in which I would have had a crucial role to play. This was during the time a certain Middle Eastern dictator had gone from being a thorn in our side to becoming a knife aimed at our nation's throat. Mr. Carabas, dismayed at the increasing likelihood of war—he had always regarded warfare as a massive failure of intelligence in both senses—had come up with a plan.

He spoke of his scheme one evening when we were by ourselves. His catering service had dropped off several prepared meals for his consumption on those nights when he wasn't out dining with friends or at Washington's better restaurants, while the cleaning woman who came in three days a week had left late that afternoon. "I'd need your assistance, Angleton," Mr. Carabas said to me as I dined on chopped chicken livers and he sipped brandy. "It would mean blowing your cover and risking your life, so I won't hold it against you if you decide not to volunteer."

I felt my whiskers twitch. "Go on, sir," I replied, feeling that I owed it to Mr. Carabas to hear him out.

His plan, to put it simply, was to smuggle me into the dictator's country with a couple of operatives who were working with that nation's resistance movement. A fast-acting and deadly toxin would be applied to my claws, and I would be turned loose near whatever palace was currently housing the tyrant. My mission was to locate that disagreeable fellow, administer the powerful and inevitably fatal poison with a few scratches of my claws, and then make my escape.

"That's the beauty of it," Mr. Carabas continued. "Whatever suspicions might be aroused afterwards, no one would be able to prove that it was an assassination. If we're lucky, the evildoer's cronies might begin to think that a usurper among them had found a way to administer poison, and never suspect an outside intelligence service at all. And there wouldn't be any of those blasted hearings with all those windbags in the House and Senate." He peered at me over his snifter. "But it's a lot to ask of you."

"I might have a problem getting close to the man," I said. "He's extremely paranoid, heavily guarded, and has a fetish for personal hygiene." I had picked up those details while eavesdropping on some roundtable discussions at Agency headquarters.

"All true enough, but he also has a great fondness for cats. Magnus Ritchard confirmed that with one of his deep cover contacts just the other day, that's what gave me the idea. Apparently there are cats in every one of the dictator's palaces and hideaways at all times."

"No doubt doubling as his food tasters," I murmured.

"That was also in the report given to Magnus," Mr. Carabas said.

"My biggest problem might be getting past the other cats without engaging in a territorial dispute. If I end up clawing one of them in a fight, and the cat keels over, that would give our whole game away."

Mr. Carabas set down his snifter as I leaped into his lap. "As I told you," he said while scratching me behind the ears, "this has to be your decision. I'll understand if you refuse."

Actually, it wasn't the dangers of the mission that gave me pause. If my human handlers could get me into the country and anywhere near the target, I knew that I could accomplish my task. What worried me more was what might happen to me afterwards. My accomplices, and probably others in the Agency, would have to be informed of my abilities if they were to trust me to carry out the mission. Could I rely on all of them to keep my secret? Would I, instead of being rewarded for my success, end up as a prisoner, a caged experimental subject at a government laboratory? Even worse, how could I be sure that the Agency would want to keep me alive after the operation was over? I would, after all, be a loose thread that could tie our intelligence service to the assassination of a foreign leader.

Another danger, however remote, was that some counterspy planted within the Agency by a foreign power might learn about me. Such a mole might try to do away with me, or might even be foolish enough to think that I could be "turned" with bribes of lobster, live mice to chase, and other such luxuries, but in any case, my life would become much more precarious.

I said as much to Mr. Carabas.

"If I could take you on this mission myself," he replied, "I would, but I've been out of that game for too long. I can promise you that I won't send you in without people I trust implicitly."

That was good enough for me. "I'm in, Mr. Carabas." I curled up on his lap and settled in for a nice long nap, dreaming of my eventual triumph.

A week later, just before Maury was to receive his law degree, Mr. Carabas suffered his last heart attack. He was already dead by the time two fellow officers found him in his office, slumped over his desk, his ever-present cup of black coffee spilled across his papers. Had he brought me to the office that day, perhaps I might have saved him; a resonant and persistent repetition of meows might have summoned others to his side in time.

I padded through the house all that night, alone and frantic, fearing for him. Latisha Knowles, our cleaning woman, arrived the next morning at her usual time; Magnus Ritchard rang the front doorbell only a few minutes later.

"There was nothing they could do for Charles," Mr. Ritchard said to Ms. Knowles before he had even taken off his coat. "He's gone—we'll have to call his son." That was how I learned of Mr. Carabas's passing. Whether he ever had the opportunity to broach the subject of my Middle Eastern mission to Mr. Ritchard or to anyone else at the Agency, I did not know.

* * * *

Maury flew home immediately to take charge of the funeral arrangements. The Requiem Mass was held at the Dahlgren Chapel on the Georgetown University campus, according to Mr. Carabas's wishes, but the majority of mourners chose to pay their respects to his son at home rather than attend the funeral itself. I well understood their reasons for avoiding the service. For such a large contingent of intelligence officers, politicians, Cabinet secretaries, and notorious figures who had been forced to testify at Congressional hearings about Agency operations to show up at the Mass might have aroused too much curiosity and attention. Even so, I wished that there could have been more of a crowd, that I might have been present at the rite. Instead, I circulated among the mourners at home, allowing them to pet me and offering what comfort I could mutely, while longing to speak to them aloud about how much Mr. Carabas had meant to me.

Maury soon discovered that his father had failed to apply his considerable intelligence to his own fiscal affairs. The family legacy that had helped to support Charles Carabas was no more. Taxes were owed, investments had failed, considerable debts had accumulated for the purchases of fine wines, cigars, trips to exotic places, and a library of rare volumes. Consultations with Mr. Carabas's executors revealed that nearly everything would have to be sold, including the Georgetown house, in order to cover everything, leaving Maury with what can only be called a modest inheritance.

"Well, little buddy," Maury said to me one late August night, after the bad news had finally sunk in, "I guess it's just you and me now." I was lying next to him, and offered him a few subdued purrs, grateful to realize that he apparently regarded me as part of his father's legacy. "Don't know what's gonna happen, but I'll always look out for you, Angleton. I know how much you meant to Dad."

I rested my head on my front paws as I considered our situation. Maurice Carabas had, unfortunately, not inherited his sire's considerable intellect. Attendance at one of the country's finest preparatory schools had not entirely prepared young Maury for his father's alma mater of Harvard, to which he was admitted only through much covert pulling of strings. He had flunked out of Harvard after two semesters, barely managed to graduate from Georgetown a few years after that, and considerably more string-pulling had been required to get him into a minor law school in the South. That he had finally succeeded in earning a law degree was either a miracle or else a function of that particular law school's lack of rigor. How he was going to establish himself in the world without his father's guidance was not a matter I cared to contemplate too deeply.

Yet Maury, I knew, had some potential. He was, as human beings measure such qualities, an extremely handsome young man. His lack of academic accomplishment had been in part caused by a deep devotion to the pursuits of tennis and golf, but such athletic skills would be useful in enabling him to meet people who might benefit him socially. And he was kind and loyal; he had readily accepted his responsibility for me, with no thought of giving me away or consigning me to a shelter.

I knew then that I could not keep my secret from him any longer. I sat up, gazed directly at him, and said, "Maurice, there is something about me that you should know."

"Hey, you can call me Maury," he said absently. A few moments later, his eyes suddenly widened and his brows shot up. "You can talk?"

"I just did, didn't I? Your father and I used to engage in many long discourses whenever we were alone. I don't suppose I need to explain to you why we thought it best to keep that to ourselves."

He was still gaping at me. "You can talk?" he said again.

"Yes, I can talk, in English and in other languages as well. Je parle français. Watakushi wa nihongo ga wakarimasu. Ich—"

"I get the picture." Maury shook his head. "I always knew Dad was smart, but I didn't think even he could teach a cat how to talk."

"He didn't teach me how to talk. He was as surprised as you were when I revealed my vocal talents. What he taught me was a certain degree of eloquence."

"Maybe some other stuff, too," Maury said. "Like, I always knew he was a spook, even if I don't know much about what he actually did, so I guess he taught you how to keep a secret, too."

"That he did," I said, "and it would be wise of you to keep this one."

"You don't have to worry about that, old buddy. If I told people I had a talking cat, I'd probably end up in the hat factory. Hell, maybe I am crazy, but if it was just me imagining this, you probably wouldn't sound so smart." He sighed. "I guess you know what we're up against, then. Dad didn't leave me a whole lot. I figure it might be just enough for me to go back to Florida and see what I can set up for myself there. There's a couple of guys I knew at law school who might be able to find me a gig in Tallahassee."

"Is that what you want?" I asked.

"I don't know. I always thought I'd end up back here, in Washington, I mean. Never really thought about living anywhere else, but we've got to be practical now." He patted me gently on the head. "I said I'd look after you, Angleton, and I meant it. I won't leave for Florida without you."

I was moved, even though the prospect of spending my remaining years in the Florida panhandle was less than enticing. An idea was forming in my mind. "But there's no reason to leave your home town," I said, "and seek your fortune elsewhere. There would be far better hunting for you in Washington than in Tallahassee."

"Maybe," he said, "but I can't afford to live here now."

"You'll have a nest egg after everything's sold. Would you like my advice?" I asked.

"Sure."

"Use the money to stay in Washington, and leave everything else to me. I've learned a few skills that might stand us both in good stead."

"Really?"

I fixed him with a stare. "Just listen to me, young Maury, and you may find out that you have more of a legacy than you realize."

* * * *

Mr. Carabas's belongings were auctioned off, the house sold, and the taxes and debts paid, leaving Maury with a slightly larger sum than he had expected. We might have invested some of the money, but Maury knew nothing of such matters. I, given the unfortunate example of Mr. Carabas, knew little more than Maury did about finances, but in any case, the plans I had for him and myself did not involve living modestly on a pittance, being bystanders at life's game instead of players. His father, my rescuer, would have pulled enough strings to get his son set up in a suitable position; in his absence, I could do no less.

"We have to move out by the end of this month," I said to him one evening in Mr. Carabas's library. The built-in bookshelves were empty, all the rare books having been sold at auction, and we were sitting on the floor, since the leather chairs and reading lamps had also been taken away by their new owners.

"I know," Maury replied as he fed me an anchovy from his pizza, "but every place I've looked at has a rent that's too high. About the only place we could afford would be some shithole in a really bad neighborhood."

"Taking up residence in a shithole would hardly improve your future prospects, Maury. I suggest instead that we move to the Watergate complex and purchase some living space there. It's come to my attention that there are some apartments available in Watergate South." I had found that out at the latest auction of Mr. Carabas's possessions, when one of the buyers had mentioned to another that he was planning to move there soon.

"The Watergate? That's way out of our league, old buddy. I can't afford a place like that."

"You have your inheritance," I said. "That could pay much of the freight, so to speak, and you could borrow the rest, and I vow to you that after the move, you'll be launched on a most promising trajectory."

"I don't think you understand." Maury swallowed more beer from his can. "That would just about clean me out."

"Only if nothing else comes along, and you'll be able to sell your place to another buyer in the future."

"Which just might pay off whatever I end up owing by then."

I accepted another anchovy, then sat back on my haunches. "Maury, think of an apartment in Watergate South not as an expense, but as an investment. If you're going to get anywhere in the world, you have to position yourself among individuals who can help you. Living at the Watergate will put you in close proximity to some influential people."

"And what if nothing else comes along?"

"Leave it to me," I said. "You promised to look after me, and I'll do no less for you. Trust me. After all, we're both in this together."

* * * *

Maury accepted my advice in the end, largely because he couldn't think of anything else to do. I assisted him with his application to the Watergate co-operative board; he easily won approval, since I was able to demonstrate, by sitting quietly on his lap during his interview and allowing the board members to pet me, how well behaved a creature I am.

By the beginning of January, we were ensconced in a one-bedroom apartment with balcony in Watergate South. By early February, with my advice on whom to call and where to submit his résumé, Maury had secured a position on the staff of one of the senators on the Intelligence Oversight Committee, a gentleman who had always treated employees of the Agency fairly and sympathetically whenever they appeared before him. Maury's salary was small, certainly not enough to cover our expenses, but he was now well situated, with his job and his residence, to meet people who could help him to rise in the world.

By late spring, however, I was coming to see that more action on my part would be needed. Maury was not the sort of fellow likely to become a trusted and influential advisor to his senatorial patron; indeed, he often brought work home with him, or emailed it to his home computer, so that I could peruse various studies and polls, read constituents' mail, and advise him on the wording of position papers. Instead of making influential contacts, Maury had made the acquaintance of a number of young ladies, most of them Congressional staffers or interns. From them, he seemed to require only that they be fond of cats and possess a quality he referred to as "bodaciousness." I spent many a night lying on his bed while he and his companion of the evening slept, trying to conjure up a plan of action.

"Maury," I said to him one evening when we were by ourselves, "it's time to cut to the chase."

"What do you mean?" he asked, feeding me a scallop from his takeout carton of Chinese food.

"At the rate you're spending money on wining and dining and tennis-playing with your young ladies, we'll be lucky if we have enough money in the end to get to Tallahassee with a low-fare ticket for you and consignment to the cargo hold for me."

"But you said I have to make an impression."

"Making an impression on young ladies nearly as penniless as yourself isn't exactly what I meant. You might at least find someone with more substantial assets."

Maury looked abashed. "It isn't as if I'm not trying. I mean, most of the time they're coming on to me, and I don't, like, ask them about their bank balances. You can't exactly expect a guy to say no when opportunity knocks."

"I suppose not, but these weren't the sort of opportunities I had in mind."

"Anyway, it never lasts," he said. "By the time I'm ready to think about getting serious, they're dumping me and going out with somebody else."

"Which means that going on in this way," I said, "with companions who inevitably tire of you, is both expensive and pointless. We have to take more drastic measures."

He quickly agreed to my tentative plan, which was hardly a plan at all. I was hoping only to scout the territory, so to speak, to see if there was any way to bring Maury to the attention of some of the wealthy and influential human beings who inhabited the Watergate complex. I did not expect an opportunity to do so to land right in front of me.

* * * *

Early the next morning, Maury and I left our building, he on foot and I in my carrying case. When he was certain that no one was watching us, he opened the case and set me loose. Since it was Saturday, Maury would be able to wait for me until I safely made my way back to Watergate South.

"Take care, little fella," Maury whispered after me as I slipped out of my carrier. "You be really careful, you hear?" He was being far too solicitous. I could easily find my way back, having studied a layout of the complex; in addition, I was wearing an ID tag that I had insisted he buy for me, one that had my name, Maury's name, and our address and phone number engraved upon its surface. Maury's father had always spared me the indignity of a collar, but it was best to be on the safe side. If I did get lost, I didn't want to give myself away by having to ask for directions.

I bounded across the grass, reveling in my freedom. Only a few people seemed to be out, jogging on the pathway near the Potomac or wandering off with guide books in the direction of the National Mall.

Birds twittered in the tree limbs overhead, and I thought of bagging one or two before resuming my reconnaissance.

Then I spied a glittering loop lying under a shrub. I scurried over to examine the object, and found what looked very much like a bracelet. There was no way to tell if the bright stones of this human limb adornment were of any value or were only cheap imitations, but something about the bracelet attracted me. I rolled around, swatting at it with my paws, and somehow managed to get it hooked around my neck.

A short, sharp, extremely hostile sound suddenly interrupted my play. My ears twitched and my fur stood up; even with my lack of experience in the out-of-doors, I recognized the sound of a dog's bark. I turned my head and moved my eyes just in time to see a large beast bearing down on me from the right, still barking, as a man ran after him waving a long leather strap.

The dog had slipped his leash and was on the warpath. I could either stand my ground and rely on my claws, or flee.

There wasn't time to disentangle myself from the bracelet. I ran, expecting the dog to nip at my tail any second, and managed to claw my way up a tree. The dog circled below, howling and barking, until his human being finally caught up with him. I watched, clinging to safety, as the man hooked the strap onto his collar and led him away.

My heart was beating rapidly. I stretched out on the limb, reluctant to venture forth again. Dogs weren't my only worry; there might also be stray cats in the area. In a desperate situation, I had a chance of intimidating a dog, but no cat worthy of the name would back down from a fight with me.

I shook myself, trying to free myself of the bracelet, then forced myself to be calm. A survey of the area revealed that I was not that far from the entrance to the Watergate complex's hotel, where a limousine was just pulling up to the entrance.

Something moved below me; a woman in shorts and a baggy shirt was jogging toward me. She stopped under the tree and leaned against the trunk.

"Jesus," I heard her say, "Daddy's going to kill me. He's just going to *kill* me." She sounded quite distressed.

"Mrrow," I said, thinking that I might be able to use a little help making my way down.

She looked up. Young Maury had always brought home attractive human females, but this one far exceeded them in beauty. Her hair was thick and dark, her eyes large and green, and her teeth were white as she smiled at me.

"You poor kitty," she murmured, and then, "Oh, my God."

"Mrrow," I said again as I crept backward along the limb. When I was halfway down the trunk, hands seized me and gently set me on the ground.

"Nice kitty." She showed me more of her teeth. "You wonderful kitty. You absolutely excellent and terrific little kitty." She reached for the bracelet and removed it from me. "You found my diamond bracelet. Daddy would have just killed me for losing it." She scratched my head; I purred, then rolled around in the grass, showing my belly. "Are you sure you'll be all right? Do you even have a home? I wouldn't mind taking you home myself."

I stretched and got to my feet. She knelt next to me and peered at my tag. "Why, you live around here. I think I'd better take you home."

I squinted at her. I was tempted to scurry away, given that I'd had so little chance to explore my surroundings. But my encounter with the dog had dampened my enthusiasm for more adventures, an extremely large male human being seemed to be watching the young lady and me at a distance, and perhaps it was wiser to take advantage of the safe passage home that this female was offering.

I allowed her to pick me up. She insisted on holding me with my head nestled against her elbow, not exactly the most comfortable position, but I was able to endure my discomfort until we reached Watergate South.

The doorman recognized me as we approached, and quickly opened the door for us. Maury was lurking in the lobby, still clutching my carrying case, as my captor entered the building. "Angleton!" he said to me. "Thank God you're safe."

"Is he yours?" the young woman said.

Maury didn't reply immediately. I had a good look at his face from my vantage point; his mouth was hanging open and his eyes were as glassy as they had been when he first heard me speak.

"Is he your cat?" the woman said. "Are you Maury Carabas? The tag says he belongs to a Maury Carabas." I wriggled around in her arms, then leaped to the floor. "Hello?" she continued. "Anybody home?"

Maury managed to close his mouth for a moment. "Hello," he said at last in a muted voice. "Yeah, he's my cat."

"It's a good thing I found him, then. You really shouldn't let him run around outside, even if he did find my bracelet for me. I was afraid I'd never see it again." Her arms tightened around me. "You should be a lot more careful with this wonderful, beautiful kitty."

"I know, but Angleton has a mind of his own." Maury still had a dazed look on his face. "What's your name?"

"Desirée."

"That's a beautiful name."

This hardly passed as witty repartee, but the young woman was now staring at Maury in the same stupefied fashion as he was gazing at her. "Maury's a nice name, too," she replied.

"I work for Senator Trilby. I'm a member of his staff."

"I'm here in Washington with my father," Desirée said. "He always stays at the hotel here when he's in town."

They continued to stare at each other for a while, while I longed to feed Maury some more eloquent lines of conversation, until he leaned over and opened the top of the case. "In you go, old buddy," he said as he took me from Desirée and deposited me in my container. "Um, I know this is kind of sudden, but after I take Angleton back to the apartment, would you like to have a cup of coffee with me?"

"Sure. I'll wait down here."

I sighed with exasperation as Maury picked up the case. Risking my hide so that he could find yet another young lady to waste his money on was not what I'd had in mind.

"You can come up to my place if you want."

"Better not." She gestured toward the doors. "One of my security people probably followed me here. He won't bother us if I wait for you here, but he'd probably want to check you out before I went off with you."

"Your security people?" Maury asked.

"My bodyguards. It's not my idea, but Daddy insists on it whenever I'm out jogging or shopping or wandering around. The only thing he gave in on is that they have to keep their distance while they're protecting me. I mean, like, what kind of social life would I have if they were standing right next to me all the time?"

Bodyguards, I thought; people of limited means usually did not hire such protection. Perhaps this young woman had more substantial resources than I realized.

"With the crime rate in this town," Maury said, "maybe your dad's got a good idea."

A man came through the entrance. Peering up through the metal bars of my carrier, I recognized the rather large individual I had spotted outside earlier.

"Jeez, Jeffrey," Desirée said to this man, "you don't have to come in here. It's cool. Like, all I was doing is giving this guy's cat back to him."

The man touched the cap over his brow with one hand. "Never hurts to double check, Ms. Morlock."

"Morlock?" Maury said.

"That's my last name," the young woman said.

"Any relation to Roland Morlock?" Maury asked.

"He's my dad."

I had to restrain myself from rolling around inside my carrier in ecstasy. A lost bracelet and an unleashed dog had led Maury and me to the daughter of the richest and most powerful media lord in the country.

* * * *

Maury and Desirée were soon keeping company, so much so that the *Washington Post*'s society pages began to take note of the fact. Whenever the two weren't spending time in the Royal Suite at the Watergate's Swissôtel, they were playing tennis, picnicking in Rock Creek Park, working out at the hotel's health club, playing golf at Burning Tree, attending yet another performance at the Kennedy Center, or jetting up to New York City for a weekend of theater performances and club-hopping. Often I accompanied them on these junkets, packed in my carrier and safely in the keeping of one of Ms. Morlock's bodyguards.

That Desirée and Maury had a certain lack of intellectual prowess in common only seemed to strengthen their bond; however vacuous they might have seemed to many of their former loves, they never bored each other. The two were together nearly every evening, and on those rare occasions when they were not, Desirée called on the telephone and engaged Maury in lengthy if often monotonous conversations. They spent their evenings at Mr. Morlock's hotel suite, where Desirée had remained even after her father returned to New York, or at Maury's apartment, where they could barely restrain themselves from expressing their affection at almost any opportunity.

The young woman's increasing fondness for Maury also encompassed me, the cat who had found her bracelet and had enabled her to meet the man who had, so she proclaimed, become the love of her life. When they were not at Maury's apartment, the two brought me to the hotel suite with them. Whenever they dined on take-out or room service food, they fed me tidbits with their fingers, and because Desirée was always dieting, I had my choice of abundant leftovers.

Even more miraculously, Roland Morlock, upon meeting Maury, took a strong liking to him. I suppose that I can claim some credit for that, as I was careful to rehearse Maury in a recitation of Mr. Morlock's prehistoric political views before he met his love's father for the first time; by repeating Mr. Morlock's various statements or else keeping his mouth shut and nodding while the great man expounded on politics and society, Maury had made a stunningly good impression on Desirée's father. It's also true that Mr. Morlock had grown increasingly distressed at seeing stories about his daughter's nocturnal shenanigans regularly appear in the publications of several of his competitors. Maury, to his mind, was a great improvement over Desirée's past suitors.

Maury's prospects had never been brighter. One of the wealthiest young ladies in the world adored him, and it was increasingly likely that their strong attachment to each other would eventually result in matrimony. Mr. Morlock, during his visits to Washington, often spoke of various executive positions that Maury might some day occupy in one of his companies.

I should have been as delighted as a cat roaming in a garden of catnip, but I had miscalculated Maury's capacity for subtlety. Knowing that Mr. Morlock was extremely wary of young men who were unduly interested in his daughter's financial assets, I had advised Maury to hint that he was a young man of considerable means. "You don't want Roland Morlock to think of you as a fortune hunter," I had told him, "especially since young Desirée, according to a recent article in *Vanity Fair*, has already had a couple of unfortunate and expensive involvements with mercenary young men of dubious antecedents. The only way to convince him that you're not after his daughter's money is to act as though money doesn't matter to you—in other words, as if you have more than enough of it yourself."

"I always foot the bill when we go out," Maury said. "I'm not exactly a cheap bastard."

"True enough," I said, well aware of how rapidly our scanty resources were being depleted, "but we've reached a point where more is required. You're already living as a young man of means might, and you have an eminently respectable family background thanks to your father, but it wouldn't hurt to drop a few hints about other assets."

"How the hell do I do that?"

I repressed a sigh, which would only have escaped me as a snarl. "You might mention your occasional enjoyment of a good horseback ride in the Virginia hills, thus leading Mr. Morlock to assume that you possess a horse or two, even a stable and a farm. You can imply that your broker was smart enough to get you out of the market just before the dotcom and telecommunications fiascos. You needn't say anything outright, or make any overt claims that could easily be checked. The trick is to leave a certain impression."

Maury not only followed my advice, but also exceeded it. Four months after meeting Desirée Morlock, he had managed to convince her father that he had a few million salted away in bonds and other investments, that the acreage of his Virginia farm encompassed a county or two, and that he had given up his late father's Georgetown home for the Watergate only because the house had evoked too many painful memories of his beloved sire. Had he been more discreet and ambiguous, he might have been safely wedded to Desirée before her father discovered his true net worth. By then, Mr. Morlock, faced with a happily married daughter, would most likely have overlooked the matter, especially since he would have had to admit to himself that he had drawn his own conclusions too readily from some rather vague statements of Maury's. He was not a man who cared to admit his own mistakes.

But he was also not a man who would allow his daughter to marry a four-flusher. The truth would come out, either through Mr. Morlock's investigations or else in some published item by an inquisitive journalist. Maury, by being too specific instead of ambiguous in his statements, would soon be exposed as an outright liar, and I had no way to avert the disaster that would ensue.

* * * *

Maury and Desirée had jetted off to Los Angeles in one of her father's Gulfstreams for a week-long vacation before Christmas. They had wanted to bring me with them, but I had explained to Maury privately that I had other fish to fry.

There was much for me to ponder in his absence. I spent a couple of days at Maury's computer, which he had left on for me, distracting myself by researching real estate listings in Tallahassee. At last I removed my paw from the mouse and closed my overstrained eyes.

The truth of our situation could escape me no longer; we would soon be penniless. The longer we stayed in Washington, and the more prolonged Maury's courtship of Desirée became, the greater the chance of exposure, and of Mr. Morlock's parting the two lovers decisively and forever.

It was time for desperate measures. Perhaps if we decamped from the Watergate and headed south, Desirée would be moved to follow Maury there, and would quickly agree to marry him so as not to lose him again. It wasn't much of a plan, but I was hard-pressed to come up with anything more promising. We might be able to scrape together enough to afford one of the modestly priced bungalows in the Tallahassee listings.

As I contemplated this half-baked idea, there was a rattling outside our door. My ears flicked as I heard the almost imperceptible sound of the lock turning. Desirée had left her bodyguard Jeffrey at her hotel suite with orders to come over twice a day to feed me and clean out my litter box, but he had already completed his rounds.

The door opened. The silhouette outlined by the lights in the hallway was much smaller than Jeffrey's large form. Someone was breaking into the apartment.

I leaped down from my chair, frantically looking for a place to hide in the large room that constituted most of our living space. It was unlikely that a burglar would go out of his way to harm me, but I wanted a good look at the miscreant in order to be able to describe him later to Maury before he contacted the police.

"Angleton," the intruder said then; I had heard that voice before. "Angleton, I know you're here." The door slammed shut behind him; heels clicked against the marble floor of the foyer. "You'd better come out."

I slipped under the dining room table, holding my breath, then crept toward our Christmas tree. An overhead light suddenly illuminated the room as I scrambled under the tree's lowest branches. "Come out, Angleton," the man said. "You can't hide from me, I'm afraid I know all about you. Charles told me your secret, just before his death, while we were planning a certain operation in the Middle East. I know all about what your role in that mission was to be."

I saw his face now, and recognized Magnus Ritchard. For such an experienced operative to get past the doorman and our building's security systems and to acquire copies of our keys was probably a simple matter. But why was he here? Perhaps the Agency had finally given the go-ahead for the obstreperous dictator's assassination, and Mr. Ritchard was here to enlist my services in that effort.

He sat down on the sofa. "Here, kitty, kitty."

I crept out from under the tree, still apprehensive. Mr. Carabas would never have confided our secret to his colleague unless he had trusted Mr. Ritchard implicitly, yet I remained suspicious. If the man wanted my help in one of the Agency's operations, surely he could have contacted me in some other way.

"Mrrow," I said.

"Don't get funny with me, Angleton. I know you can do more than meow. Charles told me all about your long conversations and how many languages you managed to pick up. I know you can understand every word I'm saying to you."

I moved a little closer and sat down a few feet away from his feet. "I know all about you," Mr. Ritchard continued, "and I'm the only one who knows, now that Charles is dead. There's something I have to discuss with you, and unless we come to an understanding, your nine lives will pass very quickly, I promise you."

My fur rose along my spine; he was threatening me. He would not have had to threaten me to enlist me in any Agency operation; evoking the memory of Mr. Carabas would have been enough to win my cooperation. Mr. Ritchard, I feared, was playing another game.

"Mrrow," I said again.

"You'd better listen, you little fleabag. This isn't about that mission Charles and I were planning. That never got past a couple of discussions we had by ourselves. This little meeting involves you and that doofus you're living with, and if you're not cooperative, a lot of very unpleasant things can happen to recalcitrant kitty cats and their masters. Nobody else in the Agency knows about you, either, so don't think you can go running to them for protection."

I stretched out, still keeping my eyes on him.

"It's very simple," Mr. Ritchard said. "You'll go on living with Maury, and every once in a while, you'll report to me. That isn't asking so much, is it? Later on, when we figure out how to make the best use of him, there'll be more for you to do, but nothing as risky as what Charles was planning for you in the Middle East. Once Maury's married to the Morlock girl, he'll start rising in her father's company, and having somebody in place to watch him and maybe to help in using him later on could be very beneficial to us." He paused. "Wouldn't surprise me if you had something to do with getting those two together."

Somehow I restrained myself from hissing at him. Roland Morlock, who never missed a chance to wave the flag either figuratively or literally, would happily have cooperated with the Agency on anything they asked of him, so why all this hugger-mugger? In any case, given Maury's precarious situation, Magnus Ritchard would have to find another way to spy on the Morlock enterprises.

"You'd better start piping up," Mr. Ritchard said, "or it won't go well for you." He glanced toward the glass-covered door that led to the balcony. "I don't think even a cat could survive a twelve-story drop. Especially if I wring your furry little neck first."

I sat up. "Very well, Mr. Ritchard," I said, "but I fear you're too late. Young Maury's marital prospects aren't looking especially good at the moment."

"Holy Christ," he said. "You sound just like Jeremy Irons."

"Not quite. I'm afraid I picked up a fair number of mid-Atlantic locutions from Mr. Carabas."

"What did you mean, Maury's marital prospects aren't looking good? Is that Morlock girl getting tired of him already?"

"All indications are that Ms. Morlock is still besotted with him," I replied, "but that may not matter in the end. Her father's probably already poking around doing background checks on Maury, and when he finds out how impoverished he is, he's not likely to consider him a fit mate for his daughter."

"There's nothing wrong with being broke."

"There is if you've led someone to believe otherwise."

Mr. Ritchard shook his head. "He can't be that broke if he's living here."

"He's living here well over his head, I assure you. Mr. Morlock is well aware that Maury's riches don't come anywhere close to equaling his own—that's not the problem. The problem is that he believes Maury to be far more prosperous than he is. When he finds out—"

"I can guess," Mr. Ritchard interrupted. "He's going to think Maury's a gold digger. He'll make sure they don't get married after all."

"Exactly." I kept myself still and restrained myself from flicking my tail, but my mind was racing. Magnus Ritchard could not be here on the Agency's behalf; he had something else in mind. I didn't know what kind of game he was playing, or who was behind him, but he wouldn't be the first mole or double agent who had infiltrated our intelligence agencies, or the first who had decided a foreign power could reward him more lavishly than his own country.

"That's too bad," he muttered ominously, and I smelled danger. He had threatened me; now that I was useless to him, he might already be plotting how to get rid of me.

"About the most we can hope for," I said, "is that when Mr. Morlock learns the truth, he offers Maury a nice chunk of change to get out of Desirée's life."

"That wouldn't exactly serve my purposes."

"What I meant is that Maury, being the kind of fellow he is, would almost certainly turn the money down. And at that point, perhaps Mr. Morlock would be moved enough by his sincerity to relent."

Mr. Ritchard scowled. "I don't know if Morlock is that sentimental."

"I am sorry to be the bearer of bad tidings," I said, "but whatever plans the Agency might have for Maury may have to be abandoned." Despite my words, I was now sure that Magnus Ritchard was not here on the Agency's business, and kept my eyes on him, watching for any sudden and threatening moves on his part. "It's a pity we can't just magically make large sums appear in his accounts."

Mr. Ritchard was silent for a while. "Is that what it would take?" he asked. "Just making it look like he has a fat wad tucked away?"

I sensed then that I was on to something; maybe I could use this man for my own ends. "Well, yes," I said. "If only Mr. Morlock's background checks could turn up a few million in accounts and investments in Maury's name, we'd be home free. But it's useless to hope. I feel badly about that, Mr. Ritchard, you know that I'd do anything I could for you and the Agency, but..."

"I might be able to handle this." He rubbed his chin. "I can get the money wired to me, since it would only be a loan. Maury won't need it once he gets past Morlock's background checks."

"True enough."

"It'd be well worth it to me. I just about promised that I could pull this off, get somebody into Morlock's group. I just didn't tell anybody how I was going to do it. I'll get the money, Angleton, and open the accounts myself, and back-date the records so it looks like Maury's had it for a while."

"That would be most advisable." I stretched myself, then settled down on the floor once more. "And I'll have to verify that those accounts actually exist."

"I'll bring you all of the passwords." He glanced at the computer. "You can go online and check out the accounts for yourself. When you let me know Maury's passed muster with Morlock, I'll close them out. And then you and I will stay in touch on a regular basis, and you'll follow my instructions, or—" He let the word hang in the air.

"I assume," I said, "that I should tell Maury nothing about this arrangement."

"You are a smart little kitty." He stood up. "Just make sure you don't let me down."

"I have no intention of doing so. Maury will be back in Washington by next weekend. When do you plan to return here with verification that the accounts have been opened in his name?"

Mr. Ritchard thrust his hands inside the pockets of his coat. "I think I can get it settled by Friday."

"Then come back here after dark. I assume that you can find your way in here again."

"See you then, Angleton. Just don't try to cross me. You wouldn't care for the consequences to you and Maury if you do."

* * * *

I slept restlessly the next day, my thoughts roiling as I tossed and turned on my favorite cushion. Magnus Ritchard had to be in the employ of a foreign intelligence service. That was the only way he could have arranged for Maury to be worth a few million on a temporary basis so quickly; the red tape required by the Agency would never have allowed for such a rapid transfer of funds. Someone wanted to plant an operative at the heart of Roland Morlock's media empire. For what purpose, I did not know, but could safely assume that the purpose was not to improve television news coverage, produce finer motion pictures, or publish only the best of the world's literature.

What could I do to foil Ritchard's plans? I could not reveal my secret to Desirée's bodyguard Jeffrey and enlist him as my protector. Maury, however devoted to me, would also be of little use in solving my dilemma. No one at the Agency was likely to take the word of a talking cat over one of their most trusted operatives, and Ritchard would probably see that I ended up in a government laboratory for my pains. I could pretend to fall in with Ritchard's plans, and string him along for a while, but there would be hell to pay when he discovered my deception; I took his threats quite seriously.

I could rely only on myself. Realizing that plunged me into a deep well of despair and helplessness. I was unable to eat, even when Jeffrey set down my favorite foods, unable to emit even the faintest of purrs while he combed my fur. Magnus Ritchard had as much as said that no one else knew about me, either at the Agency or among his foreign contacts; admitting that he would be working through a talking cat would have done little to establish his credibility.

The conclusion was inescapable: I could thwart Ritchard's plans only by getting rid of him entirely. But if I succeeded in that, I would erase any tracks that might lead his co-conspirators to me and to Maury.

The cloud of despair lifted a little at that thought. I forced myself up and padded through the apartment, working myself up to a run, flexing my muscles. My task was a dangerous one, but surely no riskier than my foray into the Middle East would have been.

After all, I was a cat, and therefore a superior creature, wasn't I?

* * * *

Magnus Ritchard returned at the appointed time on Friday. He had memorized the passwords for Maury's temporary accounts, had me recite them, then allowed me to sit on his lap while he accessed the accounts on the computer. The figures scrolling up on the monitor revealed that Maury now had a net worth of some nine million dollars.

"That should be enough to satisfy Mr. Morlock," I said as the Windows desktop reappeared on the screen. "If he completes his background checks before Christmas, and if Maury and Ms. Morlock are officially engaged by New Year's, you can close out the accounts early in January."

"It might be safer to make sure they're married first."

"They're likely to proceed to the wedding quite rapidly," I said. "Ms. Morlock is quite impetuous, and her father is increasingly anxious to see her settled." I hopped down from his lap. "If you'd care to toast our new arrangement, there's some Scotch in the cabinet over the kitchen sink. And you might set out a can of salmon for me."

"I think I'd better be on my way."

"Then perhaps you can do me a favor," I said. "I've been cooped up in here all week, and wouldn't mind getting a little air. Could you open the door to the balcony for me?"

"It's December, Angleton."

"Just for a minute or two. Cold weather doesn't bother me, what with all this fur, and I do need to stretch my legs."

"Fine." Ritchard shrugged back into his coat and walked toward the balcony, with me at his heels. He opened the door; I took a breath as we stepped outside. The weather was colder than I had expected, the balcony dusted with a light covering of snow.

I bounded across the balcony and hopped up onto the ledge. "God," Ritchard said as he came up behind me, "it's cold as hell out here." He was close enough to me now; his hands rested on the ledge next to me, and he had leaned forward slightly. I reared up on my back legs, extended my claws, and leaped at his face, aiming for his eyes.

He was too fast for me. His arm came up, swatting me, and then I was suddenly falling from the balcony. A gust of wind caught me from below; I spread my limbs as something hard rushed up to meet me. For a moment, I hung from the bare bough of a tree, until my claws lost their grip. I continued to fall, was briefly captured by another branch, and finally came to rest on a thick wooden limb.

I lay there for a long time, afraid to move, then tentatively stretched my front legs. Apparently I was unhurt; the tree had broken my fall. Relief swept through me, raising my fur; I backed halfway down the tree, then leaped to the ground.

Above me, lights shone from the concave grill of Watergate South. If I circled the building and made my way to the front entrance, either the doorman or a resident returning home was likely to see me, and my tag would tell them where I belonged. I padded over the thin layer of snow, felt the cold against my paws, then thought of Magnus Ritchard.

I had failed Maury, and wondered what would happen now. Perhaps Ritchard assumed that I had met my demise, and had already vacated our quarters. Perhaps he took nothing for granted, and was already looking for me.

In the distance, I heard the sound of many human voices. A group of people bearing objects of light in their hands came around the side of the building. They were singing, and I paused for a moment to listen to their words. "Silent night," they sang, "holy night, all is calm, all is bright."

Then a beam of light shot toward me; I froze, blinded by the light. A second later, a piercing voice called out, "It's a lost cat!"

I narrowed my eyes. "The poor thing," another person called out. The group of singers was coming toward me, and then I saw the shadowy form of another human being rush up from behind them.

"I think that's my cat," the newcomer said, and I recognized the voice of Magnus Ritchard.

I turned and ran, heedless of where I was headed, until I glimpsed a parkway and, just beyond it, the wrinkled dark surface of the Potomac. The sound of the traffic was a muffled roar. I crept down to the parkway, flattening my ears as the roaring grew louder, then looked back.

The singers were small black shapes and patches of light against the serpentine curve of Watergate South. Magnus Ritchard was a large shadow with flapping arms bearing down on me; I hadn't realized he was so close.

"Angleton," he shouted, "you won't get away from me."

Terrified, I fled onto the parkway. Bright circles of light swelled as they rushed toward me; the shrieks and roars of motor vehicles nearly deafened me. Somehow I reached the other side of the thoroughfare unscathed.

Ahead of me lay the river. I looked around frantically for another escape route. An odd screaming sound came to me, and then the sound of a loud moist slap.

I crept toward the parkway. The roaring sound was fading; vehicles slowed, then came to a stop, their eyes of light still aglow. The dark shape of Magnus Ritchard lay in the road, unmoving, looking as though a giant arm had scooped him up and thrown him there.

* * * *

I was able to make my way back across the parkway and around to the front of our building. By then, I was shivering from both nerves and the cold, and was far too weak to call attention to myself. It was my good fortune that a neighbor of Maury's found me lying there and brought me to the attention of the night doorman, who wrapped me in a blanket and got a few drops of warm soup down my throat before I fell into a deep sleep.

Maury returned home the next day. By then, I had been brought to our apartment, and Jeffrey, summoned there by our building's manager, was nursing me back to health.

"Well, little buddy," Maury said to me after Jeffrey had left us, "I heard all about your adventure. Maybe you can tell me just how you managed to get outside."

I considered how much to tell him. With Magnus Ritchard out of the way, there was no need to reveal the whole story.

"It would be wise of you," I began, "to advise the managers of this complex that their security procedures should be tightened. Somehow an intruder was able to get into this apartment. While searching the place for something to steal, he opened the door to our balcony and stepped outside. Perhaps he wanted some air, or to take in the view."

"Maybe he wanted to listen to some Christmas carols," Maury said. "The doorman said there was a bunch of carolers here from George Washington University last night. I mean, even burglars probably have some holiday spirit."

"In any case, I slipped outside while the door was open, only to be trapped on the balcony when the door was closed again behind me. Knowing that I would surely suffer from exposure to the cold air if I remained out there for too long, I forced myself to leap from the railing, hoping that the trees below would break my fall. After that, I was luckily able to get to our building's entrance."

"You're a tough little guy, Angleton." He gave me a hug. "Got to admit it. I don't know what I'd do without you. Anyway, it doesn't look like anything was stolen, not that I have that much to steal." He hugged me again. "You could have been killed. I heard there was an accident on the parkway last night. I'm just glad you're safe."

"Maury," I said, "I urge you to plight your troth to Ms. Morlock as soon as possible. I think your courtship has lasted quite long enough."

"I think so, too, and Desirée'd marry me in a second. But what happens when her old man finds out I'm broke?"

"You needn't worry about that," I murmured. "I predict that he'll welcome you into his family with open arms after his background checks are completed. Let's just say that your assets may be greater than you think."

* * * *

Maury and Desirée were married that winter, in a hastily organized but lavish ceremony at St. Patrick's Cathedral in New York, followed by a reception at the Plaza. Not long after that, Maury began his meteoric rise through the executive ranks of Morlock Enterprises. Although Maury benefitted from my advice, and was soon a well-known public figure through his frequent appearances on radio and television talk shows, celebrity-filled social galas, charity events, and political fund-raisers, it soon became clear to Mr. Morlock that his son-in-law's particular gifts were perhaps better suited to some other occupation than that of managing a media conglomerate.

Which is why now, four years after leaving Washington, Maury and Desirée and I are returning to that city. Much as I've enjoyed our time in

Manhattan, with my own suite of rooms in our domicile, I am looking forward to taking up residence on my old territory. As I was Maury's chief campaign advisor, I can claim some of the credit for his victory, although he might not so easily have won election to the Senate without the vast resources of the Morlock fortune to aid his quest.

To celebrate his victory, Maury bought me a handcrafted pair of red leather Italian boots, which may seem a rather odd, even kinky, accessory for a cat. But my back legs have never been quite the same since my terrified flight from Magnus Ritchard, and I find that a soft pair of boots eases my aches and pains considerably. I've grown more solicitous of my health lately, controlling my intake of treats, working out on my treadmill, chasing catnip mice thrown to me by Desirée. With the opportunities that now lie ahead for Maury, I plan to be around long enough to wear my boots in the White House as First Cat.

Afterword to "Puss in D.C."

When John Helfers and Martin H. Greenberg asked me for a story for *Little Red Riding Hood in the Big Bad City*, an anthology of classic fairy tales retold for modern readers, my inspiration for the story had four sources. One was a recent trip to Washington, D.C. and the second was current events; misleading reports about nonexistent "weapons of mass destruction" were at the time leading up to what would become a disastrous war with Iraq. The third inspiration was our cat Spencer, a long-furred tuxedo cat with all of Angleton's arrogance, who died in 2000 after a very long and largely happy life of some seventeen years. If Spencer had possessed the power of speech, he would have sounded a lot like Angleton, and I suspect that in his younger years he would have been more than willing to risk even such a dangerous challenge as assassinating a dictator; I had seen him confront dogs who were five times his size and even intimidate our human neighbors with his fierce green stare. And the classic fairy tale of Puss in Boots seemed the perfect way to unite all of these elements while retelling the story of the young man and the brilliant talking cat who secures their fortune.

Marty Greenberg, who died much too soon in 2011, was the founder of the book packager Tekno Books, one of the founders of the Sci-Fi Channel (now, for reasons that have always escaped me, operating under the name of SyFy), and probably the most prolific anthologist ever in the science fiction and fantasy fields. Marty and his Tekno Books colleagues, among them John Helfers, Richard Gilliam, Larry Segriff, and the late Kathleen Massie-Ferch (another fine anthologist who passed on much too soon) were largely responsible for keeping me in the writing game during some hard years, when both the pressures of the publishing marketplace and my own self-doubt came close to pushing me out of writing altogether. In addition to reprinting stories that might otherwise have been lost, Marty and his coeditors also put together anthologies of new work. They would contact writers and commission stories on various themes, meaning I could write a story knowing that it would be paid for and published when finished, as opposed to waiting long weeks (or months) for either acceptance or rejection. Knowing that anything I wrote would be accepted forced me to do my best, as I wasn't about to let either the editors, or myself, down.

Marty was also responsible for helping to create an anthology I edited, *Conqueror Fantastic*. I sent him and John Helfers a story, a historical fantasy set in thirteenth century Mongolia I had come close to selling a few times, asking if it was suitable for any anthologies Tekno Books might be putting together. It wasn't, so Marty suggested that instead I edit an anthology and include my own story in the book. *Conqueror Fantastic* was published by DAW in 2004 and enabled me to do for several writers I greatly respected what Marty had done for me: ask for a story and trust them all to give me their best. They did, as most good writers will if you trust them.

STRAWBERRY BIRDIES

As Addie finished reading her storybook, Maerleen Loegins arrived suddenly at her family's home, as if blown in on a strong wind. She rang the doorbell and in a few minutes convinced Addie's mother that she was the only person to move into their spare room. Addie had never seen her mother convinced so quickly.

"You seem older than most students," Addie's mother said. "More mature, I mean."

"I began college late," Maerleen Loegins replied, "and I am working on my master's degree, not a bachelor's." She had an odd accent and said her name in a manner that made her sound like she came from far away: "May-er-leen Low-egg-ins." That was how it sounded to Addie.

"Your master's?" Addie's mother said.

"In physics."

"That's my husband's department. Didn't know there were any women students in physics."

"I am one of two." Maerleen Loegins lifted her brows. She was short enough that Addie didn't have to crane her neck to get a good look at her face. She had large brown eyes and short glossy black hair, wore a pale blue dress, and carried a large suitcase. She looked alert and ready to take charge, unlike Addie's mother, who stood there with slumped shoulders looking as though she was ready to go back to bed.

Addie had a younger brother and two infant siblings, a boy and a girl, who were twins, so her mother had plenty to do at home, while her father was a graduate student and lab assistant in the Hayes University physics department. There, he scribbled indecipherable symbols on a blackboard and supervised students who used pieces of glass to cast rainbows. They also did experiments with something called an inclined plane, which Addie envisioned as an aircraft tilted to one side and resting on one wing. While he was engaged in these mysterious activities, Addie's mother fluttered around the house looking worried and distracted while hovering over Addie and her brother Cyril or warming up yet another bottle for one of the twins.

But now, Addie thought, they would have somebody to help out. The reason her parents had put an ad in the paper offering free room and board and a small stipend to a college student was to have someone around to look after their children, especially Cyril, who wouldn't be ready to go to school that fall, not even to kindergarten, and might never be ready.

Addie's mother looked over the letter Maerleen Loegins had handed to her. "Professor Eberhardt recommends you very highly, says he was really sorry to lose you. Why did you decide to leave?"

"His boy is going away to boarding school this autumn, so there was no reason for me to stay on."

Boarding school, Addie thought; it sounded both exciting and scary. Her mother frowned. "I didn't know Sam was going away to school. He seems awfully young for that."

"He is almost ten years old. He seemed happy about going away, although Mrs. Eberhardt does not seem overjoyed. And moving to the home of somebody in my own department seemed appropriate, even though living in the home of a history professor was most instructive."

Maerleen Loegins took a step toward Addie. "Adelaide," she continued, "do not suck your thumb." Addie jumped back and dropped her hand to her side. "It is not sanitary, and such a habit can deform your teeth." Her voice had taken on a stern, commanding tone.

"Well." Addie's mother sighed. "I'm glad we found someone so quickly. Of course my husband will have to speak to you, too, but I'm sure he'll agree…"

"Oliver Almstead? Of course he will," Maerleen Loegins said. Addie's mother looked surprised. "I spoke to him at some length this morning, Mrs. Almstead, just before coming over here. He told me that Professor Eberhardt's recommendation was good enough for him, but that he would leave any final decision to you."

"Well." Addie picked up the uncertain tone in her mother's voice. "I suppose… I'll show you the room. I hope…well, it isn't very large."

"That is quite all right," Maerleen Loegins said. "Except for a few books I must fetch from Professor Eberhardt's house, everything else I need is in here." She gestured at her suitcase.

The twins, Gail and Gary, whimpered from their room at the back of the house. As Mrs. Almstead led Maerleen Loegins toward the stairway, the two began to shriek. "Somebody sounds distressed," Maerleen Loegins said, pronouncing the word "dee-stressed."

"Oh, dear." Addie saw her mother look as though she was going to start fluttering around the house again. "Adelaide, would you mind showing Maerleen upstairs? I've got to heat up bottles for the twins." Before Addie could say anything, her mother had left her standing in the hallway by the stairs.

"Uh, just follow me." Addie led Maerleen Loegins to the narrow staircase and climbed the steps, with the woman just behind her. "That's Dad's study." She waved a hand at the closed door at the top of the stairway. "He likes some place quiet when he's home. Sometimes, when the twins are crying a lot, he even sleeps up here." Maerleen Loegins gazed at the door with a fierce look in her eyes that made Addie feel that she had said the wrong thing. "He's...he's..." Addie shook her head, not wanting to say that sometimes her father would come home with a scowl on his face and go straight to his study without saying anything to anybody. With his weekend job for an insurance company, and going to his labs and classes at the university, she didn't see all that much of him even when he was home. The only money he had was from selling insurance and from something called the G.I. Bill, which made Addie see a duck waddling toward her with a piece of paper in its bill, a sheet like the ones with numbers on them that her parents often got in the mail.

"Perhaps he needs some peace and quiet while studying," Maerleen Loegins said.

"We're not so noisy. Cyril and I aren't, anyway. Gail and Gary cry a lot, but they're only babies, and anyway you can't hear them from upstairs that much." Already Addie heard the sound of tuneless humming coming from the room at the end of the short hallway. Cyril did that sometimes, sat in their room humming and staring at the walls for hours at a stretch. She turned away from her father's study and gestured at the door on her right. "And that's your room."

Maerleen Loegins went to the door, pushed it open, and went inside, with Addie just behind her. The room had a single bed covered with a quilt, a small night table and lamp, a worn red rug, and a window hung with white cloth curtains that Addie's mother had made from sheets. Addie had wanted the room for herself, small as it was, instead of having to share a bedroom with Cyril.

"You like it?" Addie asked.

"I think it will do very nicely." Maerleen Loegins set her suitcase down by the bed. "And now you may show me your room."

Addie led her into the hall. The door to the large front room was open. The tuneless humming broke off. A small shadowy form appeared in the open doorway.

"Cyril," Addie said, "this is Maerleen Loegins. She's going to be staying with us." She wondered if Cyril would just stand there and stare at the floor, run back into the room to huddle in the corner, or start shrieking and banging his head against the wall.

"May-er-leen," Cyril mumbled.

Maerleen Loegins said, "How do you do, Cyril." Her voice was softer. Cyril backed away from them as they followed him into the room. Although he was almost six, two years younger than Addie, he was nearly as tall as she was, with hair so blond that it was almost white. He gazed past them with his pale blue eyes, then shuffled to one side.

"Strawberry birdies," he said as he plopped down on the floor. "Over there." He pointed at the wall behind them.

Addie turned, knowing what she would see. On the green surface of the sunlit wall, two rows of shadows shaped like miniature cars crawled across the wall, one row upside down, the other right side up.

"That's them," Addie said, pointing at the shadows. "That's what he calls them, strawberry birdies." She didn't know how Cyril had come up with that name, but he had his own names for a lot of things. The dogwood tree in the back yard of their next door neighbors, the Meyers, was a "brahbee" and the cribs Gail and Gary slept in were "brangbugs."

Maerleen Loegins watched the shadows for a bit, stepped over to the three front windows to look outside, then came back and sat down on the floor next to Cyril. "How often do you see them?" she asked.

Cyril shook his head.

"In the afternoon," Addie said, "when it's sunny. That's the only time we ever see them."

"Do you know what they are?" Maerleen Loegins said. Cyril did not reply. "Those little cars are reflections from the roof just outside your windows, the flat roof over your front porch."

"Cars?" Cyril said.

"Cars like the ones going by outside. The tin surface of the roof picks up the images and projects them onto the wall."

Cyril gazed at the silhouettes in silence. He would, Addie knew, keep staring at them until the shadows grew fuzzier and finally faded away. Maerleen Loegins touched him lightly on the back; he leaned into her as she looped her arm around him, surprising Addie. Cyril hated having strangers, or even people he knew, get too close to him; she had expected him to shrink back or push the woman away.

She trudged toward her bed and sat down on the pink coverlet, gazing resentfully at Cyril's bed on the other side of the room. Their father had promised to put a partition across the middle of the room, leaving two front windows for her, one for Cyril, and a clear path to the door for both of them, but he hadn't put a divider in yet and would be even busier when school started, so maybe he would never get around to that. It wouldn't be like having her own room anyway, even with a partition. Now she wished again that Cyril would go away, that their parents would send him to one of those places where, according to her mother's friends, children like Cyril were better off, and then felt shame at the thought.

Maerleen Loegins looked toward her and smiled. "Adelaide," she said, "you do not like to watch the shadows?"

Addie liked her smile, and that she had called the images on the wall "shadows" instead of "strawberry birdies," but didn't like being called by her full first name. "Call me Addie."

"Addie?"

"All my friends call me Addie. It's just Mom and other grownups who call me Adelaide."

"Then Addie it will be."

"What are you called? Are you a miss or a missus?" Addie's parents had always told her to use last names for adults who weren't relatives.

"Just call me Maerleen."

"Okay." Addie smiled. Maybe it was better to have somebody like Maerleen Loegins living here than to have her own room.

* * * *

Addie and Cyril played with the newspaper, which Cyril had brought up to their room after breakfast, while Maerleen went to her room to unpack. Addie had wanted to see what she would pull from her suitcase, but Maerleen had squinted at her in a way that said she wanted to be left alone.

"Ike," Cyril said as he tore the front page from the paper; Addie recognized the smiling face of President Eisenhower in the photo. "Ike," Cyril said again as he folded the paper into an airplane, while Addie wondered if he had somehow learned to read and was hiding it.

"I like Ike," Cyril said.

If Cyril knew how to read, even a little, he was ready for school. Maybe his head-banging, wild shrieks, and long frozen silences were only an act, so he could skip school and stay home to do whatever he wanted.

"Adelaide! Cyril!" Their mother was calling to them. "Your father's home!" Cyril dropped his paper airplane and shuffled toward the hallway, Addie at his heels. Maerleen stood outside the door to her room.

"Dad's home," Addie said to Maerleen. "That means it's almost time for supper."

"Follow me," Cyril said, the "me" exploding from his mouth as he marched toward the stairs, swinging his arms.

* * * *

Cyril ate his tuna noodle casserole in silence, shoveling it into his mouth with a spoon without either playing with his food or staring at it until their mother had to feed it to him herself. Addie peered at their father as they ate. He looked more tired than usual and was silent as their mother discussed the household duties with Maerleen. She would help with caring for the twins, look after all of the children whenever their parents were out, and do some of the dusting and vacuuming.

After supper, Mr. Almstead retreated upstairs to his study, Cyril wandered off to the living room, and Addie helped her mother and Maerleen clear the dishes from the table. Even though the kitchen windows were open to the evening air, the air inside was hot and oppressive. By the time they had stacked the dishes in the sink, the twins were crying again.

"Better check Gail and Gary," Mrs. Almstead murmured, looking even more flustered than she usually did. "Sounds like their diapers need changing."

"I shall be happy to help," Maerleen said.

Mrs. Almstead wiped her forehead with the back of a hand. "Adelaide, go keep an eye on your brother."

Addie headed through the dining room toward the front of the house. Cyril sat on the living room rug staring at the television. The sound was off; blurry black-and-white images danced on the screen. He would just sit there until he got tired enough to go to bed.

She went upstairs, wishing that Leslie Vicks was back from summer camp. She could have gone to Leslie's house to watch television, or else Leslie could have come here to sit on the front porch and spy on any neighbors out for a walk or sitting around on their own porches. Leslie always told stories about the neighbors, even if she probably made most of them up. Old Mrs. Merkel would give you the evil eye if you took a shortcut through her back yard. Leslie suspected that the young blonde woman who had just moved into the apartment on the second floor of Mr. and Mrs. Smith's house was a secret Communist spy, maybe because she had a weird accent or maybe because Leslie's favorite television show was *I Led Three Lives*. She had a crush on the actor who played the undercover FBI guy, who was always dealing with scary Communists who talked about liquidating people; Addie would imagine somebody slowly dissolving into a puddle of water. She wondered what kinds of stories Leslie might think up about Maerleen Loegins.

The door to her father's study was open. Both his desk and the cot under the window were covered with books and papers. She crept toward the door and stood there until her father looked up from his desk. "Addie? Something wrong?"

She shook her head.

He beckoned at her with his cigarette. "Come on in, then."

She shuffled toward him. "How long is Maerleen Loegins going to be here?" she asked.

"I asked her if she could stay with us at least until next summer. If Cyril's ready for…" He fell silent. "Depending on how things go, we'll see what happens after that." He stubbed out the cigarette in the ashtray on his desk, already filled with a mound of butts and ashes. "You like Maerleen, don't you?"

Addie nodded.

"I barely know her, but Morey Eberhardt has nothing but good things to say about her, and she'll be a big help to your mother. Things have been harder for her since the twins came." Addie thought of what it had been like just after Christmas, when her mother had disappeared from the house and come back a while later without her huge belly and with two new babies. Grandma Lohmann had taken the train from New York City to come and stay with them and had not left until February; all that time Addie had known that everybody was worrying about her mother. Having the twins was hard; her mother had not been her usual self. Sometimes she would burst into tears for no reason at all. Now she fluttered around and sometimes snapped at Addie, but at least she didn't cry.

Her father suddenly reached for her and pulled her onto his lap. "You're a good kid, Addie," he said, and she wondered why he was telling her that. "Never a complaint out of you. You'll be a big help to Maerleen, won't you."

"Sure."

"Things'll be different when I'm out of grad school. They'll be a lot better. You'll see." She had heard him say that to her mother only a few nights ago. "Things'll be better," he had said to her. "It'll be easier on you, too." Addie had overheard them from inside the bathroom.

"But you love teaching," her mother had told him.

"Not enough money in it, not with four kids, not with Cyril—" He had sounded angry for a moment.

"But you always said you never wanted to work on weapons research," her mother had said then.

"Maybe I can't afford to be that choosy."

Her father let go. Addie slipped from his lap. "Good night," he said, which was the signal that he wanted to be left alone. She left the room and closed the door behind her.

* * * *

Addie was in bed, and her father had retreated downstairs, by the time Maerleen came upstairs with Cyril. Addie sat up, arms draped over her knees, while Maerleen took off Cyril's t-shirt and pants and helped him into his pajamas.

"Did he give you a lot of trouble about brushing his teeth?" Addie asked.

Cyril shook his head violently.

"No, he did not," Maerleen said.

"Good about the emp, too," Cyril muttered.

Maerleen leaned closer to him. "What's an emp?" Addie asked, thinking it had to be another of her brother's made-up words.

"Maerleen put one in. Here." Cyril put his hand on the back of his head near his neck.

Maerleen said, "I did no such thing."

"Yes you did."

"I smoothed back your hair. That is all." Addie glimpsed the fierce look in her brown eyes before she turned away. "Now be quiet and behave yourself." Maerleen tucked him into bed and turned out the light on his night table. "Good night, Addie and Cyril."

"G'night," Addie mumbled.

"Sleep tight," Cyril said in a singsong voice. "Don't let the bedbugs bite."

Maerleen disappeared into the darkness of the hallway, leaving their door open as their mother always did, because Cyril was afraid to go to sleep with the door closed. Addie heard a soft click and knew that Maerleen had closed her own door.

She lay there, listening to the sound of people talking, punctuated by the occasional muted blare of a trombone. Her father was watching television, as he sometimes did before going to bed. Usually the indistinct sounds soothed her into sleep, but she lay there, awake, turning over on her stomach and then onto her side before the sounds abruptly died.

Her father had gone to bed, Cyril's rhythmic deep breaths told her that he was asleep, and yet she was still awake. That must be because of Maerleen, because someone new and strange was in their house.

Addie sat up, slipped from her bed, and tiptoed toward the doorway. There was a sliver of light at the bottom of Maerleen's closed door.

She went into the hall, expecting Maerleen to fling her door open at any second. She could always say that she was going downstairs to the bathroom. Somebody was talking behind the closed door; it had to be Maerleen, but why would she be talking if she was in the room all by herself?

Addie crept to the door and pressed her ear against it.

"…sez dee fond hem." Maerleen was almost whispering the words. "Empsen, but…neh." There was a long silence, as if she was listening to somebody on a telephone, and then, "Bay."

Addie scurried back to her room, then peered around the doorway.

There was no telephone in the room, so if Maerleen was talking to somebody when nobody was there, maybe she had some kind of secret radio device, something that a spy might use. But what would a spy want with anybody in their house?

Maerleen's door opened. Addie imagined that she would come out in a long coat, even if it was the middle of August, holding a parrot-headed umbrella like the one in the storybook Addie had been reading that afternoon. Instead, she came out in a long white bathrobe and headed for the stairs. Addie waited until her shadowy shape had disappeared below the railing along the stairwell, then followed her. Probably only going to the bathroom, she thought as she crept down the stairs, disappointed. She reached the downstairs hallway just as the front door opened.

Maerleen went outside, closing the screened door behind her but leaving the other door open. Her bathrobe was a luminescent bluish-white in the moonlight. Addie held her breath as she crept toward the doorway.

Maerleen stood on the porch, looking toward the street. A man in a pale sports jacket, a floppy dark bow tie, and dark pants stood on the sidewalk, facing the house. Addie froze, even though she was sure he could not see her through the screen. He had a mop of thick white hair, a long, thin face, and held a flat metal object that looked like her father's cigarette case in one hand.

Maerleen lifted an arm and shook her head.

"Tamara," the man called out.

Maerleen shook her head again. "Not now."

"Will see." The man nodded, looked down, and disappeared.

Addie caught her breath. He had just winked out all of a sudden, the way people sometimes did in her dreams. Maybe she wasn't really awake. But he couldn't have disappeared. He had only stepped into the black shadows under the small tree in their front yard, where she couldn't see him.

Maerleen turned toward the door. Addie scurried into the living room and slipped behind the sofa.

Maerleen's pale robe made her look like a ghost as she moved through the hallway. Addie held her breath until she heard creaking sounds from the stairway. Maerleen and the man outside obviously knew each other. Maybe they were in love. Maybe they were spies; that was what Leslie would think.

Addie crept out from behind the sofa. The front door was open. She went to close it and saw that the man was across the street now, his back to her, and then he moved away from the streetlight and disappeared again.

She closed the door and went upstairs slowly, treading lightly on the steps that creaked. She made it to the second floor without making any noise, but as she passed Maerleen's room, heard her voice behind the door.

"…don't know," Maerleen was saying. "Give me more time. Think…" Addie hurried to her room, afraid to hear anything more.

"Addie!" Cyril shouted from his bed.

"Shh!"

"Addie!" he cried out in an even louder voice.

"Shut up," she whispered. "You'll wake up Maerleen." She got into bed and pulled up the top sheet.

"She won't hear me," Cyril said in a soft, calm voice that did not sound at all like his. "And she's already awake. I heard her."

"Be quiet."

He did not say anything else. She lay there, counting her breaths, which made more sense to her than counting sheep, and at last fell asleep.

* * * *

Leslie Vicks said, "I think she's weird." Leslie had come home from camp the day before and had just met Maerleen a little while ago.

Addie sat on the front steps of her house with Leslie and Bobby Renfrew. Erastus, the Meyers' orange-furred cat, had wandered over from next door and was stretched out on the step next to Bobby. Cyril was behind them on the porch playing with Lincoln Logs; he had already put together a ranch house and a stagecoach station.

"She's okay," Bobby protested.

Leslie leaned toward Addie. Her brown hair was longer, and her bangs came down to her eyes. "I think she's up to something," Leslie whispered. "Maybe she's a spy."

Addie looked around uneasily, even though Maerleen had left right after meeting Leslie to spend the afternoon at the Hayes University library. At least that was where she had told Addie's mother she was going, but maybe she was meeting that man she had spoken to from the porch two nights ago. Maybe they were climbing the hills of the Hayes University campus to look at the gorges, or having a picnic in the park near Delphi College.

"I said maybe she's a spy," Leslie repeated. "A Red spy, from Russia."

Addie waited for Bobby to tell Leslie she was silly, with all her talk about spies. Instead he said, "Maybe a spy would come here."

"To Delphi?" Addie snorted. "Why would a spy come to Delphi?"

"I wasn't talking just about the town, I meant your house."

"Why would a spy come to my house?"

"Because your dad's a scientist," Bobby replied, "and scientists know stuff, like how to make A-bombs."

"Dad's still in school," Addie said. "He isn't a scientist yet."

Bobby squinted at her through his glasses. "But he wants to be one, doesn't he? That's what he's studying, and there's a couple of profs at Hayes who worked on the A-bomb, aren't there? Maybe the Commies want to get them on their side."

"That's silly," Addie said, but Bobby might be on to something. His father had joined the Army and died in Korea, so Bobby had good reason to worry about Commies, and his mother had a job at the town library and was always bringing books home for him to read. He was smart; he knew more than she did, anyway, with all his reading, which made her feel that she had to at least consider whatever he said.

"Maerleen isn't a Commie," Cyril said behind them.

"I didn't say it," Bobby said, "Leslie did."

"Did not." Leslie scowled. "I said maybe she was a spy."

Cyril said, "She's not a spy, neither."

Addie turned to look at her brother. He didn't sound like himself, and now he was staring right at Leslie as if he actually saw her, instead of looking down or away from her.

"How do you know?" Leslie said. "How could *you* know?"

"I just know." Cyril shrugged. "She showed me another strawberry birdie this morning."

That was impossible, Addie thought; they only saw those on the wall in the afternoon.

"She said she came down a thread looking for me," Cyril continued, "and it took a long time but she found me, and then she showed me the strawberry birdie, and then we went downstairs and she went out."

Leslie snickered. "Strawberry birdies."

"Don't make fun of him," Bobby said.

"She sounds funny when she talks. She sure doesn't sound like an American." Leslie stood up. "Let's go to my house." She waved an arm at Addie. "Come on."

Addie did not move.

"You just gonna sit there with Bobby and that stupid cat and your retard brother?"

"Don't call him a retard," Bobby said.

"Well?" Leslie put her hands on her hips. "Are you coming?"

Addie shook her head, not trusting herself to speak. Leslie stomped toward the sidewalk, looked back over her shoulder, then ran down the street.

"She's mad," Bobby said as he scratched Erastus behind the ears. The orange cat hunkered down, resting his head on his front paws. "But she won't stay mad."

Addie said, "I don't know about that. Anyway, she shouldn't have said that about Cyril."

Bobby got up. "Wanna go to Capetti's?" Capetti's Haven, a store that sold candy, paperbacks, and comic books, was one of Bobby's favorite places.

"Can't. Mom told me to keep an eye on Cyril."

"Bring him along, then."

She glanced at her brother. He seemed all right now, but he might start acting up if they went downtown, she'd have to watch him whenever they crossed the street, and she didn't feel like walking the three blocks to Capetti's just to hang around while Bobby looked at all the *Tales from the Crypt* comics his mom would not allow him to read at home.

"Nah," she said. "We better stay here."

Bobby shrugged, then hurried toward the sidewalk and down the street. Addie gazed after him until he disappeared around the corner. "You told Leslie you saw a strawberry birdie this morning," she said, "but you couldn't have."

"I did too. Maerleen showed it to me." Cyril took the ranch house of Lincoln Logs apart and put the pieces carefully back into the box, then pushed the stagecoach station under the porch swing. "Wasn't like the other strawberry birdies."

"What do you mean?"

"There was this big grey building like a church but with sand all around it, and these little tiny people standing on the steps in front, and next to that was this big long building with this big loop pointing up at the sky." He made a swooping motion with his arms. "And yesterday she showed one with all this water with patches of red stuff all over and some buildings sticking up out of the water."

"Another strawberry birdie? When?"

"Yesterday. She said something about it showing where she came from, but I didn't see any people."

He was making it up. But Cyril didn't make things up. He used funny names for things, but he did not tell stories that weren't true.

"Ask her," Cyril said. "She'll tell you." He pointed across the street. "There she is."

Maerleen stood on the other side of the street, in the yellow shirt-waist dress she had been wearing that morning. She stuffed something into her handbag, then crossed the street. Addie wondered why she had not noticed her standing there before.

"Go ahead," Cyril said as Maerleen reached the sidewalk in front of their house. "Ask her."

"Cyril says you showed him a strawberry birdie this morning," Addie called out as Maerleen approached them. "And he says it wasn't anything like the little car shadows, that he saw people and sand and a big long building with a loop, and yesterday you showed him another place and said—"

"Why did you tell that to your sister?" Maerleen glanced from Addie to Cyril.

"Because it's true." He crouched down and crawled toward the porch swing.

"What did you show him?" Addie asked.

"Think of them as being like your moving pictures," Maerleen said, "except that they are not showing images of a made-up story. They are showing something that has…that will happen."

"Maerleen?"

Addie looked up. Her mother stood behind the screen door, dressed in the sleeveless white shirt and baggy blue shorts she wore only at home. "I thought you were going to the library," she continued.

"I have finished my research there."

"Then maybe you could take Adelaide and Cyril to the park. I'd rather have them playing there than watching television here. Just keep them away from the pool." Their mother was afraid they might catch polio if they swam in the park pool.

"Then you do not need me here?" Maerleen said.

"Gail and Gary are asleep, so I'm going to take a nap." Mrs. Almstead wiped her forehead with one hand. "It's too hot to do anything else. Just bring them back by suppertime." She retreated into the darkness, leaving the door behind the screen door open.

"Then we shall go to the park," Maerleen said.

Addie did not want to go to the park, especially if they could not swim in the pool. By now the older boys would be hogging all the swings, the slides, and the jungle gym, while the girls just sat around and watched them.

Cyril put away the rest of his Lincoln Logs, tucked the box under his arm, and stood up. All he would do at the park was play with his Lincoln Logs. She couldn't go anywhere without her brother tagging along and doing something weird that made other kids laugh at him. Her face flamed. She suddenly wanted to hit him and wished he would go away and never come back.

"Adelaide," Maerleen said.

"It's Addie!" she shouted.

"Addie, why do you look so angry?"

Cyril widened his eyes. She was suddenly ashamed of her anger. "There's nothing to do at the park," she mumbled.

"Perhaps we should go there anyway," Maerleen said, "and find out what there is to do."

Addie stood up and shoved her hands into the pockets of her shorts. Erastus padded up the steps and curled up under the porch swing. Cyril looked down at the box under his arm, then put it on top of one of the wicker chairs.

"Come on, children." Maerleen slung the strap of her handbag over her shoulder; Cyril grabbed her left hand. "Come *on*." Addie felt fingers grip her right hand tightly. They were suddenly moving toward the sidewalk; Addie scurried to keep up with Maerleen, who kept glancing behind herself with a worried look on her face.

They turned right, in the direction of the park. A red Chevrolet convertible sped past them, followed by a green Pontiac station wagon, and then the street was empty of traffic. As they came to the small bridge a block from their house, Maerleen let go of Addie's hand, fumbled with her handbag, and pulled out a flat silvery object. The familiar bridge seemed to flicker and then disappeared. For a moment, all Addie saw was a distant patch of light at the end of a dark tunnel. Her stomach lurched and then, all at once, they were standing in the park next to the jungle gym.

"Here we are," Maerleen said.

But this couldn't be their park. The jungle gym was rusty, several bars were missing, and the rest of the structure looked as though it would fall apart if she tried to climb on any of the bars. All of the grass was dry and yellow, with sandy patches, even though it had been green and in need of mowing just the other day, while the swings and the slides had disappeared. The pool was gone, replaced by a broken-up pit of rubble, and the brick building next to the park was only a couple of walls of reddish rock. On the other side of the street, she no longer saw the gray house with the turret and the big white house with the wraparound front porch, but instead a high metallic wall. They were the only people in the park; she wondered why no other kids were around.

"What happened?" Addie asked. "How did you do that?" The air was strange, too, so hot and thick and sticky that sweat was already dripping from her bangs onto her face. "This doesn't look like our park."

"But it is," Maerleen replied.

"But why—"

"No one lives near here now," Maerleen said, "but it is the park."

"I don't understand."

"It is the park as I know it…as I will know it, as it will be."

"I still don't understand."

"It is what the park will be a long time from now."

"I don't like it," Addie said.

"My life and the lives of those like me are not easy lives," Maerleen said. "We did not inherit what we might have had, but even so, our lives might have been much worse. We might not have lived at all."

Cyril's face was slick with sweat. He leaned against Maerleen. She put an arm over his shoulders. He was different when he was with her—quieter, able to look into her face, not shoving her away when she reached out to him.

Maerleen's eyes widened; she suddenly looked afraid. Addie turned her head and saw a man on the other side of the park, standing near a metal pole. He wore a red and white striped jacket, white pants, and a straw hat with a wide brim. The man took off his hat, revealing a head of thick white hair.

Maerleen said, "I did not think he would follow us here."

"Who is he?" Addie asked, not wanting to admit that she had seen him before during Maerleen's first night in their home.

"A colleague. A companion." The man walked toward them. "Not yet," Maerleen called out to him.

"Then when?" he shouted back. "Why ya here? Ya supposed to…" and then came a stream of strange words. Addie made out only a few: "Shouldn't." "Boy." "Long time." "Waiting." He kept glancing at Cyril, and Addie had the feeling that they were talking about her brother. Maerleen stepped toward him; the man took a step back. "What are you waiting for?" Addie understood his words now.

"It does not matter how long I wait," Maerleen said.

The man smiled. "No, it doesn't, not to us, but it does to them." He waved an arm at Addie. "Keep waiting, move up and down the threads like you been doing, and you complicate things, you change too much stuff, you mess things up." She could understand all of his words now, even if she didn't know what they meant.

Maerleen put a hand on Addie's shoulder. "I cannot leave the girl to her unhappiness, to torment herself after what must happen. If we could only—"

The man glared at Addie. "Keep delaying, and it's worse for her, too."

"What are you talking about?" Addie asked.

"See, we came here to get something," the man replied, "and when that something, or someone, isn't here any more, it changes things." He was speaking very slowly now. "Things happen that wouldn't have happened, and things don't happen that would have happened otherwise. That's one way to put it, but maybe a better way is just to say that Maerleen came here to get something we need, and the longer she takes to get it, the more complicated things get."

"You are not very good at such explanations," Maerleen said, "and there is no need to confuse these children with them."

"There's no need for you to keep delaying."

Maerleen's fingers dug into Addie's shoulder. "But to leave her behind, to know she will not be—"

"You can't take her with you."

Don't talk to strangers. Dad had told her that many times. Don't talk to strangers and look out for your brother. This man had to count as a stranger even if Maerleen knew him, and Addie could tell that she was afraid of the man.

Maerleen grabbed Addie's hand. Everything lurched around them; Addie suddenly wanted to throw up. The jungle gym rippled, as if she was looking at it through water, then took shape as she remembered it, with shiny, unrusted bars. Her nausea eased as she breathed in some of the drier, cooler air. The park still didn't look right; the slides were farther away from the jungle gym and there were only six swings instead of seven. Except for a couple of older kids in swimsuits over by the pool, probably the lifeguards, the park was empty of people.

Addie trembled. Her legs gave way under her and she suddenly found herself sitting on the grass. "What happened?" she whispered.

"We went to the park," Maerleen said, "and my friend followed us there." Her voice was shaky. "But now we have to go home because, as you see, it's almost time for supper."

"Almos' time for supper," Cyril repeated.

"It can't be," Addie muttered. "We only just left the house." But the park wasn't as bright with sunlight as it usually was in the afternoon, and across the street a man and a woman were sitting at a table on the screened-in porch of the big white house.

She did not remember seeing a screen around that porch before. She looked up. "What's going on?" she asked.

Maerleen's face was pale. She bit at her lower lip.

"Look," Cyril said. "A strawberry birdie." He pointed across the street, at the gray house with the turret. A picture like one they might have seen at the movie theater appeared on the front of the house, near the front steps, and then sharpened into the rusty jungle gym from the deserted park they had just left. The white-haired man in the striped jacket stood next to the jungle gym, holding his straw hat over his chest.

The man waved his hat at them and then the image slowly faded away. "No," Maerleen said under her breath. She took Addie's hand, clutching her fingers so hard that it hurt, and led the children away from the park.

* * * *

Addie's father hurried across the bridge toward them, with a worried look on his face. "Figured I'd better come looking for you," he said to Maerleen as he reached down to hug Addie.

"I am sorry we are late," Maerleen said.

"Aren't that late, but their mother was getting worried."

"Can't be that late," Addie said as they crossed the bridge. "We weren't gone that long." But it was already getting dark, with cars parked on both sides of the street and in driveways, as they were when people were home from work. "We went to the park, except it was different, with—" Maerleen's hand squeezed hers, hard.

"Saw a strawberry birdie," Cyril murmured.

"Thought you only saw them on the wall in your room," Mr. Almstead said.

"Saw one at the park," Cyril said.

"You did not," Maerleen said. Her voice sounded funny, as if she felt bad about telling the lie.

"Did too, on the side of that big house."

Maerleen said, "You just imagined that you did."

"Didn't."

Addie's father halted. "Exactly what did you see?" he asked.

"A man," Cyril replied. "Maerleen talked to him in the park. Saw him in the park and in the strawberry birdie on the house."

"What man?" Now their father sounded really upset. "Have I met him?"

"He is a friend," Maerleen said in her shaky nervous-sounding voice. "You do not know him. He waved to us at the park, that is all."

"You'll have to bring him around sometime," Mr. Almstead said. "Sarah and I should meet him if—"

"He was in the strawberry birdie!" Cyril shrieked.

"Cyril!" Now her father sounded angry. Addie was afraid to look up at him. She caught a glimpse of Maerleen's face; she was biting her lip again. Addie was torn; if she admitted that Cyril was telling the truth, their father might get even more upset. Don't talk to strangers; he had told them that so many times. You have to look out for your brother, he doesn't know how to look out for himself. She had failed to look out for him today, and if she told her father that Maerleen had let them talk to a stranger, one who seemed kind of scary, maybe he would send her away from their house for good.

"I saw him!" Cyril screamed. "In the strawberry birdie!" Across the street, Mrs. Smith stood on her front steps, shaking her head.

Addie said, "I didn't see him."

"He was right there!" her brother shouted.

"He only waved at us!" Tears stung Addie's eyes. "And I didn't see your strawberry birdie!"

Mr. Almstead reached for Cyril, then backed away and thrust his hands into his pockets, looking bewildered.

Maerleen said, "Be quiet," and put her hand on the back of Cyril's head. He seemed about to twist away, then suddenly stood still; his pale eyes stared past Addie, as if he could not see her.

"Cyril," Addie said. She had been waiting for him to throw himself onto the sidewalk, or run shrieking down the street.

"How did you do that?" her father asked.

Maerleen drew away from Cyril. "How did I do what?"

"Calm him down like that." He shook his head. "You've got the magic touch." He frowned. "Now that I think of it, he's been behaving a lot better since you've been with us."

Maerleen could take good care of Cyril, Addie thought. That was what mattered, more than admitting the truth to her father.

"Emp," Cyril said. "Emp," he said in a louder voice.

"Don't you mean ump?" Mr. Almstead said. "In baseball, it's an ump. Were some kids playing baseball at the park?"

"Ump," Cyril said, shaking his head. Maerleen looked down.

Their house looked different this evening, its stucco surface more yellow than beige, and somebody had moved one of the wicker chairs off the porch. A cat with ginger and white fur was stretched out on one of the front steps. Mrs. Almstead paced across the porch, hands jammed into the pockets of baggy khaki shorts; she looked up, seemed about to run toward them, then waved and went inside.

"Mr. Almstead," Maerleen murmured, "I am sorry. Please be assured that I want only what is best for your children."

"I don't doubt it," Addie's father replied. "Anyway, I'm not about to make a federal case about your being a bit late bringing the kids home."

"Thank you," Maerleen whispered.

* * * *

The night air outside the bedroom window was cooler, a reminder that autumn was coming. Addie sat by the window next to Cyril, her hands folded under her chin and resting on the sill. Behind them, Maerleen shook out a quilt and laid it over Addie's bed.

A patch of light appeared at the edge of the roof outside the window and grew into a bright pale blue square. The white-haired man, dressed in a white jacket and blue pants this time, stood inside the square.

A hand clutched Addie's shoulder. "Go away," Maerleen said behind her.

"Not until you do what you were sent here to do," the man replied.

"Go away," Maerleen said. Her other hand rested on Cyril's back.

The square dissolved. The man took a step toward them, then winked out.

"Strawberry birdie gone," Cyril said. His voice was steady. He pulled away from Maerleen and stood up.

"What's going on?" Addie whispered, afraid.

Maerleen knelt next to her. "You want what's best for your brother, don't you?"

"Sure."

"So do I. That is why I am here, to do what is best for your brother and for many other people as well."

"Then do it," a voice said from the doorway. Addie jumped to her feet and turned to face the white-haired man. "Stop dithering."

"How did you get in here?" Addie asked.

"That's for me to know and you never to find out." The man held a flat silver case like the one Maerleen had carried around that afternoon; he quickly slipped it into a jacket pocket. "It's time." He chuckled, as if he had said something funny.

"You better go," Addie said, "or my dad'll call the police."

"Your father's in the kitchen having another drink with your mother, who's whining to him about how tired she is and how are they ever going to make it with all you kids and with Cyril the way he is while your father keeps telling her it'll all work out somehow."

Cyril squinted at the man.

"And in a few moments, your parents will go to bed and fall asleep, because your mother is exhausted and your father's had too much to drink. I went up this thread and checked on that before I ducked back here. But if Maerleen doesn't do what she's supposed to do, everything isn't going to be all right. It's not going to work out for Cyril and your mother and your father and you, and maybe not for a whole lot of other people, either. She's already off the thread we started on, and if she keeps moving across more threads—"

"You have no business saying that in front of these children," Maerleen said, and Addie saw the fury in her dark eyes.

"What's going on?" Addie whispered. She grabbed at Maerleen's sleeve. Her legs shook and she sat down, hard. "What's he talking about?"

The man stepped back into the darkness of the hallway; only his white jacket and hair were visible. "It's up to you," he said, and the white hair and jacket vanished.

"Maerleen," Addie said.

"It is all right. Allow me to ask you a question. Do you want what is best for your family, for your brother? Do you know what his life will be if I do not intervene?"

Addie turned toward Cyril. He sat down and stared out the window, ignoring her.

"I will tell you. He will eventually need to go away from your home to another place. He will not be able to make use of his gifts, his special talents. He will have to go away, and then your father will not become what he might have been. He will give up his studies and his teaching and take other work to support his family and to pay for Cyril's care. I was not able to see clearly what happens to him after that, only indications that his life would be unhappy and he would be working at what he hates but doing well at his work in spite of that. He and those working with him will bring about a catastrophe—a disaster, a war. This thread will snap, and those near it will also snap, more threads than would have been lost otherwise. That is what I am trying to prevent."

Addie shook her head, confused.

"But if Cyril goes away with me," Maerleen said, "his life will be better and so will your father's. At first, things will not be so good. Your father will be angry and worried, your mother upset and despairing. They will notify your police and search for both of us. When we are not found, they will sorrow for a while, but that will pass."

She could not know anything like that, Addie thought. Nobody could know such things. She was making it all up.

"Eventually your father will find solace in his work, in teaching the young. Your mother will rear her other children and find a purpose of her own. This thread will not break. And Cyril will have a life with us, one in which he can use his gifts instead of having them wasted."

What about me, Addie thought; Mom and Dad will blame me. They would be angry with her for not looking out for Cyril. She thought of all the times she had wished him gone, had hoped they would send him away, had longed for her own room and not having to watch out for him. They would know that she wanted him to go away, so they would be right to blame her. She was suddenly sorry for all the times she had hoped for Cyril just to disappear.

She could not let Maerleen take him. That was the only way she could make up for all of her hateful thoughts.

"What did you do to my brother?" she asked. "What's an emp?"

"It is a small thing, a device that dampens certain of his senses so that he—" Maerleen sighed. "It helps him. Without it, he would be overwhelmed by what he sees and hears and senses."

"Then why does he have to go away if you can make him better with that?"

"Because he will need more than an emp, and he will not get what he needs if he continues to live along this thread. He will not be able to use his gifts. Your father will also not do what he should do. Cyril must go with me."

This could not be happening. "You can't take him away. You can't."

Maerleen leaned toward Cyril and took his hand, pulling him to his feet. "Come with me."

"No." Addie threw herself at the woman. "Leave him alone!"

"Adelaide—"

"You can't have him!"

Maerleen let go of Cyril, grabbed Addie under her arms, and threw her onto her bed. Addie lay there, too shocked to move, as Maerleen reached for her brother again. Her left hand closed around his wrist; she held her flat silver case in her right. An opening appeared in the wall, revealing grey stone steps that led to a tall glassy door.

"Strawberry birdie," Cyril said.

Maerleen said, "I am sorry."

"You can't take him!" Addie forced herself up and flung herself at the two of them. She held on to Cyril, trying to pull him away, and then felt Maerleen's arm around her shoulders. The floor heaved under them; Addie felt sick and squeezed her eyes shut, afraid she might throw up.

The ground under her feel was still. She opened her eyes and saw a glass door. "Maerleen?" Addie whispered.

"It is all right," Maerleen replied. "No one will harm you."

Addie turned to face a barren landscape of sand and rocks that stretched to what looked like giant jagged teeth on the horizon. "I want to go home," Addie said. If Maerleen would only take them both home, she would be good and always look out for Cyril and never again wish that he would be taken away.

As she turned back, the glass door slid open. The white-haired man stood in front of them. "Ya know what ya done?" he shouted. "Do you know?" he said more quietly.

"I know," Maerleen said.

"She can't stay here and she can't go back down that thread to where she was, not now."

"I know."

"Then why did you bring her here? Why did you let her—"

"She does not deserve what would have happened to her where… *when* she was. There would have been no forgiveness for her. Even if her parents had believed she did nothing wrong, she would always have carried the blame inside herself." Maerleen knelt next to Addie. "Your brother will be well cared for here. You believe me, do you not?"

Addie nodded, forcing herself to believe it in spite of the desolation outside the glass door.

"Then you must go back now, but all by yourself."

Addie swallowed. "But he said—" She pointed at the man. "He said—I thought—"

"Do not think of what he said. Turn around."

Addie turned to her right to see a hallway with walls that seemed made of mist. She could barely make out the room at the other end of the hallway, but it appeared to have windows like the ones in her bedroom.

Maerleen said, "You must walk down that passage, now."

"Will you ever come back?" Her eyes were tearing up. "Will you bring Cyril back home, just for a little while—"

"Go." A hand pushed her forward. She stumbled into the passage. The windows rushed at her as she slid down the hallway, unable to stop herself. She rolled onto the floor, righted herself, and got to her feet.

Cyril and Maerleen were only tiny blurred images on the wall, standing at the end of a tunnel, and then they winked out.

* * * *

At last Addie got up and stumbled toward her bed. Tears ran down her face; she could no longer hold them back. Cyril could not be gone; he was downstairs watching television with the sound off or playing on the porch with his Lincoln Logs. She fell across the bed, unable to stop crying. Dimly, outside the windows, she heard the sound of a car driving by, and then a voice that sounded like Bobby Renfrew's calling out to somebody else.

She wiped her eyes. It had been night only a little while ago, and now there was sunlight outside her windows. She sat up and looked across the room. Cyril's bed was gone, and in its place stood a small bookcase and a painted chest of drawers.

"Cyril," she whispered, and then saw that the green bedroom walls were now yellow. This isn't my room, she thought, suddenly frightened;

Maerleen had sent her somewhere else. She sank to the floor and put her hands over her eyes. She was dreaming; that had to be what was happening. All she had to do was wake up and everything would be the way it was.

"Addie?"

She turned her head. Her father stood in the doorway, his tie loosened, his jacket draped over one arm. "I could have sworn—" He shook his head. "Came up to look for you a few minutes ago, and you weren't here. How'd you get past me?"

She did not know what to say. For a moment, she had the feeling that someone else was in the room with her and her father. "I was here all the time," she said, although that wasn't what she had meant to say. Maerleen took us both away, but she brought me back. That was what she wanted to say. She struggled to recall what the woman had said to her.

He frowned. "What's the matter? Is something wrong?"

She shook her head. The woman had a strange name, but she couldn't remember what it was.

"Then come on downstairs. Dinner's almost ready." He moved away from the door; she got up and followed him into the hall. The door to the room down the hallway was open; she glanced inside as they passed and saw blue curtains and a Brooklyn Dodgers pennant on the wall.

She darted into the room. A baseball glove sat on top of a dresser, and a pair of sneakers on top of a blue rug. Through the half-open doorway of the small closet, she glimpsed a couple of pairs of pants draped over hangers. This wasn't the way this room should look, she thought, but could not remember what it had looked like before.

"Your brother's downstairs," her father said.

She turned around. "Gary's downstairs," her father continued, "and I hope you're not going to get into a fight with him at dinner. You mother says you two were really going at it this morning."

She ran from the room, pushed past him, and headed for the stairs. Her hand gripped the railing as a boy appeared at the bottom of the stairwell; he pulled off a baseball cap to reveal white-blond hair.

"Cyril," she whispered. But this boy wasn't Cyril. A woman in shorts and a sleeveless white shirt appeared next to the boy; her smile was so open and her gaze so steady that it took Addie a few seconds to recognize her mother.

"Addie," her mother said, "what's the matter?"

Addie stared down at the boy. "You're not Cyril." She tried to remember who Cyril was.

"What are you talking about?" the boy shouted. "I'm Gary, your brother. Or are you too dumb to know?"

"But then what about…" Addie turned toward her father. "What about the twins?"

"What twins?" Her father looked really worried now. Addie took a step toward him, then ran past him back to her room.

She had lost something. She could not escape that thought. Maybe it was still here, somewhere in her room. She dropped to her knees and looked under the bed, but saw only a pair of sandals and a few dust balls. As she stood up, she noticed shadows on the wall. She had seen them so many times before, miniature silhouettes of cars, reflections of the traffic in the street outside her window.

She sat down on her bed and watched the shadows flicker across the yellow wall.

"Addie?" Her mother came into the room, trailed by her father and brother. "Is everything all right?"

She had gone to her room earlier to read; that was coming back to her now. "I'm okay," she replied.

"Are you sure?" her mother continued. "You must have been up here all afternoon."

"I'm fine," Addie insisted. "I was going to read for a while, but I must have fallen asleep." She looked over at the bookcase. She had taken a storybook out of the town library a few days ago; that was the book she had planned to read that afternoon.

Gary made a face at her, screwing up his eyes and sneering. Their father put a hand on his shoulder. "Come on, slugger," he said to the boy. "Might as well head downstairs and wash up before supper." The two retreated down the hallway.

The reflections on the wall had blurred. "Strawberry birdies," Addie said.

"What did you say?" her mother asked.

Addie pointed at the shadows. "Strawberry birdies," she repeated, not knowing where those words came from, but feeling that they fit the shadows somehow. The sense of something lost came over her again and then faded.

Afterword to "Strawberry Birdies"

This story is set in a college town that resembles the Ithaca, New York of my childhood, and the house where Addie and her family live is much like the house my family inhabited. (As a child, I thought of the house as being roomy and was surprised, visiting years later, to see how small it actually was.) That Ithaca of the 1950s seemed scaled to a child; downtown was only a couple of blocks from our house, the school

I attended was just down the street, and there were the steep hills and gorges of the Cornell University campus to explore. Ithaca had the virtues of a small town while being more cosmopolitan than most, given Cornell's large population of foreign students and others from all around the U.S.

I look back on that Ithaca with some nostalgia, but there were dark spots even in that pleasant place. There was the constant fear of contracting polio; some of my playmates were the kids wearing leg braces and on crutches at a rehabilitation center near our home. (I was one of the children included in the Francis Field Trial of the Salk polio vaccine, one of the largest medical experiments ever conducted; the first injection made me ill with fever and nausea, so I wasn't surprised years later to find out I'd been given the actual vaccine and not the placebo.) There were also the Cold War, Senator Joe McCarthy, and the possibility of nuclear war, all of which hung in the background of my childish life even when I was only dimly aware of them.

The character of Maerleen Loegins was inspired by Mary Poppins—not the Disneyfied depiction of the nanny by Julie Andrews, but the imposing and mysterious woman I first encountered in the P.L. Travers books. Even my family resembled the Banks family of that first volume; there were Jane Banks, the oldest (me), followed by her brother Michael (my brother Scott), and the twins, John and Barbara (my sister and brother Connie and Craig, who were also twins), making it a simple matter for me to transport myself and my own family imaginatively into the world of Mary Poppins. I recall being very disappointed when I finally saw the movie version of *Mary Poppins*; charming as Julie Andrews was, she didn't fit my image of the intimidating and sometimes frightening Mary Poppins, and the Banks household had been reduced in that movie to only two children, Jane and Michael.

The "strawberry birdies" in the story were actual shadows I used to see on the walls inside our house.

AFTER I STOPPED SCREAMING

The blonde in the big ape's hand. Long before you had Rita Hayworth on that bed in a negligée or Marilyn standing over that grate with her skirt billowing up, there were all those pictures and posters and billboards of me, the blonde in the big ape's hand.

You asked me why I became so reclusive, why I stayed out of the limelight for so long. Well, I really wasn't that much of a recluse when I was younger, I did have my friends and activities, and if you think I'm a recluse now, all I can say is that when you get past ninety, you pretty much have to keep closer to home. In my younger days, I also preferred to be around people I knew pretty well, people who were pals and wouldn't ask me all the usual questions. I would have gotten out and about a lot more if I just could have counted on strangers not to start asking me for the "real" story.

You know what I mean. Frankly, it was a relief when almost everybody seemed to forget about the whole thing, so all of this interest in the story now is kind of surprising.

No, I don't really mind talking to you, not at this point, and maybe it's time to set the record straight. I think I'm finally old enough and understand enough that I can tell you the real story, or at least my version of the real story.

I don't suppose that I really even started putting it all together until years later. Actually, I think the light started to dawn at about the time that my husband and I were celebrating our thirtieth wedding anniversary, which was kind of a miracle in itself, considering how we started out, two kids with no real prospects sailing off on the Impresario's boat to that creepy island. The early years of our marriage weren't that easy or happy, for reasons I probably don't have to mention. The Impresario was paying for my psychoanalysis the whole time my husband and I were living in Manhattan, but I didn't need an analyst digging around inside my head to know what was bugging me, and if that meant going through the rest of my life with a phobia about apes, well, I could live with that. I never much cared for zoos anyway, but I was starting to develop a phobia about bearded guys with German accents. And I was beginning to realize that if my marriage was going to have any chance of lasting, I'd have to put what happened with that big gorilla and me behind me for good.

So I did. I avoided thinking about those days at all, just pretended to myself that they never happened, and it helped, believe me. Pretty soon, I didn't wake up in the middle of the night screaming and my man was able to get a good night's sleep. But as time went by, and I picked up what you might call a different perspective, I began to see that the Impresario had actually done me a big favor, whether he intended to or not. I'd been around the track a few times, if you know what I mean, and things weren't going to get any better for me, not during the Depression, anyway. Without the Impresario, I wouldn't have been on that boat where I met my husband, and I wouldn't have had a shot later on at a career on Broadway and in pictures, even if that didn't quite pan out in the end. I wouldn't have had all those happy years in California, and I guess I don't really have to explain why we were just as happy to get out of New York. My husband wouldn't have made all that money in real estate after World War II—it didn't hurt that he got to know Ronnie Reagan while they were making all those morale boosters for the Army together—and I wouldn't be sitting here in this ritzy old age home talking to you. And now I'm old enough and I've lived long enough to understand what that big ape must have gone through. I can even have some sympathy for the old gorilla.

Yeah, you've got that right. Maybe I was picking up on that from the start, maybe that's how I was able to survive the whole experience. Things might have been tough for me, but they were a whole lot tougher for that giant ape. He'd been through some pretty hard times long before I ever got to his island.

Here's something I only understood later. The Impresario had this nutty idea—people nowadays would call it racist—that the way to capture the big ape was to attract him with some white woman. But in all honesty, a lot of those babes in that African village could have given me a run for my money in the looks department. About the only thing I had going for me there, lookswise, was being a novelty, and that novelty probably would have worn off really fast after a few more weeks in the jungle, when my roots would have started to show and I probably would have picked up one hell of a sunburn. The truth was that, for whatever reason, and maybe it was just plain loneliness, the ape would show up at the village wall, and they'd set out some poor girl or other to keep him away, and then he'd carry her off, probably worrying the whole time about how he was going to take care of her in a place where you've got dinosaurs running around, especially if she's screaming all the time. And then he'd lose her sooner or later, and he'd get even more depressed and lonely, so he'd come back for another babe, and then he'd lose her, too. Some T. rex would grab her, or a pterodactyl would carry her off, or she'd fall off a cliff.

It had to be depressing, to put it mildly. After a while, he must have felt like he was trapped in one of those nightmares that keeps repeating itself, like the ones I used to discuss with my analyst. He comes back to the village, finds another girl tied up and waiting for him, probably screaming her head off the same way I did, and the folks in the village beating their drums and waving their torches around and just basically telling him to grab the girl and go away. Off he goes, with the poor woman still screaming her head off, and maybe he just wants her to stop screaming. It's making him feel really inadequate, all that screaming and carrying on—I can tell you that I never knew a guy who didn't cringe and feel horrible if a gal started screaming whenever he so much as laid a hand on her, unless he was the kind of guy you really didn't want to know. So here's the ape, carrying still another girl off to his cave or wherever, and no matter what he does, something awful happens to her. I don't know how anybody, even a big gorilla, goes through that without becoming seriously traumatized, do you?

What about his life before that? That's a good question. I didn't start sorting that out until after the Impresario came back from his second expedition and I found out that the big gorilla's son saved his life, not that this good deed did Junior any good. I mean, I didn't know before then that the big ape had anything like a family life, but obviously he did, and obviously there was what you could call a Mrs. Giant Gorilla around, or there wouldn't have been any son. Let's be honest—a big giant female ape should have had a lot more appeal for a big gorilla than a teeny little bottle blonde from New Jersey. For one thing, besides the obvious, namely being a lot closer to his size, she probably would have been able to handle herself in that jungle. Any pterodactyl coming after her would have had his wings pinned in a big hurry. The big guy wouldn't have had to worry about how he was going to protect her, either, and—here's something else I probably wouldn't have understood if I hadn't lived this long—he must have admired her independence. They would have had what the young folks nowadays call an egalitarian relationship. I'm willing to bet that they had a pretty good time in those early years, hanging around the cave and beating up a dino now and then, and then the kid came along.

Now, much as I wish my husband and I had been able to have some kids of our own, you have to admit that having a kid can affect a marriage, and not always for the better. You know how it goes. The wife's home with the kid all day while her husband's out with the guys. Or the kid's crying all night and nobody can get any sleep, or one parent's big on whipping the kid into shape and the other one's reading Dr. Spock or whatever nice old geezer is writing about babies these days. It could be any number of things, but my guess is that the ape and his mate had a big falling-out, and it probably involved child care issues as they'd put it nowadays, and the missus finally up and left and took the kid with her. All I know is that I didn't see any little gorillas running around while I was there, and I think I would have noticed even if I wasn't exactly making careful observations, but obviously Junior had to be on that island somewhere or he couldn't have saved the Impresario later on. And a little gorilla wouldn't have been any safer there without a big gorilla to look out for him than I would have been. So since the big ape wasn't looking out for the kid, his kid's mother had to be.

He must have been thinking of her. Maybe that's why he went to the village in the first place—maybe he thought she was hiding out somewhere nearby. I can't imagine what he might have been thinking when the villagers first started tying up women outside the wall for him, but by then he might have really needed some female companionship, even if it was kind of on the small scale. And maybe he was so mad at his mate for leaving that he kind of liked the idea of having some tiny little woman around who had to look up to him. He wouldn't be the first.

And then he would lose the women, one by one. First the one big dame he cares about who can take care of herself walks out on him, and that has to be a blow to his ego, and then he can't even protect the ones who are completely dependent on him. I don't even want to think of what my analyst might have said about that. And after that, he's got my husband and the Impresario coming after him, and he gets dragged off to New York, and—well, I don't have to go into all of that.

A male archetype, my analyst called him—my analyst was actually more of a Jungian than a Freudian, if you must know. He claimed that's why there were so many stories about the big ape in the papers and the tale was so compelling and scary and the movie was so popular for so long and the big gorilla became such a famous public figure, even if you'd think having a giant ape running around in New York and then getting shot off the Empire State Building would be enough by itself to get a lot of coverage. But I don't know about this male archetype stuff, or any of that Freudian or Jungian bushwah or whatever you want to call it.

I think something else entirely was going on.

I don't know when it might have happened—maybe it wasn't until they caught him and tied him up, maybe it wasn't until he was getting shot at by all those planes—but I think at some point, the big ape realized that it was men who were responsible for all his troubles. Not his missus, who maybe just needed some time to find herself, or the African babes, or me with my screaming probably giving him a splitting headache, but guys in general. I'll bet the men in that African village weren't paying attention to anything the women there said, or they could have saved themselves a whole lot of trouble, I mean you can't tell me that it was the women who decided to send some poor girl out to a big gorilla. The Impresario sure as hell didn't listen to me when I told him that maybe it wasn't such a hot idea to walk out on that stage with my man and stand there in front of the big guy while people shot photos. And I think in the end, when the ape and I were trapped on the Empire State Building, when he decided to put me down instead of hanging on to me, he knew what he was doing.

He wasn't thinking about me or my welfare, even if putting me down did save my life. He was thinking of his mate and his son. That's my guess, anyway. He was thinking that maybe she wouldn't have left him if he'd treated her differently, if he'd done more of his share around the cave. You probably don't know this, but by the time we made it up to the top of the Empire State Building, my throat was really sore from all that screaming, and there were tears all over my face, and since I didn't have a handkerchief or anything, I was snorting like hell just to keep my nose from running. And I remember how he looked at me when I was snorting. He had this strange, sad look in his eyes, as if I reminded him of something, as if he'd heard that sound before and it reminded him of something he'd lost. I think his mate must have snorted like that. I was snorting and I think I might have picked up a few fleas, because I was scratching, too, and my guess is he was remembering how his mate would sit around snorting and scratching in their cave, and he was think-ing of her and their son and maybe about all those other women he'd lost after that. Seems to me that would be enough for him to give up on everything then and there. I really doubt it was that beauty-and-savage-beast nonsense the Impresario was so fond of quoting.

That's what everybody seems to have missed all these years. The giant ape wasn't some Freudian symbolism come to life, or an archetype, or the noble savage brought low. He was a fella who lost a dame who was his equal and lost some others who could never be his equals and then realized what it was he really wanted after all and by then it was too late, because a bunch of guys had taken away any chance of him getting it back.

I'll admit it. I'll bet he was wishing he'd done better by Mrs. Big Ape. He was probably thinking that things would have been a lot better for him if the women in the village could have gotten a word in edgewise and the Impresario had listened to me. You may think this is nuts, but in the end, I'm guessing that the big guy had finally become what you could call a kind of feminist.

Afterword to "After I Stopped Screaming"

If anyone is wondering why this story, so obviously about King Kong, never mentions the great ape's name, or that of anyone else, it's very simple: Peter Jackson had recently released his remake of the classic movie and trademarked not only the title, but also all of the names of the central characters. Sheila Williams at *Asimov's SF Magazine* suggested that we avoid any possible legal problems by ditching the names, which is how Carl Denham became the Impresario and Jack Driscoll is cited only as the narrator's husband. The narrator is of course Ann Darrow, played originally by Fay Wray in 1933, Jessica Lange in the 1976 remake, and Naomi Watts in Peter Jackson's 2005 version.

I was terrified of the whole notion of King Kong long before seeing the 1933 movie. A friend of mine in summer camp, a redheaded girl named Cordelia, regaled me and my fellow ten-year-old campers with a vivid blow-by-blow description of the entire picture. Cordelia was not only a good storyteller, she was also somebody who didn't shy away from the goriest and most disturbing details. I told myself then that this was one movie I was never going to see.

To date, I've seen both of the remakes in theaters and on DVDs, and the original movie a number of times. Turns out that Cordelia also had a gift for exaggeration.

THE ROTATOR

"To these I set no bounds in space or time;
They shall rule forever."

—Vergil, *The Aeneid*

All of this happened in worlds nearby.

* * * *

The tanks rolled down Pennsylvania Avenue and stopped at the edge of Lafayette Park, near the White House. To the east, more tanks were rolling along New York Avenue, while other tanks had also been spotted on 14th and 17th Streets and on Constitution Avenue.

They were closing the circle, surrounding the White House. No one knew where they had come from, but there they were, a procession of Abrams M1A1 tanks, all with the markings of the United States Army. No one had stopped them, and whatever the tourists and bureaucrats and police standing around in Washington's streets might think, none of the guards stationed on the White House grounds seemed to be at all concerned when the tanks rolled to a stop and two uniformed men in desert camouflage with stars on their shoulders climbed out, followed by a balding white-haired out-of-shape bespectacled man who looked a lot like the Vice President.

"What the hell?" somebody milling around in the crowd of sightseers near the Ellipse muttered. "Something's up," an old wino said to his homeless companion in Lafayette Park as they shared a bottle of Night Train. Then again, the unusual and even the unthinkable had become so commonplace by now that even the networks didn't seem to be covering the movement of tanks that had seemed to appear out of nowhere. There was no sign of satellite trucks or of any TV personalities doing stand-ups in front of cameramen.

"Who are they?" a child asked his mother as the two uniformed men and the heavyset man who looked a whole lot like the Vice President started to walk in the direction of the White House. She had no answer for him, and sometimes, especially these days, it was better just to mind your own business.

* * * *

The Vice President said, "No way around it, Mr. President." Whenever he was alone with the guy, he normally dispensed with the usual courtesies, "Mr. President" and "Sir" and the like, but this particular occasion seemed to require them. "We've got to get out of here."

"We do?" the President asked, glancing around the Oval Office. He had his usual blank what-me-worry expression on his face, the one that people who didn't know him that well could easily mistake for a sign of strength and self-confidence rooted in his religious faith and a deep inner calm.

"Yes, we do," the Vice President replied. "We've counted the votes seven ways from Sunday, and we've lost them, there isn't a chance now. The House is going to impeach both of us, and the Senate's going to convict, thanks to all those turncoat bastards who finally deserted us. It isn't even going to be close."

"Well, fuck them." The President still wore his look of serenity. "History is what's with us, and we've got the Almighty lookin' out for us, we sure as shit don't need the House and the Senate. Someday down the road, people'll know we were doing the right thing. When the history's all written, they'll—"

"That's all very well," the Vice President interrupted, "but in the meantime, we're dealing with this goddamn impeachment coming up out of nowhere. They're going to throw both of us out on our asses and put that bitch from San Francisco behind your desk until the next election." And that wasn't the worst they might be facing. He'd overheard a few low-level staffers muttering something about the World Court and war crimes tribunals and the Hague the other day when they thought he had left the room. "But I'm not waiting around to witness that travesty. We're all set, thanks to a secret project I've been keeping an eye on and shepherding along, just in case it might turn out to be useful. I'm getting the hell out of here, and you're coming with me."

The President's eyes became slits; he looked confused. "That's your idea, cuttin' and runnin'?" he asked, sounding a bit petulant. "And just where are we gonna go?"

"Well, in a way, we aren't going anywhere. In a sense, we'll be staying right here." The Vice President would have to explain the complexities of his escape plan very carefully. "Here's the deal," he continued in as gentle a tone as he could muster. "What if you could go someplace where everything's exactly the same as it is here, but where you aren't going to be impeached, where you'll still be the President right up until the end of your term?" And maybe even beyond that term, if certain irons the Vice President had in the fire got properly smelted. "I'm talking about a place where we can both avoid impeachment altogether."

"Sounds purty good." The President frowned, making his eyes look even smaller. "But it still smells like cuttin' and runnin' to me. Anyway, how the hell do we do all that? Round up the Congress and ship'em out for some enhanced interrogations?"

"We've got an even better way out than that, thanks to the research teams at DARPA." The Vice President paused. "They got up something for us called the Rotator."

"The Rotator?"

"The Alternative Stochastic Variability Actuator and Rotating Transporter," the Vice President explained, "but it's simpler to just call it the Rotator. And that's basically what it does, rotates you out of one continuum—er, place, and puts you where impeachment isn't going to happen, executive privilege is upheld, and we can do our goddamn jobs."

"You make it sound mighty simple."

"It is mighty simple. What happens in the end is mighty simple, anyway." There was no point in trying to explain the complexities of the technology and the assumptions underlying it to the President, especially since he didn't really understand them too well himself. "It's like this. We'll head out of here for the secure and undisclosed and meet there with everybody who's coming along with us. Then we get rotated, and before you know it, you're back in this office going about your business, but without impeachment pending and your poll ratings right back up where they should be. Hell, maybe we can even get them back up in the forties."

"So I'll be back here," the President said, "but in a way I actually won't be back *right here*. I'll kinda be like somewheres else that's sorta the same."

"That's it." Somehow the kid had grasped the big picture.

"And everything'll be the same as here?"

"Everything except the stuff we don't want to have happen to us."

"What about my wife?" the President asked. "I wouldn't want to get rotated unless she's gonna get rotated right along with me, and she won't be back here at the White House until the weekend."

The Vice President scowled. His own wife was coming along with him; she had made damned certain of that once he had revealed his plans to her, but he hadn't counted on bringing the First Lady along on this journey through the variant probabilities. For one thing, he didn't want anybody coming with them who wasn't absolutely trustworthy and close-lipped. This had kept the number of people to be rotated at a minimum; there was no point in getting where he wanted to go only to end up with some traitor whistle-blowing before some Congressional committee or other there. For another, he had doubts about the First Lady's ability to carry out what would need to be done after they were rotated and confronting their variant counterparts. His own wife was coldblooded enough to do what she had to do, but the First Lady probably wouldn't be up to it even with a triple dose of Xanax.

"She won't have to come along with you," the Vice President said very slowly, "because she'll already be there, see? I told you, everything's going to be the same except that everything'll be going our way and we won't have to put up with all this oversight and impeachment crap. Believe me, except for that, you won't notice any difference." The President probably wouldn't have noticed any difference anyway, given the useful bubble of obliviousness that usually surrounded him, but he had to know enough to avoid confusion.

The President's eyes got really tiny and squinty then, as they always did whenever he was trying to summon up anything resembling a thought. "And my ranch? That'll still be the same, too?"

"You'll have plenty of brush left to clear there, believe me." The Vice President cleared his throat. "Um, we'd better get going."

"Right now?"

"Yes, now." Better to get out of here fast, before any of those nerds working on the Alternative Stochastic Variability Actuator and Rotating Transporter got tempted to spill the beans to the media. He had never been able to tell the ethical ones from the opportunists.

* * * *

They were all there in the underground chamber of his secure and undisclosed location, his wife, his medical team, and those completely trustworthy souls who were to be rotated along with him and the President. The guys he needed from the Defense Advanced Research Projects Agency were there, too, along with a couple of officers who understood the research and how to operate the Rotator and other soldiers to man the tanks. He had, however, made sure that the scientists responsible for the actual research and for calculating his course were absent. He wasn't sure they had wholeheartedly approved of his plans, and they had always seemed somewhat too anxious to outline the possible drawbacks of the Rotator, what with their talk about opening doors and altering events in other continua that might be mirrored throughout a long run of variants and that maybe there were certain doors that should stay closed. All he had needed to know was that he could get to where he wanted to go, and they had assured him of that.

It was too bad, he thought, that his old buddy, the former Secretary of Defense, couldn't be here with him to take advantage of DARPA's Rotator. But there'd be somebody just like him in the next continuum, and maybe, if everything worked out, they'd be able to reappoint him to his old Cabinet position. After all, where they were going, there was even a chance that they were actually winning the war on terror and securing the oilfields, if what the scientists had told him about all the possible variants was correct.

"All we have to do, Mr. President," one of the Army officers was saying, "is go outside and get in the tanks, and before you know it, we'll be on our way to the White House."

"Tanks?" the President asked.

"To protect us while we're being rotated. You'll notice what you might call a kind of rippling in the atmosphere, but as long as you're inside the tank, you'll be protected from any ill effects when we're rolling through the gateway."

"The get-away?"

"The gateway." The officer had a patient look on his face. "The gateway through to another continuum that the Rotator's going to open up for us."

The President screwed up his eyes. "This isn't gonna be one of those deals where I have to put on a uniform, is it?" he asked.

"Not at all," the officer replied, still wearing his patient look.

"'Cause prancin' around in that flight suit on that carrier deck didn't work out so well in the end." The President let out one of those laughs of his that sounded like a mixture of a snort and a whinny.

"You won't need a uniform for this trip," the Vice President said, stepping forward, "but you are going to need this." He handed the President a Glock automatic. "Can't miss with this baby. Even I won't be able to miss my target." He allowed himself an avuncular chuckle.

The President hefted the automatic in one hand, then slapped it into the other in a way that made the Vice President grateful that the weapon wasn't yet loaded. "And exactly what am I gonna be aimin' at?"

"Well, it's like this." The Vice President paused, knowing that he would have to phrase things very carefully. "After we're rotated, we're going to run into—well, I guess you could call them our doubles."

"Our doubles?"

"Our twins." That didn't seem like the right word, either. "You could even call them our clones."

"Clones?" The President grimaced in disapproval. "Can't say I approve of that. Thought I signed a bill to make that illegal."

"I wasn't talking about that kind of clone," the Vice President said. "It's like this. You see, when we get to where we're going, there's going to be another President there—that's you—and another Vice President—that's me—sitting in the Oval Office. *Our* Oval Office. I mean, *your* Oval Office," he added, correcting himself. "And we have to take their places. I mean we have to take *our* places in their place."

The President pursed his lips and screwed up his eyes even more, looking extremely perplexed.

"Look at it this way," the Vice President said. "Think of that other guy who looks like you as an imposter. What he's doing is taking up space that's actually yours, and you can't have two people in the same place at the same time. So you're going to have to take him out."

"Didn't count on anything like that." The President stared at his weapon. "Couldn't we just send 'em back here? We'd be gone, and they could have our spots."

The Vice President shook his head. "Too complicated. Might not even work. There's no way to guarantee they'd even end up here."

"Yeah, but who cares?" The President's voice rose to a whine that could have shattered glass. "At least we wouldn't have to kill them, and they'd still be alive."

That didn't sound like the guy who had refused to pardon any of those inmates on death row while he was still Governor. On the other hand, it did sound like the guy who had made sure he had landed a cushy berth in the Air National Guard during wartime. "Too complicated," the Vice President said. "We'd have to convince them to go, maybe force them to leave. Tie up the loose ends—shoot'm and be done with it."

"I dunno."

The Vice President struggled to contain his exasperation. If the President got cold feet now, well, he wasn't about to wait around here and get impeached and removed from office, even if he did have to get rotated by himself. And if the President started blathering about the Rotator to those Fox News gasbags and all the other sycophants he had been inviting to the White House more frequently these days, they'd just assume that he had finally cracked under all the pressure.

"You're up to it," the Deputy Chief of Staff piped up. "You've got the balls for it." His eyes roved around the room, then peered at the President through his thick glasses. "Look at it this way—that look-alike'll be taking up a space that's rightfully yours. You'll need to take his place if you're going to go after all those goddamn liberals and lefties. You're the decider, not him."

"Besides," the Vice President added, glad of the help as he picked up the conversational ball that the Deputy Chief of Staff had thrown his way, "you won't be able to go after the terrorists *here* if you're impeached. But once you're rotated, you can go after them *there*."

The President's face brightened. His eyes took on a glow. "Then I guess we better get goin'."

* * * *

The Vice President had been somewhat apprehensive about being rotated, even though he had been assured that his pacemaker would remain unaffected. To his relief, the rippling of the air and the sudden feeling of disorientation passed quickly, leaving him feeling only slightly nauseated afterwards. It helped to be inside a tank, and he didn't bother to ask about looking through the periscopes to see what was going on outside.

"We're rolling down Pennsylvania Avenue, sir," the officer sitting in front of him at the commander's station announced. "We should be passing the Old Executive Office Building in about five minutes or so."

"Any sign of trouble?" the Vice President asked.

"Folks are just watching us pass," the officer at the gunner's station replied, "like we're some kind of parade."

Good, the Vice President thought. He had been wondering if they might encounter some of the groups that had been gathering outside the White House in recent days, knots of people who looked mean and angry and carried signs with obnoxious slogans like IMPEACH THE COMMANDER-IN-THIEF and REGIME CHANGE BEGINS AT HOME and MY TOYOTA GOT BOMBED BECAUSE IT'S SMALL FOREIGN AND FULL OF OIL and other phrases that dared to compare him and the President to Nazis and criminals. Apparently they'd arrived in a variant where the citizenry was more docile and less likely to cause them any trouble, which would make it easier to do what they had to do now.

At last the tank rolled to a halt. Two officers climbed out ahead of him, while another was just behind him, ready to help heave him out of the vehicle if necessary. He was panting by the time he clambered over the side. The driver was already standing below him, and held out an arm to help the Vice President down to the ground.

The sky was cloudless and blue, the morning air crisp and cool without a hint of global warming. By now, his wife would have taken care of her counterpart and, with the help of the trusted aides and Secret Service officers with her, secured the Vice Presidential residence. Other officers and aides were climbing out of tanks and sprinting across the

White House gardens, knowing that they would not be challenged; after all, the Vice President was with them.

He looked around and finally spotted the President; it was important that they head for the Oval Office together. He waited as the President trotted up to his side. "All set?" the Vice President growled.

"Yeah." The President had taken on his steely-eyed look, the expression he occasionally wore whenever that old bag who was still hanging on in the White House press corps shot off one of her more impertinent questions at a press conference.

The Vice President slipped a hand inside his pocket, feeling his weapon; too bad all those jokers who insisted on making wisecracks about all of his draft deferments would never know that he could be one hell of a brave warrior when it counted. "Then let's go," he muttered.

* * * *

He and the President were the last ones to enter the White House. They made it all the way through the hallways without seeing anything more disturbing than a glimpse of the Deputy Chief of Staff standing over his dead counterpart before the door to his office closed. It would have been a lot easier if the bodies could just fade away and disappear, the way they had done in a sci-fi TV series he used to watch, but the Rotator didn't work that way; the DARPA researchers had told him that they would have to dispose of the bodies themselves.

Two Secret Service men, two that the Vice President could trust completely, were moving down the corridor ahead of him and the President. Among other things, the pair had made sure that the Veep wasn't left holding the bag when that clumsy pal of his got in the way during their hunting excursion and ended up with a face full of buckshot. A couple of Secret Service officers were outside the northwest door to the Oval Office, and maybe it was just his imagination, but they both looked just a little bit heavier than their two rapidly approaching counterparts.

"Mr. President?" one of them said, looking puzzled. "Nobody alerted us." He tapped at his earpiece. "Thought you were still inside," and then his eyes widened as he stared at his own twin.

The President cackled. "Thought I'd slip out into the Rose Garden and catch some of that nice weather we're havin'. Decided to take the long way around and come back inside this way." He struck his chest. "Stayin' in shape. Every little bit helps."

Even as the Commander-in-Chief was yacking, the four Secret Service men were reaching for their weapons, but the two who had been rotated, knowing what was coming, had drawn theirs just a second or two faster. They aimed and fired, one round each, right at the heads of their alternate selves, and two men lay dead on the floor. The Vice President reflexively clutched at his chest, hoping his pacemaker would hold up under the strain; this was where things could have really gone wrong, and they weren't exactly out of the woods yet. The President had a sickly look on his face, as if he was about to toss his cookies.

They passed through the door into the Oval Office. A quick look around the large round space revealed that the same volumes of history the President had lately been browsing through were still on the bookshelves, the same paintings of Western scenes still hung on the walls, the same slightly uncomfortable sofas faced each other, and the same brightly colored rug with the Presidential seal lay on the floor. He stared past the sofas and the rug with the seal and saw the two men right where he had expected them to be. The President's counterpart was behind his desk and his own doppelgänger sat in one of the armchairs near a window.

The sight of his double unnerved him for a moment. He hadn't realized how bald he was getting, and how jowly his face was, but those cold glittering eyes behind his spectacles looked reassuringly familiar.

"What the fuck?" his double muttered.

The President's double stood up behind the desk. The Vice President was reaching inside his pocket for his gun when, next to him, the President shouted, "Nobody else gets to be me!"

"What're you talkin' about?" the President's double said.

"I'm the President, and you're takin' up my space!" The President whipped out his gun and fired. "I'm the President!" he shouted as his double fell across the desk, nearly drowning out the staccato sound of the Vice President's gun as he shot his own twin.

The balding man fell. A red stain was spreading across his chest. "Fuck you," his doppelgänger said with his last dying breath.

"Fuck you," the Vice President replied, aiming carefully, and shot him again.

"Holy shit," the President whispered. They sat down on the sofas, facing each other, and waited for the clean-up crew who had been rotated with them to arrive.

* * * *

It was taking the President a while to recover. The two bodies, their heads covered by black hoods before they'd been stuffed into body bags, had been taken away. The laptop the Vice President had requested had been brought to him, and still the President was sitting at his desk, staring up at the Presidential seal on the ceiling, perhaps seeking some heavenly guidance. He looked like he could use a stiff drink, and the Vice

President could have used one himself, but that would have to wait until he was back at his own place. He and his wife could toast themselves with some of that single-malt he kept in one of his underground vaults.

An hour of Googling various news sites and blogs had already told him what he needed to know. In this variant, they'd held on to a majority in the Senate and had a two-seat edge in the House—slim margins, but enough so that they wouldn't have to worry about hearings or oversight, let alone any impeachment proceedings. There would be no challenges to claims of executive privilege or declarations of extraordinary powers. They had landed in a place where their people were worthy of their efforts, where they'd be free to secure the world's resources and their own interests and cement their status as the world's one and only superpower. He thought of what the DARPA scientists had told him about the possibility of events being mirrored across the continua. That might mean that if they succeeded here, then they'd be increasing the odds of America's dominating all of the other variants as well. Maybe well out to infinity.

Master of the multiverse, he thought. The title had a kind of appealing ring to it.

The President coughed. "This is weirding me out," he said from behind his desk.

"What's weirding you out?"

"Can't figure out if I'm the President or an assassin."

The Vice President was about to reply when he heard the door behind him open. He turned to face himself, a gun in his hand, with the President standing right behind him. "What the fuck?" he muttered, and then a hammer struck him in the chest.

He fell forward, then rolled to one side. Somebody was shouting; he recognized the President's voice. "I'm the decider," he was shouting, "and nobody else gets to be me!"

The Vice President looked up and saw a dark form bending over him. "Fuck you," he managed to say, wondering how many times this was going to happen.

"Fuck you," his double responded before everything went black.

Afterword to "The Rotator"

This is another story that lacks proper names, but for different reasons than "After I Stopped Screaming:" proper names seemed redundant. When the story first came out, most readers could probably easily discern that the Vice President of the United States who is the protagonist was modeled on Dick Cheney, probably the most reprehensible person ever to hold that office. Later on, it occurred to me that not tying the characters to particular individuals might make the story more likely to survive when the Bush and Cheney administration has long since been forgotten.

Although given the damage done by that regime, it might be a while before such amnesia sets in; then again, we Americans have a marked talent for historical amnesia and moving on without learning any lessons from our experience. Only in alternative realities are some recent political miscreants ever likely to be called to account.

THE FALLING

written with George Zebrowski

She was sinking, caught in a familiar dream of flight, falling endlessly toward the ground.

Waking with a start, she stared at the ceiling and noticed again that one of the white ceiling tiles was curving at one corner, drooping ever so slightly toward the floor. That tile had always drooped, and she was still falling. Her stomach was pressing against her spine and the bed threatened to sink into the floor.

Elaine sat up, carefully putting her feet on the carpet. The sensation was still there. The whole building was sinking. Shoddy construction, she thought; shifting sand. She padded sluggishly to the window and pulled the curtain aside.

She was still five floors up; the green grass and parking lot below were exactly where they should have been. The fifth-floor windows of the condominium complex across the road still glittered with the morning sunlight, beaming the gleam at her window.

Turning away, she made her way to the bathroom, washed up, and then struggled back to the bedroom to dress. Each foot seemed to sink as she set it down; she lifted her knees high, feeling as though she was walking through mud. Her skirt pulled at her hips and her jacket seemed oddly heavy for a garment made out of cotton. She took a deep breath. She had to get out and get some air.

* * * *

A larger crowd than usual was waiting by the elevator; a few people were still in bathrobes and pajamas. "Hey, Elaine," one neighbor yelled.

She raised one arm in greeting, then let it fall to her side. She did not want to take the elevator anyway; she could sink without it. She went down the stairs clinging to the railing, feeling as if she were on an escalator and wondering why she could not force herself to move more quickly.

* * * *

A crowd had gathered on the lawn; several pairs of anxious eyes surveyed the building. "It's sinking," someone said.

"It isn't." Elaine waved a hand at the tiers of balconies and windows, which were still where they belonged.

"Something is."

She turned toward the speaker and recognized Bill Weinstein. "You feel it, too?"

"Everyone does." Bill was rubbing his chin so hard that she thought he would remove his tennis-player's tan. His wide shoulders slumped uncharacteristically. "I could barely get up."

Elaine suddenly had to sit down, and plopped onto the lawn. Others were already seated. Every building nearby had clusters of people gathering below on meager squares of grass, tennis courts, and at curbside. Few cars were passing—odd for that time of day. She looked down, feeling the ground sinking away beneath her. After staring at the grass for a long moment, she rose, brushing dirt from her skirt, wondering what the green and yellow blades were hiding.

"I can't do anything here," she said. "I'd better get over to the Center."

Bill frowned. "You're going to work?"

"Might as well. I can't afford to miss a day now, not with—" Elaine paused. The opportunity she had been waiting for all this time seemed to be sinking away, along with everything else.

* * * *

The sinking feeling traveled with Elaine across the causeway and to the Center's parking lot. Her knees shook as she got out of the car; her stomach was queasy. The air seemed thick and heavy. She looked at her watch; she had made the trip in twenty minutes, as usual, though it had seemed to take much longer.

George Rolfe was sitting in her office. "We're sinking," Elaine said, and tried to laugh.

George's drooping eyelids made his brown eyes look mournful. "Down, down, down," he said, and cackled. "We're being flushed away." Elaine imagined a whirlpool and the room seemed to spin, pulling her down.

"What's going on?"

"I don't know. It seems to be happening everywhere. You explain it."

She sat down, falling into the chair behind her desk with a thump. "How the hell am I supposed to explain it?"

"You're the psychologist, Elaine. It's a perceptual problem, a mass delusion. It has to be. There isn't any indication on any objective measuring device that shows any difference. That means it's in our minds."

"That means I won't be able to go." She was suddenly angry. "I've been waiting and waiting." Gravity had won; it was pulling at her, as if to register its triumph. She would not leave Earth; she would not get the chance to study the behavior of those in the spacelab. She would be pulled back into the mental morass of this world.

"How can you think about that now?" George's mouth sagged as he frowned; he glanced at her as if trying to decide whether to say any more. "I talked to them this morning. They feel it, too. It isn't just happening down here."

Elaine gripped the arms of the chair, seeing her chance. "Then it's even more important for me to go. I can see how it's affecting them."

"How can you think about that now?" George repeated. "Think of what you can do here. How is this going to affect people? Why do we all feel it? You have quite a fertile field for study."

She knew he was right. But she did not want to stay.

* * * *

As Elaine rose, her family seemed to sink. A scholarship had taken her out of the small valley town where she had grown up; her degrees had placed her on a pedestal, from which she could descend only with difficulty. Objectively, she had measured the degree of her alienation from those she had once loved while her father ranted about book-learning and people who got above themselves. She had watched as his coffin was lowered into the ground, and had never returned to the valley after that, the valley on the banks of two rivers which had cut their way through the surrounding hills.

She was falling. She stood on her balcony, looking down at the lawn. People were curled like shrimps in bedding and sleeping bags, afraid to stay inside. A television reporter and cameraman wandered among them, sinking even as they spoke to one group. Everything was sinking more rapidly, yet the air remained still and the railing steady. The absence of any visual sign of the falling was giving her vertigo.

Elaine turned away and went back inside. She was alone, as she usually was in the evening, having developed that habit during the years of consultations with the deluded and the unhappy. The ceiling stretched out above her, and she had the feeling that it was about to collapse, cover her in rubble. She was trapped in a room which would grow smaller, pressing her down to the floor as the walls slowly crushed her.

The telephone rang, shattering the illusion. She hurried to the bedroom and picked it up. "Hello?"

It was George. "Did you see the evening news?"

"No, I usually watch the late news. What is it?"

"It's out. Some astronomer at Cambridge leaked it. Some of the nearer stars have shifted position ever so slightly." Elaine clutched the receiver; her, hands were cold. "They've measured it. But that's not how it's being reported. The stars are falling." He laughed. "The sky is falling, the sky is falling. Call for Chicken Little." George cleared his throat.

"Oh, God." She sank to the bed. "What does it mean?"

"I don't know."

"Then it isn't a delusion."

"We're going to send up a team of cosmologists." He paused. "I'll try to squeeze you in." Her heart leaped, free for a moment before being pulled back. "They might need you up there, after all. And besides, we should try to keep things going as we planned—no use panicking. That's my argument, anyway."

"Can you—will you be able to send us up?"

"I don't see why not. Everything's working, it's just—well, we'll—"

"Thanks."

"Don't mention it."

She hung up and closed her eyes; a mistake. She was dropping more rapidly than ever; the sensation was growing stronger. She seemed to feel the air rush past her ears. She opened her eyes and focused on the curtain rod, staring at it for a long time. Depression draped itself over her.

The telephone's ring made her jump. She clung to the edge of the bed, afraid she would slide off and fall through the floor.

"Burkhart just called," George said. "You can go. Day after tomorrow. Get ready."

* * * *

Elaine had to get outside. She took two blankets out of the closet and went downstairs. She settled herself in an empty spot under a palm tree near the sidewalk. Near her, several dark shapes were bent over the gutter, and she heard the sound of retching.

The sky was black and clear; the stars twinkled, as they always had. Gradually, she became aware of how quiet it was. No one spoke; she could hear a few muffled sobs. Someone turned on a radio. "Repent," a tinny voice cried into the night. "God has given us a sign." The listener switched to another station which was playing *The Planets* by Holst, and she heard the thundering, threatening sounds of the Mars theme. Elaine pulled up her blanket and stretched out; the blanket was too heavy and she finally pushed it off, exposing herself to the thick, humid, heavy air.

Her body was tense. She was still falling, waiting to hit bottom, ready for the earth to rush up and crush her.

* * * *

Earth fell away; the wheel of the space laboratory swelled. Elaine was weightless, but still massive, still falling.

Her fellow passengers kept to their seats, then began to introduce themselves to those nearest them. The man next to Elaine was silent; his gray eyes probed her and then he sank back in his seat, as if dismissing her. His hands gripped the armrests as his legs floated up.

When they reached the wheel, they were greeted by a lean, gray-haired man and ushered through the curving pale corridor to their rooms. Elaine was abandoned by her roommate, a small, short-haired woman named Connie who waved at her bunk and muttered something about going to a meeting before leaving her alone.

Elaine slept uneasily. No one came for her when she awoke; the corridor was empty. She wandered aimlessly around the wheel until Connie emerged from one of the rooms.

"Elaine." Connie brushed the bangs back from her face; there were dark circles under her eyes.

"Who's in charge here?"

"You'd better talk to Colonel Ward," the smaller woman answered, pointing to another door.

Colonel Ward turned out to be the gray-haired man who had greeted the visitors. "Nice to meet you, Dr. Lantz. Make yourself at home." He waved at his desk before departing for yet another meeting.

Elaine spent the day looking at dossiers, which told her little about the laboratory's inhabitants she hadn't already known. They don't need me here, she thought: they probably don't want me here at all. She was just a ruse, George's way of pretending that nothing had really changed.

She was still falling; the wheel was pulling her down. She was growing used to the sick feeling in her stomach, the constant uneasiness. Words and letters danced before her eyes. She was falling so quickly now that she was afraid of what would happen when she stopped. If she stopped.

She spent a very long time scanning the small screen, gazing at data, and was startled when she looked at the clock; only two hours had passed.

* * * *

Elaine had filled the day with wandering, poking her head into rooms only to be waved away. She knew that she should have been planning her interviews, or observing the people on the spacelab; instead, she drifted.

Connie reappeared in their room after supper, throwing herself across her bunk. "Long day," she said.

"Yeah." Elaine glanced at her. "Have you noticed that, too?"

"Noticed what?"

"How long everything seems to take. My time sense is completely gone. Is that normal here?"

Connie shook her head. "Not like this. We all feel it. It's been like this ever since—ever since the falling feeling started. We've been thinking. What if everything's slowing down?"

"But it isn't," Elaine replied. "It can't be. The clocks—"

"How would we know? If everything's slowing down, there'd be no way to measure it, no way to tell. We'd never know. We're falling, and we can't measure that, either."

Connie was silent for a moment. "I had a message from home," she went on. "My mother's really sick. She can't keep anything down, she's always had inner ear troubles, and now—my father's trying to get her into a hospital. She might have a chance if they could keep her sedated and on intravenous feedings. But all the hospitals are so crowded now, what with accidents and people who are just going mad..."

Elaine lay on her bed for a long time, staring into the darkness. She was falling; she was running down. The universe would freeze around her; the air would become solid. The wheel would slow and stick. And she might never know. Would she feel it when everything stopped, or would she be trapped, unknowing, in one timeless moment? Could everything stop, or would they keep falling, slowing eternally, never reaching stillness? Terror pressed into her, threatening to break through her chest.

* * * *

Elaine wandered the wheel, a functionless cog. She scheduled interviews only to see them cancelled. Colonel Ward, with other things on his mind, was avoiding her.

Soon she was trailing after Connie, sitting quietly at the small woman's side as Connie scanned astronomical photographs, shaking her head as she did so. The universe had become a beast of some kind, and she was examining its entrails.

Connie peered at one photograph, then glanced at Elaine. "The stars in the whole southern sky are red-shifting and disappearing, as if they were exceeding the speed of light, leaving our universe."

"What does it mean?"

Connie shook her head and put her hand on her brow. "I don't know. It's nonsense—complete garbage."

Elaine sensed that the day of revelation was at hand. She fell faster as she waited.

* * * *

Everyone was crowding around the viewscreen. Voices rose, fell, and then grew silent.

Elaine felt dizzy as she held her stomach and tried to trust what her brain was telling her—that she would not hit a hard surface below and splatter her brains, break her bones, and die at any moment.

A flat, black plain, blacker than space, as opaque as nothingness, stretched out below the plane of the ecliptic. They were falling toward it rapidly. Red-shifted stars were disappearing below them, winking out on the infinite plain. Was the plain flat, or did it curve?

"All our ideas are wrong," a man near her said. His chubby face seemed frozen. "It's all wrong—our whole cosmology is wrong. We'll have to start reasoning from scratch."

She gazed at the blackness, wondering if they would ever get the chance. She had grown up out of the unconsciousness of childhood, hoping to push back the boundaries of ignorance, only to fall into the morass of unknowns that was the human mind. Scientists in other fields had seemed to be rising to ever more comprehensive explanations of nature, leaving her trapped below in a maze of increasingly inadequate theories. Now their work was also collapsing, and something inside her cheered.

"It must have taken eons for the universe to fall this far," the chubby man said as he looked toward Connie. "I think we began to feel it as we neared the floor."

"What'll happen when we reach bottom?" a bearded man asked.

The chubby man shrugged; Elaine saw that he was on the verge of breaking down. "Who knows? We can't say. Our sense of time is obviously affected by the acceleration as we near the blackness. Who knows what'll happen? I'm not sure of anything." His brown eyes glistened. "Five centuries of careful, cumulative science—all that effort to know, for nothing."

Elaine stared at the plain, where the galaxies were sinking away like chandeliers thrown into a lake of pitch. A wild new freedom soared within her.

The man next to her covered his eyes and moaned. She realized that she had deceived herself. Reality was not metamorphosing into something new; all vastness was dying, dissolving into chaos.

The falling was very fast now. They hit the black plain and sank into its thickness.

The room glowed red.

"We'll start over," Connie was saying to the chubby man. "We'll learn different laws." Her voice seemed far away.

Cave eyes stared at the screen. Coal-bright bodies drifted nearby.

Elaine's mind raced in a slowing body. She struggled to move her hand.

"Where—are—we?" someone whispered endlessly.

She strained against the bonds of slowing time.

"Maybe it's a barrier," Connie said, "and things will be normal on the other side." She did not sound convinced. "We may not be able to exist there," she added, "if the laws are different, not with the way our minds see…"

"We can adjust," Elaine suggested.

"How?" Connie asked after an eternity, her mouth a black o in the redness.

"An effort…of perception," Elaine sang, resisting the chaos which had reached into the known universe, into each human being, stirring stars and souls alike. She wondered if the earth was anywhere nearby, also sinking through the event horizon into a sea of chaos.

The falling slowed, continuing at an infinitesimal pace. Their minds were refusing to enter the alien reality. Elaine cradled her familiar self, the human inside which she had tried to understand all her life.

The slow sinking would never end, she thought. They would stare at each other forever, yearning to move as they fell into their private hells.

Light pierced the screen, filling her eyes with nameless hues and shifting shapes. There was nothing to see in the unfolding, alien space. We haven't evolved in this reality, she thought. No effort of perception would fit their minds to its strangeness, however much they hungered.

A river of stars poured out of Connie's mouth as she tried to speak.

The chubby man expanded like a balloon.

Colonel Ward lengthened into a slender pillar.

The man next to Elaine released massive tears. Each watery bladder contained tiny human shapes, mingling like bacteria.

Elaine saw terror in Connie's disembodied eyes. The unknown was no longer the knowable in disguise; it was naked and tyrannical.

They would not die and be buried in the earth; they would dissolve slowly, passing through madness before arriving at chaos.

The control room was gone. She was locked in a red solidity. Solid beams of light bored into her eyes from somewhere outside. The silence played a ghostly music in her inner ear. The familiar universe was a withered leaf, alive only in the barrens of memory.

Her heart slowed.

One beat.

She waited for the next.

Something walked through her mind.

Afterword to "The Falling"

My partner in writing and in life, George Zebrowski, had the original idea for this story, but we ended up writing it together. During our first years as writers, we'd gone out of our way not to collaborate with each other, partly because we didn't want any personal disputes to surface under the guise of editorial disagreements. I was also trying to find my own voice as a writer and had my own way of working that was quite different from his. George is a "putter-inner," somebody who writes sketchy drafts and then fills out his story; I was, and remain, a "taker-outer," the kind of writer who writes long, overly detailed and sometimes redundant prose and then has to cut the text without mercy.

In "The Falling," we were able to combine these approaches. George had done a first draft but remained dissatisfied with it; I read that draft and got intrigued. As I recall, we passed successive drafts back and forth, with my putting stuff in and George taking things out, and eventually ended up with this story, which Shawna McCarthy bought for *Asimov's SF Magazine*.

Years later, we collaborated in the same way, with George doing a first draft, my writing the next, and so on when we wrote four Star Trek novels together (one a Next Generation novel and three others featuring Captain Kirk and the crew of the original series). There again, it was George who came up with the ideas for the novels, all of them based on episodes of the series he would have liked to see; the last one we wrote centered on the character of Garth of Izar, a legendary Starfleet officer who had ended up going mad and being confined to an institution for the criminally insane. What if, George wondered, a cure had been found for Garth's mental illness? Wouldn't Starfleet have had to give him back command of a starship in order not to violate its principles? *Garth of Izar* was published in 2003 with a cover bearing a portrait of Steve Ihnat, the actor who played Garth in the original Star Trek episode, who sadly died of a heart attack in his late thirties. George had recommended such a cover, and both of us were moved when we received a letter from a member of Steve Ihnat's family in Canada, telling us how gratified his friends and relatives were to see his face on our book and know that he was still remembered.

STRIP-RUNNER

The three boys caught up with Amy just as she reached the strips. "Barone-Stein," one boy shouted to her. She did not recognize any of them, but they obviously knew who she was.

"We want a run," the smallest boy said, speaking softly so that the people passing them could not hear the challenge. "You can lead and pick the point."

"Done," she said quickly. "C-254th, Riverdale localway intersection."

The boys frowned. Maybe they had expected a longer run. They seemed young; the tallest one could not be more than eleven. Amy leaned over and rolled up the cuffs of her pants a little. She could shake all of them before they reached the destination she had named.

More people passed and stepped onto the nearest strip. The moving gray bands stretched endlessly to either side of her, carrying their human cargo through the City. The strip closest to her was moving at a bit over three kilometers an hour; most of its passengers at the moment were elderly people or small children practicing a few dance steps where there was space. Next to it, another strip moved at over five kilometers an hour; in the distance, on the fastest strip, the passengers were a multicolored blur. All the strips carried a steady stream of people, but the evening rush hour would not start for a couple of hours. The boys had challenged her during a slower period, which meant they weren't that sure of themselves; they would not risk a run through mobs of commuters.

"Let's go," Amy said. She stepped on the strip; the boys got on behind her. Ahead, people were stepping to the adjoining strip, slowly making their way toward the fastest-moving strip that ran alongside the localway platform. Advertisements flashed around her through the even, phosphorescent light, offering clothing, the latest book-films, exotic beverages, and yet another hyperwave drama about a Spacer's adventures on Earth. Above her, light-worms and bright arrows gleamed steadily with directions for the City's millions: THIS WAY TO JERSEY SECTIONS; FOLLOW ARROW TO LONG ISLAND. The noise was constant. Voices rose and fell around her as the strip hummed softly under her feet; she could dimly hear the whistle of the localway.

Amy walked up the strip, darted past a knot of people, then crossed to the next strip, bending her knees slightly to allow for the increase in speed. She did not look back, knowing the boys were still behind her. She took a breath, quickly stepped to the next strip, ran along it toward the passengers up ahead, and then jumped to the fourth strip. She pivoted, jumped to the third strip again, then rapidly crossed three strips in succession.

Running the strips was a lot like dancing. She kept up the rhythm as she leaped to the right, leaned into the wind, then jumped to the slower strip on her left. Amy grinned as a man shook his head at her. The timid ways of most riders were not for her. Others shrank from the freedom the gray bands offered, content to remain part of a channeled stream. They seemed deaf to the music of the strips and the song that beckoned to her.

Amy glanced back; she had already lost one of the boys. Moving to the left edge of the strip, she feinted, then jumped to her right, pushed past a startled woman, and continued along the strips until she reached the fastest one.

Her left arm was up, to shield her from the wind; this strip, like the localway, was moving at nearly thirty-eight kilometers an hour. The localway was a constantly moving platform, with poles for boarding and clear shields placed at intervals to protect riders from the wind. Amy grabbed a pole and swung herself aboard.

There was just enough room for her to squeeze past the standing passengers. The two remaining boys had followed her onto the localway; a woman muttered angrily as Amy shoved past her to the other side.

She jumped down to the strip below, which was also moving at the localway's speed, hauled herself aboard the platform once more, then leaped back to the strip. One boy was still with her, a few paces behind. His companion must have hesitated a little, not expecting her to leap to the strip again so soon. Any good strip-runner would have expected it; no runner stayed on a localway or expressway very long. She jumped to a slower strip, counted to herself, leaped back to the faster strip, counted again, then grabbed a pole, bounded onto the localway, pushed past more people to the opposite side, and launched herself at the strip below, her back to the wind, her legs shooting out into a split. Usually she disdained such moves at the height of a run, but could not resist showing her skill this time.

She landed about a meter in front of a scowling man. "Crazy kids!" he shouted. "Ought to report you—" She turned toward the wind and stepped to the strip on her left, bracing herself against the deceleration as the angry man was swept by her on the faster strip, then looked back. The third boy was nowhere to be seen among the stream of people behind her.

Too easy, she thought. She had shaken them all even before reaching the intersection that led to the Concourse Sector. She would go on to the destination, so that the boys, when they got there, could issue another challenge if they wished. She doubted that they would; she would have just enough time to make her way home afterward.

They should have known better. They weren't good enough runners to keep up with Amy Barone-Stein. She had lost Kiyoshi Harris, one of the best strip-runners in the City, on a two-hour run to the end of Brooklyn, and had reached Queens alone on another run after shaking off Bradley Ohaer's gang. She smiled as she recalled how angry Bradley had been, beaten by a girl. Few girls ran the strips, and she was better than any of the others at the game. For over a year now, no one she challenged had ever managed to shake her off; when she led, nobody could keep up with her. She was the best girl strip-runner in New York City, maybe in all of Earth's Cities.

No, she told herself as she crossed the strips to the expressway intersection. She was simply the best.

* * * *

Amy's home was in a Kingsbridge subsection. Her feeling of triumph had faded by the time she reached the elevator banks that led to her level; she was not that anxious to get home. Throngs of people moved along the street between the high metallic walls that enclosed some of the City's millions. All of Earth's Cities were like New York, where people had burrowed into the ground and walled themselves in; they were safe inside the Cities, protected from the emptiness of the Outside.

Amy pushed her way into an elevator. A wedding party was aboard, the groom in a dark ruffled tunic and pants, the bride in a short white dress with her hands around a bouquet of flowers made of recycled paper. The people with them were holding bottles and packages of rations clearly meant for the reception. The couple smiled at Amy; she murmured her congratulations as the elevator stopped at her level.

She sprinted down the hall until she came to a large double door with glowing letters that said PERSONAL—WOMEN. Under the sign, smaller letters said SUBSECTIONS 2H-2N; there was also a number to call in case anyone lost a key. Amy unzipped her pocket, took out a thin aluminum strip, and slipped it into the key slot.

The door opened. Several women were in the pleasant rose-colored antechamber, talking as they combed their hair and sprayed on makeup by the wall of mirrors. They did not greet Amy, so she said nothing to them. Her father, like most men, found it astonishing that women felt free to speak to one another in such a place. No man would ever address another in the Men's Personals; even glancing at someone there was considered extremely offensive. Men would never stand around gossiping in a Personal's antechamber, but things were not quite as free here as her father, thought. Women would never speak to anyone who clearly preferred privacy, or greet a new subsection resident here until they knew her better.

Amy stood by a mirror and smoothed down her short, dark curls, then entered the common stalls. A long row of toilets, with thin partitions but no doors, lined one wall; a row of sinks faced them on the other side of the room.

A young woman was kneeling next to one toilet, where a small child sat on a training seat; Amy could not help noticing that the child was a boy. That was allowed, until a boy was four and old enough to go to a Men's Personal by himself or with his father, an experience that had to be traumatic the first time around. She thought of what it must be like for a little boy, leaving the easier, warmer atmosphere of his mother's Personal for the men's, where even looking in someone else's direction was taboo. Some said the custom arose because of the need to preserve some privacy in the midst of others, but psychologists also claimed that the taboo grew out of the male's need to separate himself from his mother. No wonder men behaved as they did in their Personals. They would not only be infringing on another's privacy if they behaved otherwise, but would also be displaying an inappropriate regression to childhood.

Amy kept her eyes down, ignoring the other women and girls in the common stalls until she reached the rows of shower heads. Two women were entering the private stalls in the back. Amy's mother had been allowed a private stall some years ago, a privilege her husband had earned for both of them after a promotion, but Amy was not allowed to use it. Other parents might have granted such permission, but hers were stricter; they did not want their daughter getting too used to privileges she had not earned for herself.

She would take her shower now, and put her clothes in the laundry slot to be cleaned; the Personal would be more crowded after dinner. Amy sighed; that wasn't the only reason to linger here. Her mother would have received the message from Mr. Liang by now. Amy was afraid to go home and face her.

* * * *

Four women were leaving the apartment as Amy approached. She greeted them absently, and nodded when they asked if she was doing well in school. These were her mother's more intellectual friends, the ones who discussed sociology and settled the City's political problems among themselves before moving on to the essential business of tips for stretching quota allowances and advice on child-rearing.

Amy's mother stepped back as she entered; the door closed. Amy had reached the middle of the spacious living room before her mother spoke. "Where are you going, dear?"

"Er—to my room."

"I think you'd better sit down. We have something to discuss."

Amy moved toward one of the chairs and sat down. The living room was over five meters long, with two chairs, a small couch, and an imitation leather ottoman. The apartment had two other rooms as well, and her parents even had the use of a sink in their bedroom, thanks to her father's Civil Service rating. They both had a lot to protect, which meant that they would scold her even more for her failures.

"You took longer than usual getting home," her mother said as she sat down on the couch across from Amy.

"I had to shower. Uh, shouldn't we be getting ready to go to supper? Father'll probably be home any minute."

"He told me he'd be late, so we're not eating in the section kitchen tonight."

Amy bit her lip, sorry for once that her family was allowed four meals a week in their own apartment. Her parents wouldn't have been able to harp at her at the section kitchen's long tables in the midst of all the diners there.

"Anyway," her mother continued, "I felt sure you'd want to speak to me alone, before your father comes home."

"Oh." Amy stared at the blue carpet. "What about?"

"You know what about. I had a message from your guidance counselor, Mr. Liang. I know he told you he'd be speaking to me."

"Oh." Amy tried to sound unconcerned. "That."

"He says your grades won't be good at the end of the quarter." Her mother's dark eyes narrowed. "If they don't improve soon, he's going to invite me there for a conference, and that's not all." She leaned back against the couch. "He also says you've been seen running the strips."

Amy started. "Who told him that?"

"Oh, Amy. I'm sure he has ways of finding out. Is it true?"

"Um."

"Well, is it? That's even more serious than your grades. Do you want a police officer picking you up? Did you even stop to think about the accidents you might cause, or that you could be seriously injured? You know what your father said the first time he heard about your strip-running."

Amy bowed her head. That had been over two years ago, and he had lectured her for hours, but had remained unaware of her activities since then. I'm the best, she thought; every runner in the City knows about me. She wanted to shout it and force her mother to acknowledge the achievement, but kept silent.

"It's a stupid, dangerous game, Amy. A few boys are killed every year running the strips, and passengers are hurt as well. You're fourteen now—I thought you were more mature. I can't believe—"

"I haven't been running the strips," Amy said. "I mean, I haven't made a run in a while." Not since a couple of hours ago, she added silently to herself, and that wasn't a real run, so I'm not really lying. She felt just a bit guilty; she didn't like to lie.

"And your grades—"

Amy seized at the chance to avoid the more hazardous topic of strip-racing. "I know they're worse. I know I can do better, but what difference does it make?"

"Don't you want to do well? You used to be one of the best math students in your school, and your science teacher always praised—"

"So what?" Amy could not restrain herself any longer. "What good is it? What am I ever going to use it for?"

"You have to do well if you want to be admitted to a college level. Your father's status may make it easier for you to get in, but you won't last if you're not well prepared."

"And then what? Unless I'm a genius, or a lot better than any of the boys, they'll just push me into dietetics courses or social relations or child psychology so I'll be a good mother someday, or else train me to program computers until I get married. I'll just end up doing nothing anyway, so why should I try?"

"Nothing?" Her mother's olive-skinned face was calm, but her voice shook a little. "Is what I do nothing, looking after you and your father? Is rearing a child and making a pleasant home for a husband nothing?"

"I didn't mean nothing, but why does it have to be everything? You wanted more once—you know you did. You—you—"

Her mother was gazing at her impassively. Amy jumped up and fled to her room.

* * * *

She lay on her narrow bed, glaring up at the soft glow of the ceiling. Her mother should have been the first to understand. Amy knew how she once had felt, but lately, she seemed to have forgotten her old dreams.

Amy's mother, Alysha Barone, was something of a Medievalist. That wasn't odd; a lot of people were. They got together to talk about old ways and historical book-films and the times when Earth had been humanity's only home. They dwelled nostalgically on ancient periods when people had lived Outside instead of huddling together inside the Cities, when Earth was the only world and the Spacers did not exist.

Not that any of them could actually live Outside, without walls, breathing unfiltered air filled with microorganisms that bred disease and eating unprocessed food that had grown in dirt; Amy shuddered at the thought. Better to leave the Outside to the robots that worked the mines and tended the crops the Cities demanded. Better to live as they did, whatever the problems, and avoid the pathological ways of the Spacers, those descendants of the Earthpeople who had settled other planets long ago. They could not follow Spacer customs anyway. In a world of billions, resources could not be wasted on private houses, spacious gardens and grounds, and all the rest. Alysha Barone, despite her somewhat Medievalist views, would not be capable of leaving this City except to travel, safely enclosed, to another.

Her mother had, however, clung to a few ancient customs, with the encouragement of a few mildly unconventional friends. Alysha Barone had insisted on keeping her own name after her marriage to Ricardo Stein, and he had agreed when she asked that Amy be given both their names. The couple had been given permission to have their first child during their first year of marriage, thanks to their Genetics Values ratings, but Amy had not been born until four years later. Both Alysha and Ricardo had been statisticians in New York's Department of Human Resources; it made sense to work for a promotion, gain more privileges, and save more of their quota allowances before having a child. They had ignored the chiding of their own parents and the friends who had accused them of being just a little antisocial.

Amy knew the story well, having heard most of it from her disapproving grandmother Barone. The two had each risen to a C-4 rating before Alysha became pregnant; even then, astonishingly, they had discussed which of them should give up the Department job. Only the most antisocial of couples would have tried to keep two such coveted positions. There were too many unclassified people without work, on subsistence with no chance to rise, and others who had been relegated to labor in the City yeast farm levels after losing jobs to robots. Her parents' colleagues would have made their lives miserable if they both stayed with the Department; their superiors would have blocked any promotions, perhaps even found a way to demote them. Someone also had to look after Amy. The infant could not be left in the subsection nursery all day, and both grandmothers had refused to encourage any antisocial activity by offering to stay with the baby.

So Alysha had given up her job. Her husband might be willing to care for a baby, but he could not nurse the child, and nursing saved on rations. Ricardo had won another promotion a few years after Amy's birth, and they had moved from their two-room place in the Van Cortlandt Section to this apartment. Now Amy's father was a C-6, with a private stall in the Men's Personal, a functioning sink in his room, larger quota allowances for entertainment, and the right to eat four meals a week at home.

Her parents would have been foolish to give up a chance at all that. How useless it would have been for Alysha to hope for her position at the Department; they would have risked everything in the end.

The door opened; her mother came inside. Amy sat up. Her small bed took up most of the room; there was no other place to sit, and Alysha clearly wanted to talk.

Her mother seated herself, then draped an arm over Amy's shoulders. "I know how you feel," she said.

Amy shook her head. "No, you don't."

Her mother hugged her more tightly. "I felt that way myself once, but couldn't see that I'd be any better off not trying at all. You should learn what you can, Amy, and not just so that you'll be able to help your own children with their schoolwork. Learning will give you pleasure later, something you'll carry inside yourself that no one can take from you. Things may change, and then—"

"They'll never change. I wish— Things were better in the old days."

"No, they weren't," her mother responded. "They were better for a few people and very bad for a lot of others. I may affect a few Medievalisms, but I also know how people fought and starved and suffered long ago, and the Cities are better than that. No one starves, and we can, generally speaking, go about our business without fearing violence, but that requires cooperation—we couldn't live, crowded together as we are, any other way. We have to get along, and that often means giving up what we might want so that everyone at least has something. Still—"

"I get the point," Amy said bitterly. "Civism is good. The Cities are the height of human civilization." She imitated the pompous manner of her history teacher as she spoke. "And if I can't get along and be grateful for what I've got, I'm just a pathological antisocial individualist."

Her mother was silent for a long time, then said, "There are more robots taking jobs away from people inside the Cities. The population keeps growing, and that means people will eventually have even less— we could see something close to starvation again. The Cities can't expand much more, arid that means less space for each of us. People may lash out at an occasional robot now, since they're the most convenient targets for expressing resentment, but if we start lashing out at one another—"

She paused. "Something has to give way. Even that small band of people who hope the Spacers will eventually let them leave Earth to settle another world know that."

Amy said, "They're silly."

"Most would say so."

Amy frowned. She knew about those people; they occasionally went Outside to play at being farmers or some such thing. She could not imagine how they stood it, or what good it did them. A City detective named Elijah Baley was the tiny band's leader; maybe he thought the Spacers would help him. He had recently returned from one of their worlds, where they had asked him to help them solve a crime; maybe he thought Spacers could be his friends.

Amy knew better. The Spacers had only used him. She thought of the Spacer characters she had seen in hyperwave and book-film adventures. They were all tall, handsome, tanned, bronze-haired people with eyes as cold as those of the legions of robots that served them. In the dramas, they might be friendly to or even love some Earthpeople, but in reality they despised the people of the Cities. They would never allow Earthfolk to contaminate their worlds or the others in this galaxy. They might use an Earthman such as Baley, but would only discard him afterward.

"What I'm trying to say," Alysha said softly, "is that change may come. Whatever disruptions it brings, it may also present opportunities, but only to people who are ready to seize them." Amy tensed a little; this was the most antisocial statement she had ever heard from her mother. "It would be better if you were prepared for that and developed whatever talents might be useful. When I worked for the Department, I knew what the statistics were implying—it's impossible for even the most determined bureaucrat to hide the whole truth. I could see—but I've said enough."

"Mother—" Amy swallowed. "Are you going to tell Father what Mr. Liang said?"

Alysha plucked at her long, dark hair, looking distressed. "I really should. I'll have to if I'm called in for a conference, and then Rick will wonder why I didn't mention it earlier. I won't if you promise you'll work harder."

Amy sighed with relief. "I promise." She hoped she could keep that vow.

"Then I'll leave you to your studying. You have a little time before Rick gets home."

The door closed behind Alysha. Amy reached for her viewer and stretched out. Nothing would change, no matter what her mother said. Whatever Amy did, sooner or later she would, as her friend Debora

Lister put it, wind up at the end of the line. She would be pushed to the end of the line when her teachers began to hint that certain studies would be more useful for a girl. She would be forced back again when college advisers pointed out that it was selfish to take a place in certain classes, since she would not use such specialized training for a lifetime, as a boy would. If she moved up the line then, she would only be pushed back later, when she married and had her own children.

She could, of course, choose not to marry, but such a life would be a lonely one. No matter what such women achieved, people muttered about how antisocial they were and pitied them, which was probably preferable to outright resentment. She would have to live in one of the alcoves allotted to single people unless she was lucky enough to find a congenial companion and get permission for both of them to share a room.

Alysha had wound up at the end of the line long ago, although later than most, and she had a loving husband to console her, which was a good thing. Even couples who hated each other would not willingly separate, lose status, and be forced into smaller quarters. Of course Alysha would hope that Amy might move up the line; she had nothing else in life except her husband and daughter.

A fair number of women were like Alysha. Sublimated antisocial individualism—that was what a textbook-film Amy had scanned in the school library called it. Many women lived through their children, then their grandchildren, hoping they would rise yet knowing that there were limits on their ambitions. Their transferred hopes would keep them going, but they would also be aware that too much individual glory would only create hard feelings in others. That was one reason her parents refused to flaunt the privileges they had earned and used them reluctantly, with a faintly apologetic air.

Men had different problems, which probably seemed just as troublesome to them. Some men cracked under the strain of having a family's status resting entirely on them. The psychologists had terms for that syndrome, too.

Amy saw what lay ahead only too clearly. Perhaps she shouldn't have viewed those book-films on psychology and sociology, which were meant for adult specialists. Her parents would eventually have the second child they were allowed; except for tending to Amy and her father, and being sociable in ways that eased relations with neighbors and her husband's colleagues, there was little else for Alysha to do. Small wonder many women even had children to whom they weren't entitled. When Amy was grown, her mother would be waiting for the inevitable grandchildren, and transfer her hopes to them. What a delusion it all was, pretending that your children wouldn't be swallowed by the hives of the City while knowing that this was the way it had to be.

Happy families, as the saying went, made for a better City; mothers and wives could go about their business feeling they were performing their civic duty. Amy's mother would cling to her, and then to her children, and—

If this was how knowing a lot made people feel, maybe it was better to be ignorant, to settle for what couldn't be changed.

She folded her arms over her chest. She still had one accomplishment, and no one could take it from her; she was the best strip-runner in the City. She wouldn't give that up, not until she was too old and too slow to race, and maybe that day would never come. If she made a mistake and died during a run, at least she'd be gone before she came to the end of the line. Her parents could have another child, maybe two, and the loss of one life would make no difference in a steel hive that held so many. She could even tell herself that she was making room for someone who would not mind being lost in the swarm.

The psychology texts had terms for such notions, all of which made her feelings sound like a disease. Perhaps they were, but that was yet another reason not to care about what happened to her on the strips.

* * * *

"Amy Barone-Stein," the hall monitor said, "a person is looking for you."

Amy glared up at the grayish robotic face, a parody of a human being's. She did not care for robots, and this one, with its flat eyes and weirdly moving mouth, looked more idiotic than most. "What is it?" she asked.

"Someone outside wishes to speak to you," the robot said, "and has asked me to bring you there."

"Well, who is it?"

"She told me to give you her name if I were asked, or if you told me that you did not want to meet her. It is Shakira Lewes."

Amy's mouth dropped open. Debora Lister moved closer to her and nudged her in the ribs. Shakira Lewes had not run the strips in years, but Amy had heard of her. Kiyoshi Harris claimed she was the best female runner he had ever seen, and her last run, when she had led three gangs from Brooklyn to Yonkers and lost them all, was still legendary.

She *was* the best, Amy told herself; I'm the best now.

"Oh, Amy," Debora said "Are you going to talk to her?"

"Might as well."

"You'll miss the Chess Club meeting," the blond girl said.

"Then I'll miss it."

"I'm coming with you," Debora said. "I've got to see this."

"Miss Lewes requested the presence of Amy Barone-Stein," the robot said. "She did not say—"

"Oh, stuff it," Amy said. The robot's eyes widened a little in what might have been bewilderment. "She didn't say I couldn't bring a friend, did she?"

"No, she did not."

"Then lead us to her."

The robot turned, leading them past a line in front of a Personal, then through the throngs of students crowding the hall. Amy wondered how Shakira Lewes had made the robot do her bidding. Technically, the hall monitors weren't supposed to fetch students from the school levels except for an emergency, but this robot was probably too stupid to tell that it was being deceived. The robot's back was erect as it marched along on its stiff legs. Damned robots, she thought, taking jobs from people. The hall monitors had once been human beings.

By the time she and Debora reached the elevator banks, a small crowd of boys and girls was following them. They all clambered aboard after the robot and dropped toward the street level. When they emerged from the school, Amy saw more boys clustered around a tall, dark-skinned woman with short black hair.

"Ooh," Debora whispered. "Maybe she wants to challenge you." Amy shook her head and motioned at the robot's back. A robot could not harm a human being or, through inaction, allow a human being to come to harm; to this creature's simple positronic brain, possible harm would certainly include strip-racing.

"Amy Barone-Stein," the robot said in its toneless voice. "This is Shakira Lewes."

The boys stepped back as Amy approached. The woman was slender enough for a runner, if a bit too tall; most runners, like Amy, were short and slight, able to squeeze into even the smallest gaps between passengers during a run. Shakira Lewes had a perfect, fine-boned face; she looked a lot like an actress in a historical drama about Africa Amy had recently viewed. She wore a red shirt and black pants that made her long legs seem even longer. The boys were staring intently at her. None of them had ever looked at Amy that way, not even after hearing about her run against Bradley Ohaer's gang.

"You may leave us," Shakira said to the robot. The hall monitor turned and went back inside. The woman sounded as arrogant as a Spacer; Amy looked up at her, filled with admiration and hatred. "I've heard about you," Shakira continued. "I'd like to talk to you."

Amy stuck out her chin. "What about?"

"Alone, if we could." Alone meant walking among the crowds, standing on a strip or localway to talk, or, if one was lucky, finding an unoccupied chair or bench somewhere.

Amy said, "If you've got something to tell me, say it here."

"She's going to challenge," someone said behind Amy; she looked around. Luis Horton was with the group; he'd been mad at her ever since she beat him on a long run up to the Yonkers Sector. "She's going to challenge," Luis repeated. "Maybe Amy can't take her."

Amy said, "I can take any runner in New York."

Shakira frowned. "I said I wanted to talk. I didn't say anything about running."

"Afraid?" another boy asked.

Shakira's face grew grimmer. Amy saw where this was leading; the others expected a challenge. Normally, she would have demanded one herself, but something felt wrong. It didn't make sense for this woman, who surely had better things to do, to come looking for a run against Amy, whatever her fame. Shakira had to be out of practice, and would risk much graver consequences as an adult offender if she were caught by the police. Yet what else could she want Amy for? Perhaps something illegal—some illicit enterprise where a boy or girl who could easily shake off a police pursuit might be useful.

Amy shrugged. "Come on, guys. Anybody can see she's too old to run the strips now."

"I'm old, all right," Shakira said. "I'm nearly twenty-one."

"Lewes isn't scared," Luis muttered then. "Amy is."

Amy's cheeks burned. They were all watching her now; she even imagined that the crowds passing by were looking at her, witnesses to her shame. "I'm not afraid of anything," she said. "Make your run, Shakira Lewes—you won't lose me. From here to the Sheepshead Bay localway intersection—unless you're too old to make that long a run."

Shakira was silent.

"Now! Or are you just too old and tired to try?"

The woman's large dark eyes glittered. "You're on. I'll do it!"

A boy hooted. Even Debora, who would never run the strips herself, was flushed with anticipation. Amy was suddenly furious with them all. She wasn't ready for this run; she realized now that she had been hoping Shakira would back down. If the woman actually beat her, she would never live it down, while if Amy won, the others would simply assume Shakira was past her prime. She had risked too much on this challenge, and still didn't know what Shakira wanted with her.

"Let's go," Amy said.

"Just a minute." The woman raised an arm. "This is one on one, between you and me—and I still want to talk to you later."

"Talk to me after I beat you," Amy said without much conviction, then followed Shakira toward the nearest strip.

* * * *

Shakira strode along the gray bands, moving to the faster strips at a speed only a little more rapid than usual. Amy kept close. Most of the boys and girls had already headed for the expressway; they would greet the victor at the Sheepshead Bay destination. Luis and two of his friends were following to study a little of Shakira's skill before joining the others. There were still some gaps between passengers, but the strips were already getting more crowded.

Shakira showed her moves, increasing the pace. She did a side shuffle, striding steadily, then moving to an adjacent strip without breaking her pace; Amy followed. She did a Popovich, named after the runner who had perfected it, leaping from side to side between two strips before bounding from the second one to a third. She even managed to pull off a dervish. Turning to face Amy, she leaped into the air and made a complete turn before landing gracefully on a slower strip; a dervish was dangerous even on slow strips.

She was good, but Amy knew the moves. Show-off, she thought; the woman was only trying to intimidate her. Flashy moves were more likely to draw attention, as well as wearing out a runner too soon. She followed Shakira onto a localway, then swung off after her, leaving the boys behind. She had caught Shakira's rhythm, but remained wary and alert; some runners could lull a follower into their pace before doing the unexpected.

They danced across the strips toward an expressway. The crowds were thick on the strip next to the expressway platform. Shakira reached for a pole and swung herself up; Amy grabbed the next pole. The woman's long legs swung around, never touching the floor and barely missing a passenger, and then she was back on the strip, her back to the wind as she grinned up at Amy.

Amy gripped her pole, about to follow when a few people suddenly stepped to the strip just below her. She caught a glimpse of startled faces as her legs swung toward them; there was just enough space for a landing. A woman swayed on the strip; a man grabbed her by the arm. Amy knew in an instant that she could not risk a leap. Shakira turned, ran past more commuters, stepped to her left, and was gone.

Amy hung on to the pole; the wind tore at her legs. She hauled herself aboard, numbed by the abruptness of her defeat. She had lost before they even reached lower Manhattan; tears stung her eyes.

Someone shoved her; passengers surrounded her. "Damn runners!" a man shouted. Other riders crowded around her; a fist knocked her to the floor. "Get the police!" a woman cried. Fingers grabbed Amy by the hair; a foot kicked her in the knee. She covered her head with her arms, no longer caring what happened to her; she had lost.

* * * *

A plainclothesman, a C-6 with seat privileges on the expressway's upper level, got Amy away from the crowd before she was beaten too badly and took her to City Hall. Police headquarters were in the higher levels of the structure; Amy supposed that she would be turned over to an officer and booked. Instead, the detective led her through a large common room filled with people and desks to a corner desk with a railing around it.

She sat at the desk, feeling miserable and alone, as the plainclothesman took her name, entered it in the desk computer, called up more information, then placed a call to her father on the communo. "You're in luck," the man said when he had finished his call. "Your father hasn't left work yet, so he'll just come over here from his level and take you home."

She peered up at him. "You mean you aren't going to keep me here?"

The detective glowered at her. He was a big man, with a bald head, thick mustache, and brown skin nearly as dark as Shakira's. "Don't think I haven't considered detaining you. I shouldn't even be wasting my time with you—I have a very low tolerance for reckless kids who don't care about anyone else's safety. You could have started a riot on that expressway—maybe I should have left you to the tender mercies of that mob. Do you know what can happen to you now, girl?"

"No," she mumbled, although she could guess.

"For starters, a hearing in juvenile court. You could get a few months in Youth Offenders' Level, or you might get lucky and be sentenced to help out in a hospital a few days a week. You'd get lots of chances to see accident victims there." He pulled at his mustache. "That might do you some good. Maybe you'll be there when they bring in some dead strip-runner who wasn't quick enough. You can watch his parents cry when the hospital makes the Ritual of Request before they take any usable organs from the corpse. And you'll have deep trouble if you ever misbehave again."

Amy squeezed her eyes shut. "Stay here," the man said, even though she hardly had a choice, with the common room so filled with police. She sat there alone, wallowing in her despair until the detective returned with a cup of tea; he did not offer anything to her.

He sat down behind the desk. "Will you give me the names of any runners with you?"

She shook her head violently. Much as she hated Shakira, she would not sink that low.

"I didn't think you would. You're not doing them any favor, you know. If they meet with accidents or end up hurting somebody else, I hope you can live with yourself."

The detective worked at his desk computer in silence until Amy's father arrived. She glanced at his pale, grim face and looked away quickly. The formality of an introduction took only a moment before the plain-clothesman began to lecture Ricardo Stein on his daughter's offense, peppering his tirade with statistics on accidents caused by strip-runners and the number of deaths the game had resulted in this year. "If I hadn't been on that expressway," the man concluded, "the girl might have been badly roughed up—not that she didn't deserve it."

Her father said, "I understand, Mr. Dubois."

"She needs to learn a lesson."

"I agree." Ricardo shook back his thick brown hair. "I'll go along with any sentence she gets. Her mother and I won't go out of our way to defend her, and we probably share some of the blame for not bringing her up better and supervising her more. You can be certain there'll be no repetition of such behavior."

"I imagine you'll see to that, Mr. Stein—a solid citizen like you." Mr. Dubois leaned back in his chair. "So I'll do you and your wife a favor, and let Amy here off with a warning. She's only fourteen, and this is her first offense—the first time she's been caught, anyway—and Youth Offenders' Level is crowded enough as it is. But she's in our records now, and if she's picked up again for anything, she goes into detention until her hearing, at which point she'll likely get a stiff sentence."

"I'm grateful to you," Amy's father said.

"Listen to me, girl." Mr. Dubois rested his arms on the desk. "Don't think you can lie low for a bit and then start strip-running again. We know who you are now, and you'll be easy to spot. Not many girls run the strips." He glanced at her father. "I think I can count on you to keep her in line. Wouldn't do your status any good to have a criminal in the family."

"You can count on me, Mr. Dubois."

* * * *

Amy's father did not speak to her all the way home. That was a bad sign; he was never that silent unless he was enraged. He left her outside the Women's Personal and went on to the apartment.

She dawdled as long as she dared inside the Personal, then dragged herself down the hall, filled with dread, wondering what her parents would do to her. They would have discussed the whole affair by now, and her mother had probably mentioned the guidance counselor's earlier message.

They were both sitting on the couch when she entered; there was no use appealing to her mother for some mercy. The two rarely disagreed or argued in front of her, and in a matter this important, they would present a united front.

She inched her way to a chair and sat down. She would not be beaten; her parents did not believe in physical punishment. A beating, even with all the bruises the expressway riders had already left on her, might have been better than having to endure her father's harsh accusations and talk about how humiliating her offense was for all of them. She hadn't thought of them at all, of how upset they would have been if she were injured. She hadn't thought about how her pathological display of individualism might damage Ricardo's reputation at work, or her mother's among their neighbors. She hadn't considered how such a blot on her record might affect her own chances later, or reflected on the danger she had posed to commuters. She hadn't thought of the bad example she was setting for younger children, and had completely ignored her father's earlier warning about such activity.

By the time her father had finished his lecture, repeating most of his points several times, it was too late to go to the section kitchen. Her mother sighed as she folded their small table out of the wall and plugged in the plate warmer; her father grumbled about missing the chicken the section kitchen was to serve that night. They had been saving their fourth meal at home this week for Saturday, when Ricardo's parents were to visit with a few of their own rations; Amy had ruined those plans, too.

Amy pulled the ottoman over to the table and sat down as her mother sprinkled a few spices she had saved over the food. Her father took a call over the communo, barked a few words at its screen, and hung up. "That was Debora Lister." He moved the two chairs to the table, then seated himself. "I told her you couldn't talk."

Amy poked at her zymobeef and broccolettes listlessly. Just as well, she thought. Debora would only be calling to tell her what had happened when Shakira showed up, alone and triumphant, at Sheepshead Bay.

"You won't be taking any calls from your friends for a while," her father continued. "I'll notify the principal at school that you're not to leave school levels except to go directly home, and a monitor will note when you leave, so don't think you can wander around during the return trip. When you're not in school, you'll stay here except for going to meals with us or to the Personal. And in your free time, when you're not studying, you'll prepare a report for me on the dangers of strip-running. You shouldn't find the data hard to come by, and you'll present it to me in a week." Ricardo took a breath. "And if I even hear that you've been running the strips again, I'll turn you in to the police myself and demand a hearing for you."

"Eat your food, Amy," her mother said; it was the first time she had spoken.

"I'm not hungry."

"You'd better—it's all we have left of home rations for this week."

She forced herself to eat. Her father finished his food and propped his elbows on the table. "There's something I still don't understand," he said wearily. "Why, Amy? Why would you do such a thing? I thought you had more sense. Why would you risk it?"

She could bear no more. "I'm the best." She stood up and kicked back the ottoman. "I'm the best strip-runner in the City! That's all I'll ever do, it's all anybody will remember about me! I was the best, and now they've taken it away!"

Her father's gray eyes widened. "You're not sounding very repentant, young lady."

"I'm sorry I lost! I'm sorry I was caught! I'm sorry you had to come and get me, but I'm not sorry about anything else!"

"Go to your room!" he shouted. "If I hear any more talk like that, I will raise a hand to you!"

Alysha reached across the table and grabbed his upraised arm as Amy fled to her room.

* * * *

Her life was over. Amy could not view matters any other way. The story had made the rounds quickly. She had lost to Shakira Lewes and been picked up by the police; Luis Horton was doing his best to spread the news. A hall monitor noted the times she left the school levels and reminded her, right in front of other students, that she was expected to go straight home; a few boys and girls always snickered.

She greeted questions from her friends, even Debora, with a scowl, and soon no one was speaking to her outside of class. Nobody dared to bring up the run, or to tell her what the Lewes woman had said when she arrived at the destination. There was the inevitable conference with Mr. Liang and her mother, and an additional embarrassment when the guidance counselor learned about the report she was preparing for her father. She delivered the report over the school's public address screens, forced by Mr. Liang and the principal to repudiate the game; she cringed inwardly whenever she thought of how the students who had viewed her image must be laughing at her. Time inside the Youth Offenders' Level couldn't have been much worse.

After three weeks, her parents eased up a little. Amy still had to come home directly from school, but they allowed her to do schoolwork with friends in the subsection after supper. News of her downfall had been replaced by gossip about Luis Horton's successful run to the edge of Queens against Tom Jandow's gang. Her friends were again speaking to her, but knew enough not to mention Shakira Lewes.

She was ruined, and it was all that woman's fault. She dreaded the daily journeys along the strips, when she sometimes glimpsed other runners and recalled what she had lost. She could no longer hear the music of the strips, the rhythmic song in their humming that urged her to race. She was already at the end of the line; the last bit of freedom she would ever know was gone. She would become only another speck inside the caves of steel, her past glory forgotten.

* * * *

Amy left the elevator at her floor with Debora, then suddenly stiffened with shock. Down the hall, Shakira Lewes was loitering outside the Women's Personal.

"What's she doing here?" the blond girl asked.

"I don't know."

"I never told you," Debora said, "but when she finished the run, she—"

"I don't want to hear about it." Amy took out her key when they reached the door, determined to ignore the woman. Hanging around outside a Personal was the crudest sort of behavior.

"Hello, Amy," Shakira said.

"Haven't you caused enough trouble?" Amy snapped. "You don't belong here."

"But we never had our talk. This is the first chance I've had to find you, and I was pretty sure you'd be stopping here after school."

Amy gritted her teeth. "Now I can't even go and take a piss in peace."

Shakira said, "I want to talk to you." She lowered her voice as three women left the Personal. "Tonight, after supper, alone."

Amy's fingers tightened around her key. "Why should I talk to you?"

Shakira shrugged. "I'll be at the Hempstead G-level, at the end of the Long Island Expressway. Get off and cross the strips to G-20th Street.

I'll be standing in front of a store called Tad's Antiques—think you can find it?"

Amy felt insulted. "I know my way around. But I don't know why I should bother."

"Then don't. I'll be there by seven and I'll wait until nine. If you don't show up, that's your business, and I won't pester you again, but you might be interested in what I have to tell you." Shakira turned and walked toward the elevator before Amy could reply.

Debora pulled her away from the Personal door. "Are you going?" she asked.

"Yes. I've got to find out what she wants."

"But your parents told you not to leave the subsection. If any of their friends see you—"

"I'm going anyway. I have to go." She would settle matters with the young woman one way or another.

"To the edge of the City?" Debora whispered.

"She can't do anything to me on the street with people around. Deb, you have to cover for me. I can tell my parents I'll be at your place. I don't think they'll call to check, but if they do, tell them I went to the Personal."

"If my father doesn't get to the communo first."

"I'll just have to take the chance," Amy said.

Debora let out her breath. "She may want to challenge you again. What'll you do?"

"I'll worry about that when I get there." She had already made her decision. If Shakira wanted another run, she couldn't refuse, and she'd make sure some of the boys she knew were waiting at the destination as witnesses. Whatever the risk, it was a chance to restore her lost honor.

* * * *

Amy was on G-20th Street by seven-thirty. Shakira, as she had promised, was waiting in front of the antique store, which had an old-fashioned flat sign in script. There weren't many stores in the shabby neighborhood, where the high metallic walls of the residence levels seemed duller than most, and no more than a few hundred people in the street. Amy felt apprehensive. Sections like this one were the worst in the City; only badly off citizens would live here, so close to the Outside.

Shakira was gazing at an attractive display of old plastic cutlery and cups in the store window. Inside the store, the owner had made one concession to modem times; a robot was waiting on the line of customers. "Didn't take you long to get here," the woman murmured.

"I shouldn't be here at all," Amy said. "I'm not supposed to leave my subsection, but my parents think I'm with a friend." For once, they hadn't asked too many questions, and had even seemed a little relieved that she would be gone for the evening. "I told them I'd be back by ten-thirty, so say what you have to say."

"I didn't want to make that run, but you insisted, and I still have my pride." Shakira looped her fingers around her belt. "Then, once I was running, old habits took over. Maybe I wanted to see if I still had my reflexes."

"You must have had a good time bragging about it later."

"I didn't brag," Shakira said. "I just met the kids and told them to go home. I said it was tough shaking you, and that you were one of the best runners who ever tailed me."

Amy's lip curled. "How nice of you, Shakira. You still beat me."

"I saw what happened, why you didn't jump back on the strip. Some runners would have risked it anyway, even with less room than you had. They would have jumped, and if a couple of people got knocked off the strip, too bad. I'm glad you aren't that antisocial."

"What do you want with me, anyway?" Amy asked; A few women stopped near her to look in the store window, but she ignored them; even in this wretched area, people wouldn't be crass enough to eavesdrop.

"Well, I heard about this girl, Amy Barone-Stein, who could run the strips with the best of them. I still know a few runners, even though most of my college friends would disapprove of them. I thought you might be a little like me—restless; maybe a bit angry, wondering if you'd ever be more than a component in the City's machine."

Amy stepped back a little. "So what?"

"I thought you might like a challenge."

"But you said before that you didn't want to make that run."

"I'm not talking about that," Shakira said. "I mean a real challenge, something a lot harder and more interesting than running strips. It might be worthwhile for you if you've got the guts for it." Amy took another step backward, certain that the woman was about to propose a shady undertaking. "You see, I'm part of that group of Lije's—Elijah Baley's—the people who go Outside once a week. His son Bentley is an acquaintance of mine."

Amy gaped at her, completely surprised. "But why—"

"There are only a few of us so far. The City gives us a little support, mostly because of Lije—Mr. Baley—but I suspect the City government thinks we're as eccentric as everyone else does, and that we're deluded to think we can ever settle another world."

"Why bother?" Amy said. "The Spacers'll never let anyone off Earth."

"Lije left, didn't he?"

"That was different, and they sent him back here as fast as they could. I'll bet they didn't even thank him for solving that murder. They'd never let a bunch of Earthpeople on one of their worlds."

"Not one of theirs, no." Shakira leaned against the window. "But Lije Baley is convinced they'll allow settlers on an uninhabited world eventually—maybe sooner than we think—and that they'll provide us with ships to get there. But we can't settle another world unless we're able to live Outside a City."

Amy shook her head. "Nobody can live Outside."

"Earthpeople used to. The Earthpeople who settled the Spacer worlds long ago did. The Spacers do, and we manage to—for two or three hours a week, anyway. It's a start, just getting accustomed to that, and it isn't easy, but any settlers will have to be people like us, who've shown we can leave a City."

"And you want me in this group?" Amy asked.

"I thought you might be interested. We could use more recruits, and younger people seem to adapt more quickly. Just think of it—if we do get to leave Earth, every single settler will be needed, every person will be important and useful. We'll need people willing to gamble on a new life, individualists who want to make a mark, maybe even folks who are just a little antisocial as long as they can cooperate with others. You could be one of them, Amy."

"If you ever leave."

Shakira smiled. "What have you got to lose by trying?" She paused. "Do you have any idea of how precarious life inside this City is? How much more uranium can we get for our power plants? Think of all the power we have to use just to bring in water and get rid of waste. Just imagine what would happen if the air were cut off even for an hour or two—people would die by the hundreds of thousands. We'll have to leave the Cities. They can't keep growing indefinitely without taking up land we need for farming or forests we need for pulp. There'll be less food, less space, less of everything, until—"

Amy looked away for a moment. Her mother had said the same thing to her.

"There isn't a future here, Amy." Shakira moved closer to her. "There might be one for us on other worlds."

Amy sighed. "What a few people do won't make any difference."

"It's a beginning, and if we succeed, others will follow. You seemed to think what you did was important when you were only running the strips." The young woman beckoned to her. "Here's my challenge for you. I'm asking you if you'll come Outside with me."

"With those people?"

"Right now. Surely a strip-runner who used to risk life and limb isn't afraid of a little open air."

"But—"

"Come on."

She followed Shakira down the street, helpless to resist. The woman stopped in front of an opening in the high walls. Amy peered around her and saw a long, dimly lit tunnel with another wall at its end.

"What is it?" Amy asked.

"An exit. Some of them are guarded now, but this one isn't. There really isn't any need to watch them—most people don't know about them or don't want to think about them. Even the people living in this subsection have probably forgotten this exit is here. Will you come with me?"

"What if somebody follows us?" Amy glanced nervously down the street, which seemed even emptier than before. "It isn't safe."

"Believe me, nobody will follow. They'd rather believe this place doesn't exist. Will you come?"

Amy swallowed hard, then nodded. It was only a passageway; it couldn't be that bad. They entered; she kept close to the young woman as the familiar, comforting noise of the street behind them grew fainter.

Shakira said, "The exit's at the end." Her voice sounded hollow in the eerie silence. Amy's stomach knotted as they came to the end of the tunnel.

"Ready?" Shakira asked.

"I think so."

"Hang on to me. It'll be dark Outside—that'll make it easier for you, and I won't let go."

Shakira pressed her hand against the wall. An opening slowly appeared. Amy felt cold air on her face; as they stepped Outside, the door closed behind them. She closed her eyes, terrified to look, already longing for the warmth and safety of the City.

A gust of wind slapped her, fiercer than the wind on the fastest strips. She opened her eyes and looked up. A black sky dotted with stars was above her, and that bright pearly orb had to be the moon. Except for the wind and the bone-chilling cold, she might almost have been inside a City planetarium. But the planetarium had not revealed how vast the sky was, or shown the silvery clouds that drifted below the black heavens. She lowered her gaze; a bluish-white plain, empty except for the distant domes of a farm, stretched in front of her. Her ears throbbed at the silence that was broken only by the intermittent howl of the wind.

Open air—and the white substance covering the ground had to be snow. The wind gusted again, lifting a thin white veil of flakes, then died. There was space all around her, unfiltered air, dirt under her feet, and the moon shining down on all of it; the safety of walls was gone. Her stomach lurched as her heart pounded; her head swam. Her grip on Shakira loosened; the pale plain was spinning. Then she was falling through the endless silence into a darkness as black as the sky…

Arms caught her, lifting her up; she felt warmth at her back. The silence was gone. She clawed at the air and realized she was back inside the tunnel.

She blinked; her mouth was dry. "Are you all right?" Shakira felt her forehead; Amy leaned heavily against her. "I got you inside as fast as I could. I'm sorry—I forgot there'd be a full moon tonight. It would have been easier for you if it had been completely dark."

Amy trembled, afraid to let go. "I didn't know," she said. "I didn't think—" She shivered with relief, welcoming the warmth, the faint but steady noise from the street, the walls of the City. She tried to smile. "Guess I didn't do so well."

"But you did. The first time I went Outside, I passed out right after taking my first breath of open air. The second time, I ran back inside after a few seconds and swore I'd never set foot Outside again. You did a lot better than that—I was counting. We must have been standing there for nearly two minutes."

Shakira supported her with one arm; they made their way slowly toward the street. "Can you walk by yourself?" the woman asked as they left the tunnel.

"I think so." Shakira let go. Amy stared down the street, which had seemed so empty earlier, relieved at the sight of all the people. "I couldn't do that again, Shakira. I couldn't face it—all that space."

"I think you can." Shakira folded her arms. "You can if you don't give up now. We'll be going Outside in two days. You'll have to wear more clothes—it'd help if you can get gloves and a hat." Amy shook her head, struck by the strangeness of needing warmer clothes; the temperature inside never varied. "It's winter, so we'll only take a short walk—we won't be Outside very long. I'd like you to come with us. I'll stay by the exit with you, and you needn't remain Outside a second longer than you can bear. Believe me, if you keep trying, even if you think you can't stand it, it'll get easier. You may even start to look forward to it."

"I don't know—" Amy started to say.

"Will you try?"

Amy took a deep breath, smelling the odors of the City, the faint pungency of bodies, a whiff of someone's perfume, a sharp, acrid scent she could not place; she had never noticed the smells before. "I'll try." She drew her brows together. "My parents will kill me if they ever find out. I'll have to think of an excuse—"

"But you must tell them, Amy."

"They'll never let me go."

"Then you'll have to find a way to convince them. They have to know for two very good reasons. One is that it'll cause trouble for Lije if kids come Outside without their families' permission, and the other is that they just might decide to join us themselves. I'll come by your place for you, so you'll have to tell them why I'm there. You can give me your answer then."

"There's something else," Amy said. "That Mr. Baley—he's a detective. When he finds out I got picked up, he may not want me."

Shakira laughed. "Don't worry about that. I'll tell you a secret—Lije Baley was a pretty good strip-runner in his day. I heard a little about his past from my uncle and another old-timer. He won't hold that against you, but don't say anything to the others about it." Shakira took her arm as they walked toward the strips. "We'd better get home."

Amy glanced at her. "You wouldn't want to try another run?"

"Not a chance. You've had enough trouble, and you've got more to lose now. Maybe some dancing, but only if there's room, and only on the slow strips."

* * * *

The sturdy walls of her Kingsbridge subsection surrounded Amy once more. She had nearly forgotten the coldness, the wind, the silence, the terrible emptiness of the Outside.

Yet she knew she would have to go Outside again. The comforting caves of steel would not always be a safe refuge. She would have to face the emptiness until she no longer feared it, and wondered how the City would seem to her then.

She waited by the apartment door for a few moments before slipping her key into the slot. Her parents might be asleep already, and she could not tell them about this event at breakfast in the section kitchen. She could tell them tomorrow night, and would try not to hope for too much.

The door opened; she went inside. Her parents were still awake, cuddling together on the couch; they sat up quickly and adjusted their nightrobes.

"Amy!" Her father looked a bit embarrassed. "You're home early."

"I thought I was late."

He glanced at the wall timepiece. "Oh—I guess you are. I hadn't noticed. Well, I'll let it pass this once."

Amy studied the couple. They seemed in a good mood; her mother's brown eyes glowed, and her father's broad face lacked its usual tenseness. She might not get a better chance to speak to them, and did not want her mother finding out from Mrs. Lister at breakfast that she hadn't been at Debora's.

"Um." Amy cleared her throat. "I have to talk to you."

Her father looked toward the timepiece again. "Is it important?"

"It's very important." She went to a chair and sat down across from them. "It really can't wait. Please—just let me talk until I'm finished, and then you can say whatever you want." She paused. "I wasn't at Deb's. I know I wasn't supposed to, but I left the subsection."

Her father started; her mother reached for his hand.

"Not to run strips, I swear," Amy added hastily. She lowered her eyes, afraid to look directly at them, then told them about her first meeting with Shakira, the run that had ended in disaster, the encounter on the street in Hempstead, what Shakira had said about the group that went Outside, and the challenge she had met that night by facing the open space beyond the City. She wasn't telling the story very well, having to pause every so often to fill in a detail, but by the time she reached the end, she was sure she had mentioned all the essentials.

Her parents said nothing throughout, and were silent when she finished. At last she forced herself to raise her head. Her father looked stunned, her mother bewildered.

"You went Outside?" Alysha whispered.

"Yes."

"Weren't you terrified?"

"I was never so scared in my life, but I had to—I—"

Her father sagged against the couch. "You deliberately disobeyed us." He sounded more exasperated than angry. "You lied and told us you'd be with Debora Lister. You left the subsection to meet a dubious young woman who's a damned strip-runner herself, and—"

"She isn't," Amy protested. "She doesn't run any more, and she wouldn't have with me if I hadn't insisted—I told you. That was my fault."

"At least you're admitting your guilt," he said. "I let you have your say, so allow me to finish. Now she wants you to traipse around Outside with that group of hers. I forbid it—do you hear? You're not to have anything more to do with her, and if she calls or comes here, I'll tell her so myself. I'll have to be firmer with you, Amy. Since you can't be honest with us about your doings, you'll be restricted to this apartment again, and—"

"Rick." Alysha's voice was low, but firm. "Let me speak. If joining those people means so much to Amy, then maybe she should." Ricardo's face paled as he turned toward his wife. "I know she disobeyed us, but I think I can understand why she felt it necessary. Anyway, how much trouble can she get into if a City detective's with them? They seem harmless enough."

"Harmless?" her husband said. "Going Outside, deluding themselves that—"

"Let her go, Rick." Alysha pressed his hand between both of hers. "That young woman told her the truth. You know it's true—you can see what the Department's statistical projections show, whether you'll admit it to yourself or not. If there's any chance that those people with Elijah Baley can leave Earth, maybe it's better if Amy goes with them."

Amy drew in her breath, startled that her mother was taking her side and confronting her father in her presence.

"You'd accept that?" Ricardo asked. "What if the Spacers actually allow those people off Earth—not that I think it's likely, but what if they do? You're saying you'd be content never to see your daughter again."

"I wouldn't be content—you know better than that. But how can I cling to her if she has a chance, however small, at something else? I know what her life will be here, perhaps better than you do. I'd rather know she's doing something meaningful to her somewhere else, even if that means we'll lose her, than to have to go through life pretending I don't see her frustrations and disappointments."

Ricardo heaved a sigh. "I can't believe I'm hearing you say this."

"Oh, Rick." She released his hand. "You would have expected me to say and do the unexpected years ago." She smiled at that phrase. "How conventional we've become since then." She gazed at him silently for a bit. "Maybe I'll go with Amy when she meets that group. I should see what kind of people they are, after all. Maybe I'll even take a step Outside myself."

Her husband frowned, looking defeated. "This is a fine situation," he said. "Not only do I have a disobedient daughter, but now my wife's against me, too. If my co-workers hear you're both wandering around with that group of Baley's, it may not do me much good in the Department."

"Really?" Amy's mother arched her brows. "They always knew we were both a bit, shall we say, eccentric, and that didn't bother you once. Perhaps you should come with us to meet Mr. Baley's group. It'd be wiser to have your colleagues think you're going along with our actions, however odd or amusing they may find them, than to believe there's a rift between us." Her mouth twisted a little. "You know what they say— happy families make for a better City."

Ricardo turned toward Amy. "You'd do it again? Go Outside, I mean. You'd actually go through that again?"

"Yes, I would," Amy replied. "I know it'll be hard, but I'd try."

"It's late," her father said. "I can't think about this now." He stood up and took Alysha by the arm as she rose. "We'll discuss this tomorrow, after I've had a chance to consider it. Good night, Amy."

"Good night."

Her mother was whispering to her father as Amy went to her room. Her father had backed down for now, and her mother was almost certain to bring him around. She undressed for bed, convinced she had won her battle.

She stretched out, tired and ready to sleep, and soon drifted into a dream. She was on the strips again, riding through an open arch to the Outside, but she wasn't afraid this time.

* * * *

The City slept. The strips and expressways continued to move, car- rying the few who were awake—young lovers who had crept out to meet each other, policemen on patrol, hospital workers heading home after a night shift, and restless souls drawn to wander the caverns of New York.

Amy stood on a strip, a sprinkling of people around her. Four boys raced past her, leaping from strip to strip; for a moment, she was tempted to join their race. She had come out at night a few times before, to prac- tice some moves when the strips were emptier, returning to her subsec- tion before her parents awoke. More riders began to fill the slowest strip; the City was waking. Her parents would be up by the time she got back, but she was sure they would understand why she had been drawn out here tonight.

Her parents had come with her to meet Elijah Baley and his group. The detective was a tall, dark-haired man with a long, solemn face, but he had brightened a little when Shakira introduced her new recruits. Amy's mother and father had not gone Outside with them; perhaps they would next time. She knew what an effort it would be for them, and hoped they could find the courage to take that step. They would be with her when the group met again; they had promised that much. When she was able to face the openness without fear, to stride across the ground bravely as Shakira did, maybe she would lead them Outside herself.

She leaped up, spun around in a dervish, and ran along the strip. The band hummed under her feet; she could hear its music again. She bounded forward, did a handspring, then jumped to the next strip. She danced across the gray bands until she reached the expressway, then hauled herself aboard.

Her hands tightened around the pole as she recalled her first glimpse of daylight. The whiteness of the snow had been blinding, and above it all, in the painfully clear blue sky, was a bright ball of flame, the naked sun. She had known she was standing on a ball of dirt clad only in a thin veil of air, a speck that was hurtling through a space more vast and empty than anything she could see. The terror had seized her then, driving her back inside, where she had cowered on the floor, sick with fear and despair. But there had also been Shakira's strong arms to help her up, and Elijah Baley's voice telling her of his own former fears. Amy had not gone Outside again that day, but she had stood in the open doorway and forced herself to take one more breath of wintry air.

It was a beginning. She had to meet the challenge if she was ever to lead others Outside, or to follow the hopeful settlers to another world.

She left the expressway and danced along the strips, showing her form, imagining that she was running one last race. She was near the Hempstead street where she had met Shakira.

The street was nearly empty, its store windows darkened. Amy left the strips and hurried toward the tunnel, running along the passageway until her breath came in short, sharp gasps. When she reached the end, she hesitated for only a moment, then pressed her hand against the wall.

The opening appeared. The muted hum from the distant strips faded behind her, and she was Outside, alone, with the morning wind in her face. The sky was a dark dome above her. She looked east and saw dawn brightening the cave of stars.

Afterword to "Strip-Runner"

When I began reading science fiction regularly, one of my favorite novels was Isaac Asimov's *The Caves of Steel*, a book that could only have been written by a confirmed city-dweller. (Except for the years he taught at Boston University's School of Medicine, Dr. Asimov lived in New York City all his life.) During my teens, I entertained the idea of writing my own story set in that world and centering it around a female strip-runner, because even then the lack of important female characters in the novel bothered me. The only major woman character in *The Caves of Steel* was Lije Baley's wife, Jessie, who was portrayed as a wife and homemaker, apparently the only position married women in this future society could hold. This restrictive view of women wasn't uncommon, unfortunately, in science fiction written during the 1950s, and I assumed this might have been an unconscious default characterization on Asimov's part.

In the late 1980s Marty Greenberg, after obtaining Isaac Asimov's permission, offered several writers the chance to write stories set in the various Asimovian fictional universes as a tribute to the Good Doctor, to be published in an original anthology, *Foundation's Friends*. At last I had the chance to fulfill my adolescent ambition of writing a story set in the New York City of *The Caves of Steel*. I reread that novel, following it with rereadings of all the robot novels through *Robots and Empire*, and realized that given the assumptions Asimov had made about his future New York City (a shortage of jobs, an overcrowded city with little privacy, rationing, and a strong emphasis on cooperation embodied in the phrase "Civism is good. The Cities are the height of human civilization"), it was probably logical that women's roles be more limited in this world. But Asimov, toward the end of his "Robot" series, had given Lije Baley a way out of his more restricted existence, which enabled me to give Amy Barone-Stein a way out of hers.

A SMALLER GOVERNMENT

"My goal is to cut government in half in twenty-five years, to get it down to the size where we can drown it in the bathtub."
—Grover Norquist

Hector was sitting on his usual bench in Lafayette Park, across the street from the White House, freezing his ass off in the cold wintry air. On a bench nearby, the Homeless Lobbyist was consulting with the Homeless Philosopher. The Philosopher was expounding to the Lobbyist and anyone else within earshot about something he called the ethics bank and moral bankruptcy problem, although he wasn't being all that coherent. Now he was saying something about physical manifestations of moral lapses and chickens coming home to roost.

The mention of chickens reminded Hector that he hadn't chowed down in a while. He was thinking that maybe it was about time to head for the shelter when the night air rippled. Then there was a loud whooshing sound, followed by a thunderclap.

"Shee-it!" the Homeless Lobbyist exclaimed.

"What the hell?" the Homeless Philosopher asked. For a moment, Hector had wondered if the rippling air and the whooshing noise were only symptoms of some weirdassed case of the d.t.s, but the Lobbyist and the Philosopher had apparently seen and heard the same thing.

Then the bright lights across the way went out, and the White House disappeared.

"Shee-it!" the Homeless Lobbyist shouted again. He dropped his brown paper bag and the bottle inside shattered.

Hector sat there, too surprised to move. After a few moments, the low rumble to Hector's right grew into a roar. A convoy of tanks rolled past the Eisenhower Executive Office Building and stopped in front of the park. A couple of soldiers climbed down from one of the tanks, while other members of the armed services fanned out across the park.

"Come on," the taller of the soldiers said as he approached. To Hector's left, the Lobbyist and the Philosopher were being dragged away by several other soldiers.

"What the hell's going on?" Hector asked. "Where'd the White House go?"

"Didn't go anywhere." The soldiers grabbed him by the arms.

"It disappeared, for Chrissake." He twisted in their grip. "Was sittin' right here, and it fuckin' disappeared!"

"Not exactly," the shorter soldier replied.

* * * *

The Secretary of Commerce was with the Senator and the Congressman in a relatively comfy secure and undisclosed location. The Secret Service had brought in some snacks, plates of little puffed pastries with shrimp and crabmeat, diminutive tarts, and tiny cocktail wieners impaled on toothpicks. The Secretary could have used a cocktail himself, but the only beverages in evidence were coffee, tea, bottled water, and assorted soft drinks.

He sat back with a cup of coffee, figuring he'd need the caffeine to stay awake throughout the State of the Union address. The President was not only long-winded, but also had a voice that had become noticeably whinier and more high-pitched since his inauguration a year ago. If he had sounded like that during the campaign, thought the Secretary, he would never have made it past the first primary. Then again, the President had a lot on his mind, enough to give anyone a whiny voice and rapidly graying hair. His predecessor had left him with cesspools on all fronts.

"Did he get Joey to polish the speech this time?" the Senator asked. She was an imposing woman from Connecticut who belonged to the other party.

"I dunno," the Secretary replied; he wasn't exactly in the inner circle and didn't even know who among the President's speechwriters had sketched out the first draft.

"Sure hope he did," the Congressman muttered; he was a barrel-chested man of the Secretary's own party from Illinois. "Or else we're in for a long fuckin' night."

On the large plasma screen, tuned to C-SPAN to spare the Secretary any media gasbagging from the major networks, the President was still gladhanding his way toward the dais, shaking hands and clutching shoulders. The Secretary had finished his coffee and was munching on a tiny cocktail frank by the time the President was handing copies of his address to the Vice-President and the Speaker of the House.

The screen abruptly went blank.

"Fuckin' C-SPAN," the Congressman said. "If you ask me, they got too many damn glitches lately." The Secretary reached for the remote on the coffee table and switched to CNN.

"…just disappeared." A blond news babe was on the screen. She looked a bit green around the gills, but not because of any issues with the screen's color contrast controls. "And now a report's coming in from our White House correspondent. The White House is gone, too."

"Holy shit," the Congressman said.

In the corner of the room, two of the Secret Service agents were cupping their ears, clearly intent on whatever was coming in through their earpieces. The Secretary switched to Fox.

"…reports from all over the city," the voice of a male correspondent intoned. The dark and murky image on the screen showed tanks rolling past Lafayette Park. The Secretary was seized by a powerful surge of emotion compounded of both ecstasy and terror. He, the Senator, and the Congressman, those chosen this time to be tucked away in the customary secure and undisclosed location while the rest of Washington's potentates were at the Capitol, might be all that was left of the government.

He tried for NBC but found himself back at C-SPAN. The President was still at the podium, with no words coming out of his mouth, while the look on his face was that of a man about to be arrested. A big bruiser wearing an earpiece was passing a piece of paper to him.

"I don't get it," the Congressman said.

Three of the Secret Service agents stepped in front of the screen, blocking the Secretary's view. "What's going on?" he asked.

The agent tapped his earpiece. "You're not going to believe this, Mr. Secretary," he began.

* * * *

The Secret Service officer had performed some odd actions in the course of his duties. He had ridden in the freight elevators of hotels where the President was staying, the only elevators that could be truly secured, with him and his fellow agents packed as tightly around their charge as passengers on a low-fare flight. He had rerouted traffic during rush hours to allow for the Presidential motorcade, closely observed annoyed chefs in restaurant kitchens, had forced the cancellation of long-held reservations at resorts where Air Force One was headed, and generally made an unholy nuisance of himself in the course of protecting the Commander-in-Chief. But looking out for the big guy during the State of the Union address was, generally speaking, a piece of cake, because security was so tight throughout the Capitol and in D.C. at that time.

But now, looking around at the assembled dignitaries in the House chamber, he could see that pretty much all of them suspected that something was up. One of his fellow agents had discreetly passed a note to the President just before he was to begin his opening remarks, and so far the President was doing a decent job of huddling with the Vice-President and the Speaker as if he just had a few last-minute items to iron out, but the Supreme Court Justices were definitely looking restless, while the Joint Chiefs of Staff looked like they had bigger than usual ramrods up their asses. Camera crews from the networks were still going about their business, and he wondered what the TV audience, that small percentage that even bothered to watch the State of the Union, was seeing.

"C-SPAN's just about to cut off its cameras," a voice said in his earpiece, answering his question, "and all the networks have gone to their anchors for special reports. We've got the Capitol and the White House surrounded, so nothing's going to get through." There was a pause. "Okay, guys, time to tell you just exactly what's going on, but brace yourselves."

Terrorists, the officer thought. They'd finally done it, struck at a time when the whole country, or at least that segment of it that wasn't in the middle of watching ESPN, HBO, or rented DVDs, would be transfixed with terror, glued to their screens the way they'd been during those dark days in September at the turn of the century. All of the Secret Service agents inside the chamber—those by the doorways, at the end of the aisles, in the balcony with the First Lady and honored guests, and standing near the President—stood at attention while continuing to scan the room, heads turning from side to side.

"It's like this," the voice in his ear continued. "The Capitol, like, suddenly got real small, and so did the White House. What happened was this weird rippling in the air kind of deal, and then suddenly stuff shrank. I'm talking about the White House, the Capitol, the House and Senate Office Buildings, and pretty much everything on either side of Pennsylvania Avenue. Basically, the White House is now about the size of Malibu Barbie's beach house, and the Capitol dome isn't much bigger than a goddamn teacup."

The Secret Service officer pondered this statement. If the Capitol was so tiny, how could all of them still be inside it? The answer came to him just before the voice provided further illumination.

"And it looks like all of you...us...shrank right along with everything else."

* * * *

Pennsylvania Avenue was still the same size, despite the shrunken size of the bordering real estate. Rows of troops, along with police called in from surrounding counties of Maryland and Virginia, had been stationed around the Capitol and were lined up on Constitution and Independence Avenues, ready to protect the Lilliputians trapped inside the

Capitol Building from any Brobdignagian constituents seeking redress for real or imagined grievances. There was a rumor that some residents of Anacostia were preparing to converge on the Capitol.

They could stamp us all flat, the First Lady thought. She stared at her hands, which seemed the same size they had always been, but if everything here had shrunk proportionately, then everything should still look the same. If she went outside, she would notice the difference. Any eagle soaring overhead would probably look like an Airbus.

She sat in an office just outside the House chamber, along with the President, the Vice-President, the Vice-President's wife, the National Security Advisor, the Domestic Policy Advisor, and several Secret Service agents, her jaws aching from the smile she had struggled to keep in place even after she had been led out of the chamber and ushered to this temporary sanctuary. Her husband, as usual when things got really heavy, had a bewildered expression on his face, as if hoping that, real soon now, somebody would tell him exactly what to do.

"So what the hell happens now?" the Vice-President asked, looking even more morose than usual. "Can't park our asses here forever."

"True enough," the Domestic Policy Advisor muttered as he rubbed his bald pate, "but we're safer staying here for the moment. Easier to protect us."

The First Lady shuddered, then thought of all the time she had spent refurbishing the White House, rescuing it from the tacky excesses of her predecessor and restoring the residence to its former glory, only to have it all taken from her, reduced to the size of a dollhouse. But perhaps all of her efforts weren't necessarily wasted.

"Couldn't we all just go back to the White House?" she asked. Her husband gazed at her as if clutching a life preserver; the Vice-President glowered at her as though wanting to push her overboard. "I mean, it's teeny now, but so are we, apparently, and I'm sure we could be just as well protected there." The staff had to be as tiny as they were, at least those who were still there attending to their nighttime duties, so life could go on, even if on a somewhat smaller scale.

"That's all well and good for you," the Vice-President's wife murmured, "but where are we supposed to live? If we set foot inside our house, it's a toss-up which of our cats gobbles us up first." The Vice-Presidential residence had apparently escaped shrinkage, along with most of Washington, but that was small consolation to the First Lady. The Rayburn, Longworth, and Cannon House Office Buildings, along with the Russell, Dirksen, and Hart Senate Office Buildings, were the size of a set of children's blocks, while the Supreme Court Building could now rest easily on scales held by any good-sized statue of Justice.

She should be grateful that the F.B.I. Building hadn't shrunk during the daytime, when many more people there would have been in their offices, and that the Pentagon and the C.I.A. remained untouched, even though nobody there had been able to prevent what seemed a massive breach of national security.

"I have an idea," the Foreign Policy Advisor said. "Couldn't we just, well, like, go about our usual business?" She cast a wide-eyed glance around the room. "I mean, apparently the broadcast wasn't affected, at least not until the cameramen were told to shut it down, so wouldn't we still look the same on TV?"

"That won't do us any good the next time we hold a summit," the Vice-President growled.

"Or a state dinner, for that matter," the First Lady said.

The Vice-President frowned even more. "Some superpower we'd look like."

A door opened and a man wearing the dark suit and earpiece of a Secret Service agent lunged into the room and slammed the door behind him. "Got some news," he said.

"Hope it's good news," the President said, looking a little less lost.

The Vice-President scowled. "In this context, about the only thing that might count as good news is getting low bids from Mattel and Toys 'R Us for future government services."

"Better news than that," the agent replied.

* * * *

The House Sergeant-at-Arms made the discovery. He was standing in a doorway at the East Front of the Capitol because, after all the strangeness of the evening, he needed a smoke. Luckily, his cigarettes had shrunk along with him, while the few inches of snow that had been predicted for that evening had failed to materialize; he would not have wanted to confront a glacial mass in order to enjoy a cigarette.

He stood above the stairway, puffing away, until someone tapped him on the shoulder. He turned to find that the Mayor of Washington, D.C. had also stepped out for a smoke. The two men smoked together in silence, gazing out at the mountainous dark forms of tanks and forests of trousered legs that surrounded the Capitol. Finally the Sergeant-at-Arms said, "Think I'll take a walk."

"Man, maybe that ain't such a good idea," the Mayor said, "you bein' sized so small as you are."

"I advise against it," a member of the Honor Guard said behind them. "You wouldn't want to get gooshed." Another serviceman nodded his head.

"Nobody's going to goosh me with all those tanks around, and my doc keeps telling me I need more exercise, what with my cholesterol and all," the Sergeant-at-Arms said.

"If you're worried about your cholesterol," another young military man muttered, "then you ought to quit smoking."

"Watch out for pigeons," the Mayor added.

The Sergeant-at-Arms descended the steps, breathing in the cold night air between drags, and wondered how that was possible; maybe the molecules of air around him had shrunk along with the Capitol. He dropped his butt, ground it out with his foot, and tried to recall what one of his high school science teachers had said about a square cube law or whatever it was. If people were the size of grasshoppers, they'd be able to hop around like grasshoppers.

He was envisioning tiny members of Congress leaping high in the air from the Capitol steps, flapping their arms to ward off flies that would be nearly half their size, when the air seemed to ripple around him. For a moment, as his body vibrated, he felt a not unpleasant electrical sensation as the ground shifted under his feet.

Three uniformed policeman ran toward him, followed by a man in a long tweed coat, and then the Sergeant-at-Arms saw that the tanks, although still imposing, were now their normal size. The men coming toward him were of normal size, too; in fact, two of them were considerably shorter than he was.

"What the hell did you just do?" the man in the tweed coat asked.

"Came outside for a smoke and took a walk," the Sergeant-at-Arms replied.

"What you did," one of the cops said, "was just pop up out of nowhere. Maybe we better take you in for questioning." The policeman gestured toward the barricades and at the tiny Capitol dome inside them, which glowed under its small floodlights, its tiny flags on its east and west sides still proudly flying.

"I'm the House Sergeant-at-Arms, I can show you my ID." He was about to reach inside his jacket pocket before realizing that this might not be such a good idea with armed cops standing around.

"Wait a minute." The tweed-coated man scratched his head. "Maybe we'd better try an experiment." The man clapped a hand on the Sergeant-at-Arms's shoulder and shoved him toward the miniature Capitol. He felt the vibrations and then the prickly electrical sensations again as the Capitol abruptly loomed up before him in all of its majesty.

"So *that's* how it works," the man in tweed said softly.

The two tiny men turned around in unison to face six legs as big as sequoias. Far above them, a voice as loud as God's exclaimed: "Jesus H. Christ!"

They moved toward the policemen. This time, the Sergeant-at-Arms felt himself suddenly shooting up like Jack's beanstalk, or maybe Alice in Wonderland after eating that weird cookie in that Disney flick that was a favorite of his daughter's. He was again looking down at two cops who were shorter than he was.

"What now?" the Sergeant-at-Arms asked.

"Evacuate the Capitol," the man in the tweed coat said.

* * * *

It had taken a couple of weeks, but everything was almost back to normal, or at least as normal as anything could be under the circumstances. The President's Chief of Staff stood at his office window, gazing below at the cordon of tanks and soldiers around the tiny White House. He'd had to move himself and the rest of the staff over to the Eisenhower Executive Office Building, which had caused a fair amount of hard feeling. Those who had lost their cherished offices in the West Wing were not happy about their relocation to the E.E.O.B., while those who had earlier been exiled to that Siberia resented having to move their operations to the New Executive Office Building, the State Department, and the campus of George Washington University, where some basement offices had been turned over to them.

His first trip down Pennsylvania Avenue, three days after everyone had been evacuated from all the shrunken buildings, had been a sobering experience. The reduction of the F.B.I. Building had been almost as disturbing to see as the tiny Capitol. There had been talk of bringing out essential records, which would have restored them all to their normal size once they were carried outside the Peewee Zone, the appellation that had unfortunately adhered to the region of shrinkage. The problem was figuring out what was essential, since just about everything was considered essential by somebody in authority, and then finding places to store the whole shebang. In the meantime, F.B.I. agents could no longer access their files and computers, Senators and Representatives were cut off from the tiny records in their offices, the Supreme Court Justices could no longer peruse their now minute law volumes, and documents in the National Archives and at the Federal Trade Commission were unreadable to anyone over three inches in height.

At least the Lincoln Memorial, the Smithsonian Institution, and other national treasures had escaped; he would not have been able to bear seeing the Washington Monument reduced to the size of a pencil. It was also their good fortune that the offices of the Internal Revenue Service, not far from the Zone, had not been affected. But to have so many sites of power reduced to the size of scattered toys had been a heavy blow. The Chief of Staff thought of his recent conversation with the Canadian Ambassador, whose embassy on Pennsylvania Avenue was one of the shrunken structures. "So now you know how we feel sometimes, eh?" the Ambassador had said in his usually bland voice.

The phone on the desk behind him beeped. He turned to pick up the receiver. "The First Lady's Chief of Staff is here," his receptionist's voice said.

"Send her in." The door opened; a tall and emaciated woman in a red suit strode inside and sat down in the worn leather chair on the other side of his desk. "How are things going over at Blair House?" he asked. The First Family was now in residence at the guest house across the street from the Eisenhower Executive Office Building.

"About as well as you'd expect," the First Lady's Chief of Staff replied. "In other words, they totally suck. Everybody's bitching. The First Lady still thinks that she and the President should have moved into the Vice-President's residence."

"You know how the Vice-President felt about that." Actually, it had been the Vice-President's wife who had pitched a fit at that suggestion, but the Veep hadn't looked overjoyed at the idea of sharing their quarters with the First Family, either. "The set-up we've got now is about the best we can do in the interim."

The interim, he thought; he was still imagining that the tiny buildings would somehow balloon to normal size. He wished that they'd appointed a real science advisor to the President's staff instead of that Bible college biologist who had been put in to appease the more rabid of their constituents. Maybe they should put out some feelers to some of those strange institutes of nanotechnology that were popping up around the country. He didn't know much about nanotechnology except that it had something to do with very tiny things.

"I suppose you're right," the First Lady's Chief of Staff murmured, "but after all the work we put in fixing up the White House—" She paused. "That's what I'm here about. The First Lady is getting very concerned about the condition of the furnishings there."

The Chief of Staff scowled at his colleague. "What can possibly happen to them now?"

"Tiny bits of dust. Tiny spiders weaving their webs. Teeny little moths, teeny little bacteria in the kitchens, eensy-weensy dust bunnies in the Lincoln Bedroom and the Oval Office and everywhere else—you name it." She sighed. "We want to send in a cleaning crew."

The Chief of Staff was suddenly wary. "We can't," he managed to say.

"Come on, we already know that people can shrink going into the Zone and expand on their way out. Just shrink 'em in and grow 'em out."

He wondered how she had found that out. The Secret Service had sent some agents into the F.B.I. Building and both buildings of the National Gallery of Art under cover of night, making sure that they were unobserved by anyone except a few guards, and they had gone inside and emerged again with no apparent ill effects. "Who told you that?" he asked, vowing silently to punish the leaker. It occurred to him then that, if they could ever find a way to control the shrinking process, tiny little buildings might make for very effective and easily guarded prisons. That would also settle the hash of any whistle-blowers who crept in to expose abuses in the system.

"Let's just say I have my sources, and this place leaks like a sieve." The First Lady's factotum leaned forward. "So whaddya say?"

"It's too risky. Maybe the next time somebody'll go in and stay tiny when they come out. Or maybe they'll suddenly blow up when they're inside and mess up the whole damned place."

"You don't have any reason to think that'll happen."

"I don't have any reason to think that it won't." He was silent for a bit. "Wait until we've run a few more tests."

His counterpart leaned back. "Okay, okay." She let out her breath. "But don't take too long. You have no idea how messy things can get when you haven't cleaned in a while."

She was worse than his mother.

* * * *

By cherry blossom time, it was clear that people could go into the shrunken artifacts and come out again, shrinking and then expanding, with no apparent problems. The Metro under the Zone was running again; as long as passengers boarded and exited the trains at stops outside the Zone, it didn't much matter if they shrank in the interim, and nobody noticed much difference during the ride anyway. By Memorial Day weekend, tourists were returning to visit all of the famous sites, including the cute little Capitol and diminutive White House, although no visitors were allowed inside while skeleton staffs of agents, law clerks, and Congressional aides scanned and photographed the most essential of the small documents inside the Zone and emailed copies to the larger world outside; wireless Internet access was apparently unaffected by the differences in scale.

Which was all very well, the Senator from Montana thought, but having to put up with a shithole of an office in the Ford House Office Building instead of her nicely appointed and roomy space inside the Hart Building was really getting on her nerves. That all of the Congresspeople were even more crowded in the offices over at the O'Neill House Office Building, since they had conceded one of their two remaining unshrunken buildings to the Senate, did nothing to assuage her annoyance.

One of her aides sat in a corner, pecking away at a laptop; another aide was pouring himself a cup of instant coffee at the counter near the microwave. "Pour me a cup of joe, too," the Senator said. The young man poured, stirred, and set the cup on her desk with a flourish.

The Senator looked around resentfully at her crowded domain. "I don't know how much longer I can take this," she added. "Got a good mind to announce I'm not running again and that I'm resigning from public service and hauling ass back to Butte."

"I thought you hated Butte," the young woman with the laptop said.

The Senator had made her remark about Butte only for rhetorical purposes, because it sounded better than saying that she was thinking of resigning and then getting into the lobbying racket. Fortunately, K Street lay well outside the Peewee Zone. "At least I'll have enough space to turn around in back home," the Senator replied. Using "home" as a synonym for "Montana" was another rhetorical flourish; she had been living quite contentedly in her house in Virginia's much tamer horse country for over a decade. "Look, the fact of the matter is that the rest of my staff inside Hart has a lot more room right now than we do."

"They should be done with copying and emailing everything we need pretty soon, Senator," the male aide said.

That was the problem, the Senator thought, gazing at the pillars of printouts still standing on her desk for lack of enough filing cabinets. They would finish retrieving everything she really had to have within a week or so, and then she would have the impossible task of finding space for those staffers here. "Somebody should do something," she muttered.

The female aide looked up from her laptop. "Why don't you introduce a resolution?" she asked.

"A resolution about what?"

"Resolved, that the Senate will return to its offices and chambers by Election Day in order to more effectively continue to serve the American people. I mean, if everybody's staff can go in and out and get bigger and smaller as needed, there's, like, no reason why the whole Senate can't do the same. And if you introduce a resolution, somebody in the House will probably introduce one, and then maybe everything can finally get back to normal."

There was some logic to that, but something inside her resisted the suggestion. "It's absurd," the Senator said. "We can't have little tiny Senators and Congresspeople debating and passing laws inside the Zone and having them signed by an itsy bitsy President. Who the hell would take us seriously?"

"What difference would it make?" the male aide asked. "There's nothing in the Constitution or the rules of the Senate that says you have to be a certain size to hold hearings and pass laws. Besides, everything would still look the same on TV."

Her aides had a point. The Senator finished her coffee, then said, "Maybe you could start drafting that resolution, but let's change the date. We'll be back to business as usual by the Fourth of July."

* * * *

Shrinkage had done nothing to improve the slovenly ambiance of the White House Press Room. The same crappy chairs were still there, the White House Correspondent noticed as he filed in behind some other newsfolk, the same outdated equipment, the same wires all over the floor, even the same coffee and food stains on the tabletops, but the shabby familiarity of it all was oddly reassuring. The White House Correspondents' Dinner, even though postponed to a later date than usual, had been a reassuring affair this year as well, drawing nearly the same number of Hollywood celebrities as in the past. It had helped that the comedian providing the entertainment had been warned not to make any jokes about size or smallness unless he wanted everybody in the press corps and all of their famous friends to boycott his show permanently and also bring some pressure to bear on his bosses. The guy had been relying far too much on such humor for his program anyway.

The Correspondent, whose name everyone tended to forget more and more often since his network's ratings had tanked, had not been a happy camper when the head of the news department had told him in no uncertain terms that if getting tiny was what was needed to cover the President, then tiny was what he would get unless he preferred to lose his job. It wasn't as if he would have to stay tiny, except when he was inside the White House or doing standups outside of it; the network had nixed any footage that showed any of their newspeople towering over either the official residence or the Capitol. And there was no danger that anybody going into the Zone wouldn't be able to get big again outside of it. The President had been living inside the White House for over a month now, and he was still able to resume his six feet of height for trips to Camp David.

There were also the Correspondent's home in Georgetown, his Manhattan digs, his son's tuition at William and Mary, and the financial arrangements with his first and second ex-wives to consider. Anyway, he told himself, everything was pretty much photo ops these days. As long as everything looked a certain way, people in front of their TVs would come away with the impression that nothing essential had changed. Eventually most of them might forget that any shrinkage at all had occurred.

He sat down in his usual seat in the front row as the camera crews finished setting up and his colleagues settled in around him. What mattered was acting as though everything was still the same, and now that he was here, it was easier to feel that way, especially since there were no windows in the Press Room to reveal the size of everything outside these tiny walls. They were all in this together, he and the President and everybody else in Washington who mattered; he had to look at it that way.

The President's Press Secretary entered the room, smiling as he approached the podium, then resumed his usual bland expression. "I have a few announcements to make," he began, "and then you can ask your questions."

The Correspondent already knew what those announcements would include. His sources had told him that, in addition to the usual bromides about staying the newest course in the Middle East, the growing strength of the economy as indicated by the latest statistics, and more insistence that the investigation of the shrinkage incident was continuing to go forward, the President's staff had decided to have the British Prime Minister visit the President at his summer home instead of at the White House. Apparently even a close ally would not shrink in order to schmooze.

He settled back in his rickety chair; his spirits lifted just a bit. In spite of everything, the useless ritual of the White House daily briefing was comforting.

* * * *

A small Congressional investigative committee, both in numbers and size, met to inquire into what had happened.

"Any ideas about who did this to us?" the Chairman asked. The eyes of his four fellow Senators and their five House colleagues remained devoid of inspirational sparks.

Moments passed. "A terrorist," the Senator from Maryland said at last. "Some joker of a tech-terrorist." He slapped the table with one meaty hand.

"Right," muttered the Congresswoman from Florida. "He's, like, riding around in some, uh, conveyance, picking on national symbols to shrink—er, diminish."

"Sure, like Captain Nemo sinking warships with his submarine." The Chairman snorted. "If you ask me, maybe we'd better bring in some of those nano-whatever-they-are scientists. They might be able to tell us something."

"Or else they might be behind all of this," the Senator from Maryland muttered. "There's some mighty suspicious characters among scientists. A lot of them aren't even Americans."

"In terms of environmental impact," the Senator from Kentucky intoned, "we might leave a far less large footprint on the Earth if we remained at a smaller level. Perhaps we should be asking the EPA to address the environmental effects of shrinkage."

"We're here to figure out how to find the guys that did this," the Senator from Maryland said, "not to ride your hobbyhorse."

"We couldn't get shrunk any smaller, could we?" the Chairman asked. "I mean, we're already so small." He sighed. "We have to get to the bottom of this." He did not say that he suspected what the others were already thinking, that this might be only the beginning. There were a whole lot of places that the joker, or jokers, might be planning to reduce.

* * * *

Hector wasn't on his usual bench, and neither were the Homeless Lobbyist and the Homeless Philosopher. The benches where they usually sat were now behind a protective cordon of soldiers, and there were rumors that more of the park would be declared out-of-bounds. At this rate, he and the Lobbyist and the Philosopher would soon be living in the middle of H Street.

But Hector understood. The Secret Service had to think about security, and there had been stories going around about people who were angry enough over various issues to want to rush the place and stomp on everything, the White House and the Capitol. In a way, he couldn't really blame them for feeling that way, but if they had talked to the Homeless Philosopher, they would have realized that such hopes were futile.

"See, it's this way," the Philosopher had explained to him during a recent seminar and consultation over a pint of rye. "You got this here Zone where everything shrinks, so even if people got past them soldiers and the cops and the Secret Service and everybody else, they'd get small as soon as they got inside the Zone. So how the hell could they stomp anything? They'd just be milling around on the lawn until they got arrested. Jeez, they couldn't even lob a few big rocks at the place, 'cause the rocks'd shrink on their way in."

"So why are they beefing up security so much?" Hector had asked. "If there's anything to your goddamn premise, they could just station a few guys here and there and save some bucks. It's not like the deficit's gonna shrink."

"Oh, there's probably good reasons for all the protection," the Philosopher had replied. "You still gotta worry about terrorists. Teeny tiny terrorists could still do a hell of a lot of damage, 'specially if they're aiming at tiny targets. But if you ask me, I think they beefed up security out of habit. It's what they do, whatever the reason—anything happens, get more security, it doesn't matter what. More of the same. Problem solved. Makes 'em feel important." That had seemed like fallacious reasoning to Hector, but he had been too far in the bag by then to offer a convincing refutation.

The Homeless Philosopher suddenly stood up. Even in the evening light, Hector could see that the Homeless Lobbyist was trying to restrain the other man. The Philosopher knocked the Lobbyist's arms away, staggered toward the line of soldiers, then drew himself up. "Little bastards!" he yelled. "Little pricks! You're bigger than they are! Shit, *I'm* bigger than they are! So why don't you act like it?"

The soldiers were taking aim. Shut your piehole, Hector wanted to shout, but fear constricted his throat.

"Little bastards!" The Philosopher was not about to quit. "You were always small, goddamn it! You were always little guys. You didn't shrink, you diminished yourselves! You fucking did it to yourselves!"

Several soldiers were moving rapidly toward the Philosopher, but at least they had lowered their rifles. "You diminished yourselves!" the Philosopher cried as the soldiers dragged him away. In their boots and gear, they seemed so much bigger than his friend.

Afterword to "A Smaller Government"

Stories about shrinkage have a long history in science fiction, going back at least as far as the early twentieth century and including such stories as "He Who Shrank" by Henry L. Hasse, published in 1936 and the classic 1957 movie "The Incredible Shrinking Man," based on the novel by Richard Matheson. However impossible they may be, these stories challenge us to consider, even visualize, the scale of the universe around us, which is a reality from the smallest to the largest.

A satirical treatment of the theme can of course also expand our minds.

This story was written for *Fast Forward 1*, an anthology edited by Lou Anders, who may hold the record for fastest decision by an editor on any of my stories; he accepted "A Smaller Government" in one day.

NOT ALONE

"I don't know about Jerome Sivan," Agnes Mead said, after I'd told her that I'd already agreed to be one of his subjects. "Saw him on a C-SPAN debate this weekend, and he just tore this minister apart. The way Sivan attacked religion, he looked like a missionary in reverse." Agnes sounded worried, almost frightened. "It's all superstition to him, just an adaptation we picked up in order to survive. He says faith's totally outlived its usefulness."

The man she described didn't sound like the kindly professor type I had met. Jerome Sivan had turned out to be a slightly plump bearded man in a rumpled jacket and baggy slacks. He'd smiled warmly at me, ushered me to an armchair, then sat down behind his desk.

"You've read the material the receptionist handed you?" he asked.

I nodded, although the brochure hadn't told me much more than the newspaper ad, just that the medical school needed subjects for a new study. Dr. Sivan had been doing his experiments for a couple of years by then, as I found out later, but hadn't yet published any results.

"We're working on ways to lower tension and stress," he told me. That was supposedly the purpose of the study, but I wouldn't have known the difference if he'd admitted he was doing something that involved the brain and temporal lobes and magnetic induction and what-have-you. "Of course we'll need your informed consent, but I don't expect there'll be any physical or mental problems later on."

I was a bit taken aback. "Oh, I didn't think…"

"Well, I don't expect problems, but there are no absolute guarantees. That's why you should take your time to think things over." He sounded awfully reassuring, and there was also the fact that all of his subjects would get a small fee, which I could use since I was still looking for a new job, and free medical follow-ups for at least a year after that. There weren't going to be any shots or experimental drugs, either, so it was hard to see what could go wrong.

He didn't mention anything about his personal beliefs, because that would have affected his results. I found that out later. I found that out too late.

"I'll think it over," I said, even though I'd already made up my mind to go ahead.

"You do that," he replied.

* * * *

I'd always thought of myself as religious. I went to Mass and said my our Fathers and Hail Marys and never doubted that God was around looking out for me, but I didn't really think about God that much. Once in a while, it would occur to me that there had to be something more, something overwhelming that could take me out of myself, make me actually see the face of God, but then the next day would come, and I would forget about all of that. Maybe I'd have some kind of overpowering mystical experience someday, but if I didn't, in the meantime I would just do the best I could.

Better not to think about all of that, anyway, I decided, because I'd been waking up in the middle of the night more often and lying there, paralyzed with terror, wondering if anybody could be sure of anything at all, thinking that maybe there was nothing else except us and the world and the rest of space, that there was no meaning to any of it. That was what Jerome Sivan believed, according to Agnes. How could he live like that? How could anybody, thinking that we were alone, with no purpose? That was the kind of idea that kept me lying there, awake in the dark with what felt like a vise constricting my chest, unable to move until Tom snorted in his sleep or turned over on his side and I could put my arms around him and fall asleep again.

* * * *

I went to the medical school for my first session, not knowing what to expect. Jerome Sivan met me at the entrance, told me to call him Jerome instead of Dr. Sivan, and led me down a long hallway to a small room. The door had padding on one side, and the walls of the room made me think of a padded cell. A console sat in one corner, and two lounge chairs with thick leather cushioning were on either side of a table that held what looked like a transparent football helmet.

"You'd better put these on," Jerome said as he handed me a pair of ear mufflers. "You'll need them. It can get kind of noisy in here, that's why we had to put the lab at the end of this wing."

That explained the padded walls. For a moment, I was tempted to leave, but I'd signed the release and didn't like the thought of breaking my promise, so I put the mufflers over my ears and settled myself in the smaller chair. Jerome adjusted the helmet on my head; surprisingly, it was so light that I could hardly feel it at all. Two thin wires seemed to be resting just above my ears, under the mufflers.

Jerome left the room. I closed my eyes and waited. There was a low roaring sound as the floor began to shake under the chair. I clung to the chair arms, wondering how this was going to help anybody overcome tension and stress.

And then God was in the room with me. I not only knew it, I could feel it. God was with me and inside me in the room and the air and the city outside the medical center and everywhere. I felt God's presence and the purest happiness I'd ever felt, ecstasy and wonder and joy and eternity and love. This was what it would be like to be in heaven, I thought. I wasn't all alone, I'd never be alone again.

I don't know how long I was there, but the feeling of joy stayed with me even after Jerome came back into the room, removed the helmet, and helped me to my feet. "Feel all right?" he asked.

"I'm fine."

"Will you be able to drive home?"

"My husband's picking me up on his way home from work."

Jerome insisted on accompanying me to the lobby, but didn't ask me about any reactions, saying that he'd get a full report from me next time. Maybe my face told him everything he needed to know.

Tom was over an hour late getting to the center and muttered something about an accident on a nearby road. "Sorry about that," he said.

"No problem." I hadn't even noticed how late he had been until I'd looked up at the clock near the reception desk.

We drove home in silence. Tom didn't have much to say and I was content not to talk.

* * * *

That deep happiness was still with me even after days had passed. Everyone around me—Tom, my friends, the neighbors—all seemed like shadows, or ghosts. I would walk outside my house and feel as though I was flying above it; my neighbors would greet me and I would suddenly have an almost overpowering desire to share my joy with them. Days went by when I lost track of time, when I'd begin to load the dishwasher or take out the vacuum cleaner and then forget what I was doing. I would be going back to the medical center in a week, and that was all that mattered. I'd be close to God again, and all I'd have to do in return is tell Jerome exactly what I saw and thought and felt.

* * * *

Tom said, "I'm worried about you." He had found me standing by the washing machine, my hands resting on the laundry basket, and all I could recall was that I'd gone down there sometime during the morning. He led me up the stairs and sat me down at the kitchen table. "What's wrong?"

"Nothing's wrong." Happiness welled up inside me. The feeling of love for Tom and our home and our city and everything else in the world was suddenly so powerful that I nearly wept. I tried to tell him what I felt, how I saw things now, what the difference was between just thinking something's true and really feeling it inside yourself. I couldn't go on as I was, acting as though this world was all that mattered.

"You hardly ever leave the house. You sit around with that vacant look on your face." He clutched at my hands. "It's that study, isn't it, all those sessions with Dr. Sivan, that's what's doing this to you."

"You don't understand."

"It has to stop, do you hear me?" Tom's eyes were slitted with anger, his face growing red, but his rage seemed like a distant storm that would soon pass. He couldn't see that our old life was impossible for me now.

* * * *

I went in for my last session, not knowing that it would be the last. I closed my eyes and felt the room shake and reached out toward the light, but eternal joy suddenly turned into a sharp bright stab of pain.

Jerome was leaning over me. I had never seen how ugly his face was before, how pitted and pockmarked his forehead was. The air seemed thicker, harder to breathe, the padded walls drab and dark. It was impossible for me to move. A feeling of dread came into me, worse than any of the fears that used to haunt me in the middle of the night.

Jerome got hold of Tom, and somehow Tom got me home. The study was halted after that; there would be no more sessions for any of the subjects. The medical school sent me a form letter explaining that they regretted any unforeseen circumstances while pointing out that the release I had signed absolved them of any responsibility. I wondered how many others had ended up the same way—dead inside, with a soul that was no more than a burned-out husk.

* * * *

Jerome insisted on visiting me, even though I hadn't asked to see him. Tom met him at the door, ready to throw him out of the house, but settled for glowering at him while Jerome explained the true purpose of his study. It had nothing to do with relaxation techniques; what he was actually doing was proving that he could produce mystical experiences in anyone, that it was just a matter of stimulating the temporal lobes of the brain. Some subjects had felt the presence of God, and others would talk about love or transcendence or an invisible presence, but any such sensations were the result of electronic pulses and no more.

"What I didn't anticipate was that a few of you would burn out," Jerome went on. "I never intended anything like that to happen. But you have to see—this doesn't change anything, not really. Think of yourself as being rid of a delusion. That's all your beliefs about God are, you know. You can learn to live without them—you'll be better off in the end."

He couldn't see it, couldn't understand what I had lost. Without my faith, I was lost; that was what I'd been taught and what I had believed, when it was simply something I had taken for granted and later on, after my experiences in the lab had convinced me of its truth. I felt nothing, and wondered if I ever would again.

Without faith, I was damned. That had always been my assumption, faith was the buoy I had clutched to keep from drowning in doubt. I stared at Jerome and realized then that not all emotion was lost to me, that I could still feel rage. Damned I might be, but I would not be alone, not in this world or the next. Jerome was damned, too. I clung to that thought, and felt a tiny flicker of joy.

Afterword to "Not Alone"

This story was a challenge for me, given that my stories tend to be longer rather than shorter. I wrote it for Damien Broderick, who was then fiction editor for the Australian popular science magazine *Cosmos*, and the word limit for stories there was about 2,000 words. That was the first challenge. The second was that Damien, a formidable writer and intellect himself (he is a prolific writer of science fiction and nonfiction, inventive speculator about the future, recipient of the Distinguished Scholarship Award given by the International Association for the Fantastic in the Arts, and was termed "the Australian polymath" by the late Sir Arthur C. Clarke), was a demanding editor and had no compunction about offering stern criticism and asking for rewrites. In my case, as I recall (my memory of rewrites tends to be hazy, maybe because memories of intense pain have a tendency to fade over time), "Not Alone" required several rewrites. Not that I'm complaining; if you're lucky enough to have a demanding editor and enough discernment to know when the editor's giving you good advice (as opposed to trying to get you to write a different story altogether), your story can only benefit, as this one did.

THE DROWNED FATHER

The airline had promised reimbursement for his ticket, but Lucas was still irritated as he boarded the bus. From here, it would take three hours to get to the airport in Norris, and he wouldn't be home until at least two in the morning, assuming that he could get a cab in any reasonable amount of time.

A quick glance around the bus's interior revealed worn seats. Lucas took a book from his carry-on, hoisted the bag into the overhead bin, then sat down. Maybe he would get lucky and have two bus seats all to himself.

People wrestled their luggage through the aisle and settled into the seats around him. Lucas was grateful that he had brought only a carry-on; most of his fellow passengers had looked extremely unhappy while being told that their checked-through baggage would catch up with them in a day or so. He flicked on one of the overhead lights and opened his book; if anyone sat next to him, he meant to look busy and avoid conversation. He had just reached the end of the novel's first chapter when the pilot announced that they would be landing in Alton instead of at the airport in Norris because of an engine problem, but not to worry, they would all be taken care of and after all their personal safety was what mattered to the airline.

A valise hit the seat next to him. Lucas looked up to see a slender blond woman in a dark blue blazer, then lowered his eyes to his book, ignoring her as she secured her bag overhead and slammed the bin's door shut. She sat down, fidgeted as she settled a large purse on her lap, then heaved a sigh.

"I don't have any luck with planes," the woman said. "Last time it was three hours late taking off and we had to sit there the whole time on the tarmac."

Lucas said nothing.

"Next time I'll drive, I don't care how long it takes. Beats going through all that airport security."

Lucas peered at her from the sides of his eyes, noted that her attractive face was fine-featured, with a model's prominent cheekbones, and that she had far too much eye makeup on, then returned to his book.

The bus trembled and growled as it rolled away from the airport. "Whatcha reading?" the woman asked.

He closed the book and turned it to show her the spine.

"*All's Well*," she said, reading the title, "by Mack Vernon." She let out a breath.

"I started reading his novels a couple of years ago," Lucas said. "A friend of mine loaned me the first book in his Loren Reynolds series, and I was hooked."

"That was *Good Intentions*," she said, surprising him by knowing the title of the first volume.

"That's it," Lucas said. "After that, I got *Early To Bed* and *All's Well* from an online book dealer, but even without the dust jackets, they cost me a pretty penny. This dealer has a paperback of *Idle Hands*, too, but he's asking a hundred dollars for it, which is kind of rich for my blood, even if Vernon may be one of the best suspense writers ever. I just hope I can find the rest of the series without having to pay a fortune."

"He only wrote seven of them," the woman said, "so you've only got four more to buy, and they can't all cost that much."

She was holding his interest in spite of himself. "You wouldn't happen to have any of his books, would you?" he asked.

"Afraid not. Once…" She fell silent and looked away.

He opened his book and tried to focus on the page.

"What do you think of Atlanta?" the woman asked, clearly intent on keeping their conversation going.

"I was in Sarasota. Atlanta was just where I changed flights."

"Down there looking for a job?"

"No," he replied. Old memories were coming back to him, of sitting in other buses and expounding on his own fictitious accomplishments.

Actually, I'm a writer, he would say to the passenger next to him when asked about what he did. He would make up titles, tell stories about working with editors who in real life had rejected everything he had ever submitted to them. Sometimes the other passenger, having only a vague idea of what writers did and inflated notions about the glamour of the literary life, wanted to hear elaborate tales of pending book contracts and trips to Manhattan and writers' workshops and book signings and speaking gigs and queries from Hollywood, until the life he had conjured up while traveling seemed more real to him than his actual life. If he talked it up enough, he had once thought, maybe it would someday become a reality; he might wake up one morning to find his writing done, and volumes of his published work sitting on his bookshelves.

"As a matter of fact, I'm retired," he said to the woman.

"You don't look anywhere near old enough to be retired," she said.

"I took early retirement." He had been practical, postponing his dream of writing for a steady job and a pension. Now, with his fixed but dependable income, he had all the time he could want to read and travel and tell himself that it still wasn't too late to go back and write, that lots of writers didn't get anywhere until their middle years, that he had been smart to make the choices he had, and that one of these days, now that he could afford it, he would sit down and write the stories that he knew he still had inside himself.

He lifted his book and held it closer to ward off any more discussion.

"I was visiting my sister in Decatur," the woman said. "My half-sister, actually. Mom got married again after she and my dad broke up."

Lucas peered at her over the book. She looked older than she had seemed at first; there were lines etched around her eyes and her mouth, and a bit too much fleshiness under her chin. About forty, he guessed, maybe even a little older.

At last he closed the book, leaned back against his seat, and closed his eyes, hoping that she would take the hint. He had finally kicked the habit of long discussions in transit with strangers; you never knew where they might lead. People unburdened themselves of confidences they probably wouldn't have entrusted even to close friends, or simply made up stories, safe in the knowledge that they would probably never run into their fellow passengers again. He knew that game; playacting, that's what it was, and maybe some amateur psychoanalysis, too. Maybe most of the dialogues he had engaged in on trains and during flights had been mostly lies on both sides.

The woman said, "As a matter of fact, *he* was my father."

Lucas opened his eyes. "Who was your father?"

"Mack Vernon." She waved an arm at him. "The guy who wrote that book."

She had seen the name on the spine and decided to impress him with a fictitious father. That she knew the titles of a couple of books and that there were only seven volumes in the Loren Reynolds series didn't prove anything.

"Then do me a favor," Lucas said. "Don't tell me what happens in *All's Well*. I'm only on the second chapter."

"I never read any of his stuff."

Sure, he thought. That was an easy way to cover herself, in case he wanted to discuss the earlier books. He suddenly decided to trip her up, show her that she couldn't put one over on him. "Bet you appreciate all the money he made, though."

She offered him a lopsided smile. "He was almost always broke."

"Still, you must have been sorry when he died."

"He should have been more careful," she said. "If he'd been anywhere else except that cabin, maybe somebody would have found him. He didn't have to drown in that shallow little creek."

She knew that much, but then anybody who knew anything about his novels was likely to have known about that tragic accident. The tale of Mack Vernon's untimely death after what had apparently been a difficult and financially challenged life was the first story Sam Wilton had told Lucas about the author, a tragic event that was still mourned by a devoted coterie of fans.

Twenty years ago, after what had been a life of critical neglect and poor sales, the first of Mack Vernon's Loren Reynolds novels had been optioned by a movie producer. Flush with money for the first time in his life, Vernon had bought a summer cabin in his beloved Adirondack Mountains, the setting for most of the Loren Reynolds books. Less than a month after he had moved into his remote refuge, two backpackers had found him lying face down in the stream near his isolated cabin, a broken whiskey bottle at his side. Maybe he had been celebrating his good fortune, and maybe it was just as well he hadn't lived to see the screen version of *Good Intentions*, which Lucas had rented on videotape after reading the novel, much against his friend Sam's advice. The middle-aged and somewhat grizzled freelance investigator Loren Reynolds had been transformed into a muscular young hunk, his storefront office that doubled as a used bookstore had become an antiquarian bookselling operation with a wealthy clientele, the small upstate New York town in which he lived had been transplanted to the northern California coast, and the production had been graced with the title of "Lethal Intentions," entirely missing the point of all the titles in the series, which had been drawn from well-known old adages that also served as epigraphs for each novel. The whole cinematic mess had gone straight to video and had never been released in theaters. Had he not already been an admirer of the book, he would never have been able to sit through the movie.

"He had no sense at all," the woman continued, "especially about money. As soon as he brings in some serious cash, does he invest it? Does he do anything smart with his dough? Of course not. He goes and buys a cabin up in the woods. Doesn't even occur to him that maybe he should put something away for a rainy day."

Maybe she was Mack Vernon's daughter, but he still had his doubts. There had been no mention of children, or even a marriage, in any of the material about the author Sam had e-mailed to him over the past months, although that might not mean anything; Mack Vernon had gone out of his way to avoid publicity, leaving it to his steadily increasing numbers of posthumous readers to dig up the details of his life. Maybe the woman was planning to pass herself off as Mack Vernon's only heir and therefore as someone entitled to any future income from his books. Given the reputation the Loren Reynolds series was rapidly acquiring, marked most recently by major pieces in the *New York Times Book Review* and the *New Yorker*, it was probably only a matter of time before some publisher bought up the rights to the books and reissued them in new editions. She might be rehearsing a scam on him.

No, Lucas thought; that was the kind of story he might have concocted about this woman back when he had allowed his imagination to run rampant, when he was still trying to write. She was probably just entertaining herself, as he had done back in the days when he had regaled strangers on buses and trains with tales of his nonexistent publications. It was a good thing he had not followed Mack Vernon's path in life, that he had listened to the parents who had told him to stop fooling around with his writing and finish college and settle down. His tedious years in a local office of the state tax department had left him with the security of a pension and the likelihood, given his good health and sound habits, of two or even three decades of leisure. He had not actually given up his dream of being a writer, but had only postponed it.

She said, "He was just an accident waiting to happen."

Lucas closed his book. "Accidents can happen even when you're careful," he said, "and at least he missed the hash those movie people made of his book."

"I heard that movie was a turkey."

"Just about unwatchable. I think it actually won some sort of award for being one of the worst movies ever made."

"So you know about my father. Didn't think there was hardly anybody around who still cared."

"Oh, there's a lot more interest in his novels lately," Lucas said, "even a couple of articles about him. That's why my friend Sam had to loan me the first Reynolds book. He said I'd have a heck of a time finding it what with all the interest in the series. He just finished putting up a Mack Vernon Web site a little while ago, and he got so many hits during the first month that he had to get a new server."

"Really," the woman said.

"People keep asking when somebody's going to reissue his books." A puzzled look crossed the woman's face. "You know, bring his novels out in new editions now that he's getting more attention and so many people are trying to get copies. I can't believe that whoever his agent is now isn't trying to capitalize on it, that someone wouldn't have contacted you by now for permission to reprint them."

The puzzled expression was replaced by a glassy stare.

"You would be the one to contact, wouldn't you?" he asked. She shrugged. "Were you his only child?"

She looked past him to an invisible audience outside the window, as if hoping for a hint on how to answer a question that might be a trap. "Yeah."

"Then you'd be the heir to everything, wouldn't you? Unless your father left the rights to someone else. Maybe you ought to get after some information about his agent, let him know that there might be some kind of a book deal there."

"I don't know anything about that," she said.

"What about his papers, his contracts? What about—"

"Don't know anything about his papers," she interrupted. "He wasn't exactly the most organized guy in the world. All he left me was whatever else he was supposed to get paid for that movie, which turned out to be a big fat zero."

"What about that cabin he bought?" Lucas asked.

Her eyes narrowed. For a moment, she looked angry. "What about it?"

"That must have gone to you, too. Just about everybody who's a fan of his knows about that cabin, about how he'd wanted one all his life, a retreat just like the place Loren Reynolds had. Kind of ironic and sad that he didn't get to enjoy it that long."

"Had to sell it," she said, "but it was such a run-down old shack that I didn't get that much for it. And that was it. He'd spent everything else."

She seemed to have an answer for everything. According to his friend Sam, there had been recent rumors of a pending book deal for reissues of the Loren Reynolds novels, but nothing had come of that, and there was speculation that there had been problems in clearing the rights to the books. Vernon's original agent had died a few years ago, while the agent's former associate had opened up his own literary agency and taken on new partners before retiring himself. The cabin had been in a relatively inaccessible region of the Adirondacks, meaning that it probably wouldn't have attracted wealthy buyers looking for a summer place near a resort town. He couldn't find any holes in what the woman had said so far.

"You know," he said, "I could put you in touch with my friend. He's in touch with a lot of Mack Vernon fans, and even a couple of his former editors, so one of them's sure to know who's handling your father's books now. You could find out if there might be something coming to you. It could turn out to be a lot of money."

"Sure," she said. "Lots of zeroes."

"Look into it," Lucas said. "I mean, what have you got to lose?"

She looked away from him. She might be a fraud, as he suspected, or she might already know that she had no rights to any profits from her father's published work. Mack Vernon wouldn't be the first writer to die unexpectedly and leave his literary estate in a tangled mess, or to have signed his rights over to someone completely unprepared to handle them.

"You don't know what it was like," she said then. "He might have been around, but he was never there, not really. My friends used to ask me what it was like, having both my mom and my dad around the house all day, but most of the time it was like he wasn't really there. He'd go into his room, to his desk and his typewriter and his coffee pot and all his books, and he'd close the door. The only times he'd come out were for meals or to go to sleep or to get into an argument with Mom where they'd scream at each other because after a while the only way she could even get him to talk was to get into a fight with him, and when I came out of my bedroom he'd shout at me to go back to bed if I knew what was good for me. That was when he was home. Then he'd go off for a few days, or a couple of weeks, or even a month or more sometimes, and half the time Mom didn't even know where he was. Doing research, he'd say, but he always came home looking like he'd been on a bender."

Lucas made a noncommittal noise in his throat.

"I had to be really quiet when I got up, because he always slept late, and when I got home from school I had to tiptoe around and whisper and never knock on his door unless it was an absolute emergency and if any of my friends came over, I had to tell them to shut up and be quiet and not disturb him."

"He was probably just trying to concentrate on his work," Lucas said. "Distractions can really derail somebody who's writing, knock a particular phrase or idea right out of your head, even make you lose a whole day of work if you really get thrown off your stride."

"Anyway, that was before Mom went back to work because he just couldn't make enough, but then things got even worse, because then he was the only one there when I got home from school and I couldn't do anything. Couldn't watch TV, because it was in the room next to his. Couldn't bring any friends home because they'd make too much noise and then he'd come barging out and swear at everybody so pretty soon nobody came over because they all thought he was crazy. After that, the only time he'd say anything to me was when he'd open his door and yell at me to shut the hell up because he was trying to work. Nine times out of ten I had to go down the block to the deli to get some sandwiches or salads because Mom was too tired to make dinner when she got home and he couldn't be bothered to cook anything."

Lucas kept his face still, trying to think of how to stem her flow of recriminations.

"After a while," she said, "he was staying in his room almost all the time, I think he was even sleeping in there sometimes. Mom would come home and bang on the door and start yelling at him to come out and that if he weren't such a lazy bum he could make enough so she wouldn't have to go back to her shitty job. And he wouldn't come out. He wouldn't even tell her to go away. He'd just stay in there while she screamed and pounded on the door."

Lucas was now having more trouble believing that her tales might be entirely fictitious. She didn't seem like someone creative enough to invent such a detailed story, and there was an undercurrent of rage in her voice that was setting off all his mental alarm bells. He shrank back in his seat, almost afraid to look at her.

"So about a year and a half after Mom went back to work, she came home and got out our suitcases and packed my stuff and said she'd been sneaking her own stuff out of the house for a couple of weeks already because she'd rented an apartment and that was where we were going to live from now on. So we took everything out to the car and he didn't even come out to see what we were doing. That was when I was twelve. Mom got a divorce a year later, and a year after that she married my stepdad. Not that he paid much attention to me, either, but at least he paid the bills."

"Guess you had it tough," Lucas said, not knowing what else to say.

"Trouble with Joe—that's my stepdad—the thing is, he was pretty good to my mom, and my sister could wrap him around her little finger, but I was just kind of in the way as far as he was concerned, I mean, I wasn't his kid. And my father didn't care, he didn't even bother to ask for custody, not that I would have wanted to live with him anyway, but he could have tried."

Maybe some enterprising fan of Mack Vernon's had already found out about any marriage, divorce, and daughter. Not that it mattered; by the time he discovered whether or not there might be any truth to her story, they would long since have gone their separate ways.

"He didn't bother with visitation, either," she said. "He could have had me every other weekend and for two months in the summer, but he never asked for me, and he even stopped making phone calls, not that he ever had much to talk about except what book he was working on and how everything was going to pay off for him someday. He never paid any attention to me when I was around, so I sure as hell can't be surprised that he ignored me after Mom and I moved out."

"I guess not," Lucas said as she took a deep breath.

"He tried to make it up to me later, when I was out of school and working. I was waitressing at a coffee shop, and he'd come in and buy a cup of coffee and try to talk to me during my break, or he'd catch me outside when I was leaving and take me out to dinner somewhere, so we could sit there while he went on and on about how he was different now and he'd make it up to me and what a lousy father he'd been and how bad he felt about everything."

"Then he was sorry," Lucas said.

"Oh, he was sorry, all right, when it was too late to matter, when he couldn't do anything for me anyway. Just about the last time I heard from him, he called me up to tell me about *Good Intentions* selling to the movies, about how he was going to get a place in the mountains and I could come up to visit, as if I'd have time to hang around with him in some ratty old shack in the woods where he'd just ignore me or go on and on about his goddamn books. He wasn't really that sorry. Everything was always all about him in the end."

"Well." Lucas cleared his throat. "Could you excuse me for a minute?" He leaned forward in his seat, feeling that he had to get away from her torrent, if only for a few moments. "Have to use the rest room."

She nodded, got out of her seat, and stood aside. He set down his book and slipped past her, then stumbled to the back of the bus.

The rest room, he saw with relief, was empty. He went inside, secured the door, sat down on the closed toilet seat, then took a few deep breaths, wishing that he had never taken the copy of *All's Well* out of his carry-on. He might have been getting some much-needed rest by now instead of listening to a stranger complain about her life.

"You aren't really that sorry." Terri had said that to him, just after announcing that she wanted a divorce. "You won't notice anything different when I'm gone, you never paid any attention to me anyway." Lucas hadn't tried to stop her from leaving, largely because he had realized even then, hurt and humiliated as he had felt at the time, that there was some truth to his wife's statement. He had known even then that he preferred his own company to that of anyone else. That was part of what he thought of as his writer's temperament, standing a bit aside, being an onlooker to life, needing enough solitude to be able to hear his own thoughts. He still had that kind of temperament even now, and he treasured it.

Mack Vernon had clearly shared some of that emotional distance from those around him, along with a need to retreat from others; there was something of that quality in his character Loren Reynolds. Lucas congratulated himself again for having extricated himself from a marriage that had been a mistake and not weighing himself down with other obligations. Mack Vernon probably shouldn't have had any children, either, but whatever his faults, he had apparently regretted his actions. Surely by now his daughter should have been able to take some pride in his work, in the novels that might finally secure his place among the masters of suspense, perhaps even among America's major literary figures. That accomplishment surely outweighed anything else he might have owed to his embittered daughter.

If, he told himself, there was any truth to her story.

Maybe there wasn't. Vernon's protagonist Loren Reynolds was a loner, as were so many fictional detectives, but his relationship with his adult daughter Frani was portrayed as warm and affectionate. Frani hadn't put in much of an appearance in the first two novels, but she had already been on her way to visit her father in the first chapter of *All's Well*, and the *New Yorker* article Lucas had read had hinted that Frani Reynolds played a major role in the last two books of the series. Not that he would make the mistake of confusing an author's fiction with the actual events of his life; Vernon might have been writing about what he hoped his own relationship with his daughter might have been, depicting the kind of parental bond he had failed to forge in his own life.

Lucas frowned. The article in the *New Yorker*, like everything else written about Mack Vernon, had mentioned how little was known about the author except that he had been born in Buffalo, dropped out of college during his sophomore year, been constantly short of money, lived most of his life in upstate New York, been a heavy drinker if not an alcoholic, and had in midlife lived with three different women, all of whom were reluctant to talk about him, for varying lengths of time. Somehow Lucas found it hard to believe that a writer for that magazine, with all of its resources, wouldn't have been able to dig up information about a daughter, if there was one.

He forced himself to stand up and leave the rest room. The woman, he noticed, had moved to his seat; as he came closer, he saw that she was sitting there with his copy of *All's Well* propped against the purse on her lap. Her hands were hooked around the book like claws, one hand at the top and the other on the bottom, as if she were about to tear the book in two.

She started as he sat down; the fierce look in her dark eyes faded. "Okay if I sit by the window?" she asked politely.

"Fine," he replied, wanting to grab the book from her.

"We can switch back later if you want." She handed the book to him. "He dedicated this one to me, as if that was going to make any difference. I remember when he first showed it to me. It says, 'To Lindy: may it all end well for you.'"

Lucas opened the book to the dedication page, which he had only glanced at before. "Ah, yes."

"I didn't even know what it meant. 'May it all end well for you.' What kind of thing is that to write to a little kid?"

"Maybe he thought you'd appreciate it when you were older," Lucas said. "Look at it this way, Lindy. You had a major American writer dedicate a book to you."

"Don't call me Lindy." He could barely hear her voice above the bus's motor; her face had grown pale. "I hated that name, my name's Rosalind, but he always called me Lindy. I'd tell him to stop it and he would and then he'd forget. I must have told him a hundred times to call me Rosalind, but he didn't listen. He never listened. And then he has to go and put Lindy in that goddamn dedication."

Lucas said. "I won't call you Lindy." He attempted another smile. "It's just the opposite with me. My name's Lucas, but I always tell people to call me Luke."

"He didn't listen. Didn't care what I wanted to be called."

She would ruin the pleasure he took in the work of Mack Vernon; pretty soon, he wouldn't be able to pick up a Loren Reynolds novel without recalling her harsh words and hoarse voice. He could almost hate her for that, for spoiling something he had come to value so much.

"Look, your father might have had his faults," Lucas said, "and I won't try to justify his behavior, but you could still be proud of him, couldn't you? It's got to be some consolation that he did his work and there are more and more readers who admire it. You're not the only person who has issues with your father, but at least yours actually accomplished something." He tried to keep his tone light, but exasperation had crept into his voice. "Maybe he just had to save whatever was best in him for his readers. More and more people are finding out how good a writer he was, and if that doesn't mean anything to you, think about what kind of money you might get for new editions of his work. Maybe I could help you out. There are ways to find out who's representing him now."

If her estrangement from her father had left her unaware of what might be coming to her, he would be doing her a big favor. Far more important, he would be making Mack Vernon's work available to all the readers desperately seeking the increasingly hard to find copies of the Loren Reynolds series. Vernon had left her the cabin and whatever he might have been owed for "Lethal Intentions," so chances were that he had left her the rights to the novels as well. Sam would just about bust a gut if Lucas could put him in contact with Vernon's daughter, and once they found out who represented the books…he might get something out of this encounter after all.

His thoughts were racing ahead of him. There might even be a finder's fee of some kind, although just helping to get the novels back into print would be enough of a reward in itself. It might even be enough to inspire him to get back to his own writing. He could begin by writing an appreciation of Mack Vernon for Sam's Web site; better yet, he could write about Lindy—or Rosalind—and her early life with her father. That kind of human interest piece would be a natural for a major magazine, especially if it ended with Rosalind finally forgiving her father for the pain he had caused.

"Think about it," he continued. "Readers all over the country would be grateful to you, and you can't tell what might happen later on. With new editions out, there'd be even more interest in your father's writing. Somebody might even decide to make another movie from one of his books, something truer to what he wrote."

She turned away and pressed one hand against the window, as if trying to escape from the bus.

"I can give you my card," he said, "and then—"

"I don't need your card," she said without turning around. "I can't do anything about his goddamn books."

Lucas was again thinking that she was a fraud, that she was just stringing him along. She probably knew just enough about Mack Vernon to add a few convincing details to her lies, and if her anger seemed genuine, that might be only because her real father had resembled the Mack Vernon she had described. She might only be using a dead man whom she had never known to fill a role in her own personal psychodrama.

He sat there for a while, clutching his book, but apparently she had nothing more to say. Maybe he would be able to get some rest after all.

He closed his eyes and drifted as the bus rumbled on through the night. Usually, if he put his mind to it, he could fall asleep just about anywhere, but he remained conscious of the woman next to him; he sensed the tension in her, the anger, a bitterness about her life that apparently ran so deep that she could not even carry on a conversation with a stranger without spewing her resentments.

"Some ratty old shack in the woods." That was what she called the modest refuge Mack Vernon had found for so brief a time, and now Lucas found himself growing increasingly angry with her for being so quick to slander Vernon's reputation and insult the sanctuary of a man she might not even have known, just for the sake of putting one over on a stranger. She claimed to have inherited Mack Vernon's cabin, an easy enough story to make up, as his only surviving child probably would have inherited the place even if he had left no will; but she had also claimed that there had been no more money coming to her in payment for the movie rights to *Good Intentions*. She could not conceivably have known that unless someone had informed her of that fact.

His eyes shot open. Then she had to have been lying from the start, because anyone who would know enough to tell Mack Vernon's daughter what was owed or not owed for film rights either had to be an agent or someone, perhaps Vernon's lawyer, who would be able to put the daughter in touch with any agent. All of which meant that the woman's claim of not knowing anything about the writer's agent or his papers was probably the only truthful part of her story. She didn't know anything about his literary estate because she had never known Mack Vernon at all, and had picked up what she did know second-hand.

Lucas felt confused and disappointed; his fantasy of revealing a previously unknown daughter of Mack Vernon to the world had abruptly evaporated. But at least he could congratulate himself for not being completely taken in.

He suddenly wanted to get back at her for her deception. Mack Vernon, who had written so movingly and profoundly about a man struggling to help and protect other people even while longing to retreat from them, deserved no less.

"You know," he said, "I wasn't telling you everything before, when I told you I was retired. I mean, I am retired, but I have another profession, so to speak. I've had a few short stories published, and I've been working on a novel, now that there's time enough to write it, and a couple of major agents are thinking of taking me on as a client."

She shifted in her seat, then turned toward him. "Oh, really?"

"Usually I keep that to myself. I don't care to have everybody know all the details of my life. But I can make an exception for you, given who you are."

"So you are a writer," she said.

"Well, yeah, even if I haven't been at it that long, and if I can do half as well as your father, I'll consider myself lucky. It may sound like bragging, but frankly I think what I'm writing now has bestseller potential, and if I'm successful enough, I'm going to do everything I can to get Mack Vernon as much attention as possible. In fact, my real ambition is to write the kind of fiction he might have written."

She stared at him, unblinking.

"It's hard to measure up to his standard," he said, "but that's what I'm aiming for, nothing less than to be the literary heir of Mack Vernon."

He went on to mention an upcoming nonexistent piece that the *New York Times Book Review* had commissioned from him, then recycled a few other lies about editors and sojourns in Manhattan that he had tested on fellow travelers years ago. She listened without interrupting, without even fidgeting; maybe she had already guessed that he had caught on to her deception.

"So that's it," she said when he was finished. "You think Mack Vernon's such a big deal because you want to be just like him."

He had to give her credit for keeping up her front. "That's why you really ought to take my card," he said, "and let me know if you want me to help put you in touch with his agent." He reached into the front pocket of his jacket for his wallet and removed one of his cards with a flourish.

She gazed at him without speaking.

He thrust the card at her. "Take it."

She took it from him with two fingers, stared at it for a few seconds, then opened her purse and dropped the card inside. Maybe she was already thinking of all the money that might have been hers if she had actually been Mack Vernon's daughter.

"Look," he said, "I don't want to force any help on you, but do let me know if you want me to try to locate your dad's agent. Even if there's some kind of problem with the rights, he should be able to straighten it out, especially with all that's at stake."

"All the money, you mean."

"Not just the money," Lucas said, "but the chance to bring a lot more attention to the work of such an important writer. You might become pretty important yourself. I wouldn't be surprised if you had people contacting you for interviews as soon as they find out about you."

"Money's the one thing I don't have to worry about any more. Maybe my marriages didn't work out, but at least my exes were a lot smarter about money than my father ever was. And I kind of like to keep my business to myself, too, so I'm not interested in any interviews, either."

"Suit yourself," he said, "but sooner or later, somebody's going to do something about getting those books back into print. And if his agent and his lawyer can't figure out how to do it, eventually some fan of Mack Vernon's is just going to scan all the books and put them in electronic formats and post them on the Internet and dare somebody to come and sue him. Normally I wouldn't approve of that, but if it's the only way to make his work available to more readers…"

"Makes no difference to me."

"But it will." He wondered if he could needle her enough for her to admit that she had been lying. "Even that would be enough to call more attention to your father. I really don't think you can stop it. He's too good a writer to stay buried for long."

She was staring straight ahead; the small hands on top of her purse were fists.

"So you might as well let me see what I can find out about his agent and what might be done. At this point, I'm about ready to try to contact the agent myself."

"Go ahead," she said in a tiny voice.

"Maybe I will." Not that it would matter; by the time he proved her story was false, she would have disappeared into whatever kind of life she led.

"I'll tell you what the hardest part was," she said. "He didn't *need* anybody. Maybe he'd use them for a while, but he didn't really *need* them. He didn't need my mother, and he sure as hell didn't need me. Think of what that's like, knowing when you're a little kid that your father wouldn't even notice if you went and dropped off the face of the earth."

Lucas said, "Must have been tough." He folded his arms across his chest and closed his eyes.

"He lived for himself," she added, "all the time. Those books of his, that's all he cared about."

"I'm sorry," he said, like a ghost come back to haunt her.

"There was no him, never any of *him*." She shifted in her seat, and he knew that she felt trapped, wanting to escape him.

* * * *

Lucas had stolen some sleep by the time he got off the bus. The small Norris airport, as he had expected, was nearly empty. A uniformed representative of the airline, a round chirpy woman, was there to greet those who had missed connecting flights. Most of the passengers trailed after her while Lucas strode in the other direction, toward the main entrance.

He did not see the small blond woman anywhere now. She had still been in her seat when he left the bus, her face turned toward the window. Maybe she was feeling embarrassed about their conversation, about her attempt to pass herself off as the daughter of Mack Vernon.

He hurried through the glassy doors of the entrance to find that there were no taxis outside. Lucas sighed and went back indoors, sat down in one of the seats near the entrance, and fumbled in his pocket for his cell phone.

"Waiting for somebody?"

He looked up to see the blond woman. "No," he replied. "I have to call a cab."

She stepped closer to him, peered down at him with narrowed eyes, then set down her small suitcase. "I could give you a lift."

"You live in Norris?"

"No, up in Bayley, but I didn't want to fly out of there on one of those dinky little planes."

"You sure it isn't too much trouble?" Lucas asked. "It'll take you at least an hour to get to Bayley from here."

"It doesn't matter. I'm not in any rush." She seemed another person now.

"That's awfully kind of you." He was beginning to feel a bit guilty about trying to expose her lies. "My place isn't that far, it shouldn't take longer than twenty minutes or so."

"Then come on," she said as if they had just met.

* * * *

Her SUV was parked near the airport entrance. It took them only a few minutes to get to the nearest highway. "You can stay on Route 8," Lucas told her, "until exit 5, and my house is only a few blocks from there."

She did not reply. She had been silent during the short walk to the car and hadn't spoken since then.

"I really do appreciate this," he said.

"I had to take this road anyway. It's not just for your convenience." There was a sharper edge to her voice. "Maybe you should have just parked your car at the airport."

"Believe it or not, it's considerably cheaper to pay for a cab than to park a car there for a few days." The lights above the guard rail on his right streaked past as the car picked up speed; he wanted to tell her to slow down.

She said, "There's something I didn't tell you before."

So now she was going to admit that she was lying, he thought, and wondered why. Maybe she wanted to become better acquainted with him, and figured that she would now have to reveal her deception. Well, he didn't want to get to know her better; he didn't want to know her at all. It had taken him long enough to get his life exactly the way he wanted it, without other people trying to make claims on him. Right now all he wanted to do was get home and crawl into bed with his copy of *All's Well*.

"What I didn't tell you," she continued, "is that I already heard from my father's agent. About four or five months ago, I got a call from the lawyer who handled everything when my father died, said he had a hell of a time finding me, maybe because of all the name changes. I mean, I used my stepdad's last name until I got married, and I'm still using my third ex's name because I didn't want the hassle of changing it back, so it took him a while. He said this agent really wanted to talk to me, so I said, sure, I'd give him a call, thinking maybe some money finally came in for that movie."

Lucas glanced at her, amazed that she was still weaving her fabric of lies. He almost had to admire her for keeping the game going.

"So I called him, and he went on and on about how there was all this interest in my father's stuff and people calling him a literary treasure and publishers wanting to bring out the Loren Reynolds books again and even a book of his short stories and luckily they still had all the copies in the files from his old agent, the books and stories and contracts, but they needed my permission because he'd signed everything over to me. I didn't know what he was talking about. I mean, I knew my dad had done what he said, signed everything over to me, but I didn't know all the details about his contracts and all of that. So I told him I didn't know anything about it and he said I didn't have to know, all I had to do was sign what he sent me and he'd make sure everything was in order and if I had any questions about anything, I could run them past my own lawyer. 'Yeah, well, you let me know,' I told him, and then I hung up, figuring that was the last time I'd hear from him, but he called back a week later and said he just about had an agreement nailed down and there'd be a good chunk of change in it for me. And that was when I told him I didn't give a shit, that I wouldn't sign anything no matter how much money there was, that as far as I was concerned he could take all my dad's stuff and burn it."

That rant rang true. Lucas took a breath. "But...but why?" he managed to say.

"I told you why, on the bus. I told you. You just weren't listening, because you're just like him, another guy who doesn't listen to anybody. So the agent calls me back a week later, and I say I'm still not interested and frankly I have my doubts about all these people being so hot after his stuff. And that was it, I thought, but he keeps bugging me, keeps calling me up and leaving messages on my machine until I finally have to go visit my sister just to get the hell away from him. And now you tell me the same things he did, about all these people wanting to read my dad's books and that there's articles about him and how you want to be just like him. Well, don't bother trying. You're him already. Been him a long time."

Exit 5 was coming up. He wanted to tell her to get into the right lane or she'd miss the ramp, but was afraid to speak. The car suddenly swerved to the right, throwing him to the side; his shoulder strap tightened against his neck.

"You know what he did after he got that shack in the mountains?" she continued as they sped down the narrow ramp of the exit. "He called me up and said I should come up there to see him, as if I'd want to hang around that place while he ignored me or went on and on about his books, and then he said he had something to give me, to make up for being such a shitty father. And you know what he was going to give me, what my great big present was going to be?"

"No," Lucas croaked as the car bounced over a speed bump onto the road that led to his house. His body tensed; he felt melded to his seat. She was still driving too fast, especially in this neighborhood of small houses and narrow serpentine streets. He wanted to tell her to slow down, but the words would not come.

"His books," she said. "That's what he wanted to give me, a set of his books, he was going to autograph them all and then I'd have my own freakin' first editions of the Loren Reynolds series."

She paused. Lucas rushed to fill the silence. "Hope you still have them," he said anxiously as the row of books flashed in his imagination. "They'd be worth a lot now." The car screeched to a sudden stop, whipping his body toward the windshield, then throwing him backward. He sat there, gulping air, afraid to move.

"That's all you care about, isn't it," she whispered, "him and his books. He said he wanted me to have them and that maybe someday I'd read them and then maybe I'd understand him because he'd put so much of himself into them, and before I can even say anything, he hangs up on me. And that was the last time I ever talked to him. He never listened to me, and then he goes and falls into that stupid river and drowns. I never got a chance to tell him what I thought, and when I'm finally ready to tell him, he goes and dies on me."

Lucas was silent.

"All he cared about was himself and being alone and writing his goddamn books." Her voice was rising. "He didn't care about me, all he cared about was making himself feel better by giving me his books, as if that was going to make any difference. And you're just like him."

He fumbled at his seat belt. "Look, thanks for the ride." He struggled for breath, afraid that she would hit the accelerator again. "It's close enough to my home, I can walk from here."

"You're just like him," she repeated. "All he cared about was his books. Well, I don't care how much that agent can get, I won't sign anything he sends me, not ever. You won't see me with a bunch of people who only want to talk to me because of my father. You and all those people who think he's so great will just have to get along without his books."

He tried to open the door, heard a click, then pushed his unlocked door open. He swung his legs over the side of the seat. His feet hit the ground hard as he slipped out of the car; he nearly fell to the pavement.

"Don't forget your suitcase," she shouted after him. The rage in her voice stabbed at him. He opened the other door and pulled his bag from the back seat. "You're just like him, you got what you needed from me and now you're going to run off to be alone with your writing and your books." She was screaming now; a light went on in one of the houses that lined the road. "You ought to thank me, you know."

"I did—"

"Not for the ride, for the story. That's all anything is to you, stuff you put into a story. Isn't it? That's all this is to you, something you can write about. Go ahead, write whatever you want, I don't care. He's dead, and sooner or later all those people who think he's so great will forget all about him and his books."

"You're wrong!" he shouted.

"Hah!" she screamed at him, happy in her revenge.

But in time they would forget, he thought. Other writers would come along to distract Mack Vernon's fans. Lucas slammed the car door shut, grabbed his bag, and jumped back just in time as the car lurched forward. He stood alone in the darkened street as she fled from the drowned father who had eluded her.

Afterword to "The Drowned Father"

This story had its origins in an actual incident. Some years ago, on a bus trip to New York City, my partner George Zebrowski struck up a conversation with a young woman in the seat next to his. Her father happened to be a writer whose name George recognized, and she soon revealed how little she thought of her father's profession and his writing. To say that George, a writer himself, was dismayed by the bitterness she expressed would be putting it mildly.

The story intrigued me. As someone without children, I often wondered if I would have been able to say to any child of mine, as writers surely have to do often, "Go away and don't disturb me while I'm writing." Heartless as it sounds, that kind of ironclad rule is necessary to get any writing done, since the writing (unless you're a writer prosperous enough to rent an office outside your dwelling) usually has to be done at home. Now I began to wonder how some of the children of writers might be affected by this parental choice of profession, one that requires a certain level of selfishness and self-absorption. This may seem a quaint concern in an age when people routinely post photos of their children and tales of their exploits on various social media, but I used to worry how children who saw themselves reflected in a writer/parent's work might react; embarrassment, resentment, and bitterness might be only too appropriate. As Joan Didion famously put it, "Writers are always selling somebody out."

My earlier drafts of this story turned it into a tale of suspense and ultimately murder, but that kind of plot seemed to mute what was at its heart, the pain of a neglected child and the father who had tried to reach out to her in the only way he could, along with the disillusionment of a reader foolish enough to confuse a writer's work with the writer's life.

THE TRUE DARKNESS

The shrieking wind went mute. Lydia's ears throbbed in the silence. Matt reached for the remote just as the TV screen went black and the overhead lights winked out.

Matt did not curse the darkness.

Lydia lifted a hand to her face. The living room was so dark that she couldn't see her own fingers. "Isn't there a flashlight by the bookcase?" she asked. Matt had been looking for his nail clippers over there earlier, shining a flashlight under the bottom shelf and behind the books; she had reminded him that he wouldn't have lost the damned clippers in the first place if he didn't insist on clipping his nails while he watched TV. "Think you left it there before."

"If I can find it." She felt the shifting of his weight on the sofa. "Jesus, can't see a thing." His voice was above her now. "This must be the third power failure we've had. Better call and find out how long it'll be."

"Even if we manage to call through, they won't tell us much," she said.

"At least we'd have an idea."

Lydia leaned forward, felt around on the coffee table for her cellphone, flipped it open, and thumbed a button. The tiny screen should have been glowing by now. "My cell's not working."

"What do you mean it's not working?" Matt's voice was a bit more distant.

"Just what I said." She paused. "Where's your iPhone?"

"Think I left it upstairs."

"I could try the phone in the kitchen."

There was the sound of a thump. "Ow!" Matt said. "Just bashed my knee."

Action and reaction, Lydia thought, yet another example of Newton's third law of motion. She said, "Be careful."

"Found the flashlight." A small round circle of light appeared, moved up and down, then went out. There was something wrong with the flashlight, too. Everything around it, except for the patch of light, had remained completely black.

The floor creaked and then she felt the weight of her husband against her left side. "You don't have to sit right on top of me," she said.

"Sorry." He moved away from her. The disk of light reappeared, but failed to illuminate anything around it. "This is really weird," Matt continued. "This flashlight is screwy." His voice was shaky.

"Guess I should try calling," she said, "even if they don't tell us much." She had stored the number for National Access Incorporated in both her cellphone and the landline phone in the kitchen after the last power failure. She fiddled with the cellphone again, but nothing happened. "I'll try the phone in the kitchen."

"Take the flashlight."

She felt the cool metal cylinder against her palm and closed her fingers around it, then pushed against the slide with her thumb. At first she thought that the flashlight had died, and then she turned the cylinder toward herself and saw the small circle of light.

Her face felt cold; it was harder to breathe. She aimed the flashlight away from herself and saw the light disappear.

She heard Matt catch his breath, but he said nothing. During the last power failure, Matt had cursed National Access for a minute or two, cursed some more while trying to locate a flashlight, had tried and failed to get a call in to the power company, then had suggested that they relax and finish their wine and he would tell her about his latest project while they waited for the power to come back on. It wasn't like him to sit there saying nothing at all.

Lydia stood up. Even with the flashlight on, she had to feel her way toward the kitchen. She crept through the dining room, expecting at almost any moment to get to the doorway and then around the corner to the countertop where the phone was located, but the kitchen felt far away, almost unreachable. Before she could take one step, she had to take half a step, then half of that half-step, then half—

Stop it, she told herself. The minutes seemed to crawl by before she finally touched the edge of the kitchen counter.

Late that afternoon, a middle school kid had called the library to ask what Zeno's paradox was; Lydia had taken the call.

"You don't need a reference librarian to answer that question," she had told him.

"But I don't understand the answer I found," the boy replied, sounding close to tears. A homework assignment, she thought, probably one he had put off doing until the last minute, and maybe his computer wasn't working and he couldn't go online to search for more information.

"Well, let me put it as simply as I can," Lydia said. "Zeno's paradox states that an arrow will never hit its target, because it has to fly half of the distance to it first, and then half of that distance, and so on and so forth, so the arrow will never reach the target at all, because it has to traverse—move through—an endless series of halves."

"But that doesn't make any sense."

"Having to cover endless half-distances and never able to get where it's going is a way of saying that motion is impossible. Or an illusion. Think about it."

"Thanks, lady," the boy said, sounding unconvinced.

At least she had made it to the kitchen, unlike the arrow forever kept from its target by halves. The power had only gone out for an hour last time, and for about half an hour a month ago, but there had been a high wind warning up earlier in the evening. There had been more such warnings lately, perhaps a sign of increasing climate change since this region had rarely been swept by such strong winds in the past, and the wind had been howling for at least a couple of hours, to the point where she had started to worry about the roof and the tree limbs that might come crashing down on the house. That was one thing they hadn't had to worry about while living in the city, where the nearest trees of any great size were in the park a block and a half away.

She slapped the countertop. Her hand found the telephone; her thumb pressed the "Talk" button. Instead of a dial tone, all she heard was a distant whistling sound.

Lydia leaned against the counter. The silence outside was unnerving. No police sirens, overheard conversations, car alarms going off, or people calling out to one another or gabbing on the sidewalk. She bit her lip, tried the phone again, set it down, then turned off the flashlight. The darkness and silence pressed in around her; she turned on the flashlight again. The patch of light shone up uselessly at her, illuminating nothing, as though the light was being blocked by an invisible barrier, or else struggling to penetrate the ether scientists had once believed filled all of space.

She made the journey back to the living room and sat down on the sofa. "Any luck?" Matt asked.

"I couldn't even get a dial tone." She waited for him to curse or say something, but he was silent. "Wasn't there supposed to be a full moon tonight?" She had noticed that earlier, on her office calendar at the library. Matt kept up on things like that.

"Yeah."

"So you'd think we'd see some light through the blinds, wouldn't you?"

"I was thinking the same thing. Maybe it's gotten really cloudy. Maybe the clouds are really thick. That's what I've been telling myself."

His hand slipped around her wrist. "But that doesn't explain the flash-light. Light doesn't work that way."

"I know."

She turned off the flashlight. They sat there in silence. This was what it must be like to be blind, Lydia thought. At last she said, "Maybe we should see how the people across the street are doing." They had been living in this house for almost four months now, and she had still not met any of their neighbors, but Matt must know something about them by now, since he ran his business from home. "I mean, this is the third power failure since we moved here. Maybe they can tell us how often this happens."

"They've got three kids," Matt said. "At least I think all of them are their kids, the ones I saw playing on their lawn the other day. Hard to believe anybody can afford three kids these days." He sounded a little more like himself. "Guy's name is Olaf. He looks like an Olaf, too. He's a big blond-haired guy who's built like a linebacker and his wife is this little tiny thing with black hair."

"What's her name?"

"Don't know. I only talked to the guy for a few seconds. He asked me what I did, and I told him Web site design and computer workshops for individuals and groups, and he asked if maybe I could design a Web site for him if he ever quits his job and starts a landscaping business. And that was it." He sighed. "I could head over there, see if he's found out anything."

"I'll come with you." She fumbled for his hand, afraid of sitting alone in the dark; his fingers closed around hers.

They moved slowly toward the front door, clinging to each other. After long moments, Matt let go of her and then she heard the door creak open. The still air seemed even colder than it had been earlier, when the wind had started to pick up. It was as dark outside as inside the house; the other houses on their street were completely invisible.

"Matt," she whispered. Even the thickest cloud cover wouldn't have turned the sky this black; there would have been some sign of the full moon, a soft silvery glow behind the clouds, a break through which she could have seen stars.

A speck of light suddenly appeared in the blackness. "Olaf?" Matt called out. "That you? It's me, Matt Polgrave from across the street."

"Matt?" That was a man's voice, sounding very faint.

"Olaf?" Matt replied.

"Yeah, it's me. This flashlight isn't working." The speck of light disappeared. "Maybe it's the batteries. I knew I should have picked some up on my way home."

"My flashlight's got the same kind of trouble," Matt said.

"Vicky tried calling National Access, but she couldn't get through. National Asshole, I call them. We'll probably be the last ones in town to get our power back on."

Olaf was very likely right about that, Lydia thought. They were on a cul-de-sac in the middle of nowhere, or so it had always seemed to her, since it took her a good five to ten minutes just to get to the highway and another half an hour after that to drive to work. "We'll be able to have two cars," Matt had told her before they moved, "and we won't have to worry about parking." She would have preferred just the one car and the parking hassles and her former ten-minute walk to her job at the library. She had felt freer in the city, with the sounds and movement of so many other people around her. Here, she often felt cut off, embedded, trapped. Inertia had become the ruling principle of her life.

"This is the third time since we moved here," Matt said to Olaf. "How often does this happen around here, anyway?"

"Not this often. Not until the last few months, anyway."

Another point of light appeared far to Lydia's left, then vanished. Another neighbor, she thought, somebody else she didn't know who was probably bewildered by the totality of the darkness. She began to wish that she had made more of an effort to meet the people here, that Matt had been more outgoing. It had been mostly his idea to move out of the city, to get away from worrying about burglaries and getting mugged and hassles with parking the car and to have more space for his computers and his workshop and all the other stuff that had cluttered and finally overflowed their condominium and the small office he had rented down the street.

"Want to come over?" Matt asked.

"I'd probably get lost crossing the street," Olaf said. "Can't see a goddamn thing. Anyhow, I better get back to Vicki, she's got a thing about the dark."

"See you," Matt said, and laughed.

"That's a good one." Olaf's voice sounded even fainter.

"Step back," Matt said to her, and Lydia knew that he was going to close the door. She felt her way back through the doorway and had to grope her way back to the sofa, brushing her hand against the bookshelves as she passed them and taking tiny steps so that she didn't hit her legs against the coffee table.

She felt as though she would never get to the sofa.

Her leg bumped up against an obstacle that felt like the sofa. She turned and sat down. Matt plopped down next to her.

"He was right," she said.

"Who?"

"Olaf. About getting lost crossing the street. I read this article the other day that says if people don't get certain kinds of cues, they end up walking in circles, that's how people get lost in the woods. We could go out the front door now and end up just circling around to the back of our own house."

Matt said, "You're creeping me out."

She had thought she was making a joke. Now she knew from the flat tone of his voice that he was really frightened. She felt around the coffee table for her cellphone, found it, and pressed a button with her thumb; it still wasn't working.

"The radio," Matt said. "You know, that old one we took with us up to the lake this summer. I think I left it in my workshop."

"What about it?"

"We could tune into one of the local stations, find out what's going on. Might as well find out if it's a major blackout." He brushed against her as he stood up. "Think I can get to the basement," his voice said overhead. "I'll take it slow."

* * * *

The first power failure they had experienced in this house had happened in the middle of dinner, and the power had come back on just as Lydia was lighting a candle for the table. The second had actually turned into a pleasant experience, giving her a chance to talk to Matt while they finished some wine instead of her having to sit through a DVD of a crappy action movie.

This power failure was different. This darkness didn't feel like only the absence of light. She could imagine it as something seeping into the atmosphere, thickening the air, leaking through crevices in the walls and windows and billowing throughout the house until they were drowned in the blackness.

"Planck's constant," Betsy Dane had told four high school students earlier that week, "is a physical constant, symbolized by h, used in quantum mechanics to denote the sizes of quanta." Lydia and Betsy, a newly hired librarian, had spent half an hour helping the students locate references for a science project. Quantum mechanics, to Lydia's surprise, had turned out to be a subject that greatly interested her coworker, who had minored in physics in college. But quantum mechanics was not what she needed to dwell on at the moment. It only reminded her that the normal, usually unexamined daily assumptions she made and acted upon—that there were such things as continuity and causation—might be illusions, that the light and space she sensed were only the product of her own perceptions, the way her senses ordered the world, and not a kind of absolute reality that existed independently of her relationship to physical phenomena.

I have to stop this, Lydia told herself. The lights would come back on any minute now.

She got up and walked slowly to the kitchen. There was a box of kitchen matches in the second drawer from the top of the counter, and there might be a candle in there as well. She found the drawer handle, pulled out the drawer, and found the box of matches. Leaning against the counter, she opened the box and struck a match.

The tiny flame danced, a spark against the darkness, but her hand and the match she held were invisible to her. Her hand shook. She blew out the flame and dropped the match on the countertop.

She shuffled back to the living room and sat down, then pulled on the sweater she had shed earlier. The living room felt cold for this time of year, and without any power, they could not turn on their furnace.

Matt was certainly taking his time looking for the radio; it felt as though he had been downstairs forever. There was no reason they had to sit here doing nothing just because of a blackout. They could drive to someplace where the power was still on and stay overnight at a hotel. She could always call in sick tomorrow, since she had some days off coming to her. If they stayed anywhere near downtown, she could even walk to work.

"Matt?" she called out, in case he had come back upstairs and she just hadn't heard him. "Matt?" The air seemed thicker, harder to breathe, but that had to be her imagination. She waited silently for a few more moments. "Matt?"

"Found the radio," he said from the direction of the dining room. "Couldn't hear anything downstairs, though. Maybe we can pick up something up here." There was doubt in his voice.

"I'm over here," she said, worrying that he might lose his way even along the short distance to the front of the house.

He thumped down next to her, at her right this time. "I know it's on," he said, "and I found the tuner dial, but nothing's coming in."

"Maybe the battery's dead."

"I know it's not dead, because I put in a new battery just the other day."

"I went to the kitchen again," she said, "and lit a match, and even..." She sighed. "Even the flame wasn't acting right."

"What do you mean?"

"I could see the flame, but nothing else, not even the match."

"What's so strange about that? You're not going to get much light from a match anyway. You're too suggestible. The flashlight doesn't work, so now you're imagining that fire doesn't, either."

She wanted to accept that. She always had been suggestible, even gullible at times.

"I mean, you're too damn suggestible." He seemed intent on establishing that fact, an assumption that would cut off other possible theorizing about their situation. "Damn radio." She heard him sigh. "Maybe there's nobody on the air," he continued, "because this is a really big outage, like the one that knocked out the whole East Coast a while back."

It isn't just an outage, she thought; she knew that and was sure Matt knew it, too, deep down, however much he resisted the fact. Flashlights that cast no light, a darkness so pervasive that nothing was visible, even the feeling that air was beginning to congeal around her—this was more than just a power failure.

"Matt," she whispered, "I was thinking. We don't have to stay here, you know. Let's go somewhere else."

"We'd feel awfully stupid when the power comes back on, driving around and wasting time and gas when we could just be patient." Matt had always been practical. Living in this house gave them more space for less cost than they'd had in the city, even with the second car; keeping their old furniture and making use of old appliances like the radio was economical; and there was no point in going on a vacation somewhere else this year when they could enjoy their own back yard. Of course Matt had wanted to leave the city, she thought. The house gave him even more of an excuse to keep to himself, to anchor himself to one place, to surround himself with certainty, to become almost immovable.

"I'll keep fiddling with the radio," he said. "Think you can make it to the front door, see if anything's going on outside?"

"Sure." The power would come back on any second now. The world would become continuous again.

She got up and inched toward the front door, hands out, until her fingers found a surface. She pressed her palms against the door, found the doorknob, and pulled the door open.

She stepped outside; the darkness took her, starless, cold. She wrapped her arms around herself. As she turned to go back inside, she glimpsed a faint glow to her right. The glow became two globes of light; there was the sound of a motor. A car was coming down the small hill at the end of the cul-de-sac, and it seemed to be moving very slowly, maybe no more than five miles an hour.

She retreated inside, closed the door, and shuffled back to the sofa. "It's still just as dark," she said, "but somebody was driving down the hill at the end of our street. The headlights—they were doing the same thing as our flashlight. I mean, I could see them, but I don't know how the driver could see the road or anything else." They wouldn't be able to drive out of here, with no way to see where they were going.

"Nothing," Matt said, and she knew that he was referring to the radio. "Everything's out."

She sat down. Maybe they should get out of here, whatever the risks. Anything would be better than sitting helplessly, passive victims of whatever was going on outside. Maybe the blackout, or whatever it was, had taken out the whole country this time. Maybe all of North America was dark and cold. Maybe terrorists had finally managed to knock out the entire grid. Maybe somebody had finally started a nuclear war. Thoughts of terrorists and nuclear war didn't frighten her as much as they might have. At least they were familiar possible causes of potential disasters.

"Hey!" That was a woman's voice, and very faint. "Hey!"

"Did you hear that?" Matt asked.

"Yes." Lydia was already up, shuffling toward the door. She pulled the door open and leaned outside. "Hello?"

"I'm here," the voice said. Lydia guessed that the woman had to be somewhere near the edge of their lawn. "In my car."

"I'm Lydia Polgrave," Lydia said. "My husband Matt and I live in the two-story brick house next to the white Colonial at the bottom of the hill." It suddenly seemed ludicrous to be introducing herself to someone she could not see.

"I know the house. My name's Gretchen Duhamel, and I live in that gray shingled job with the screened-in porch at the end of the road." The alto voice was strong, almost reassuring. Lydia tried to visualize this woman she had never seen. She sounded like a tall woman, maybe somewhat overweight, with a short, no-nonsense haircut. "Can't see a darned thing, so it probably isn't a good idea to keep driving. Only trouble is, I don't know if I could even find my way home now, in the car or on foot."

Lydia thought of asking her inside. Under the circumstances, Matt was unlikely to object, and might even welcome the company. Even the presence of a stranger would be better than sitting there stewing by themselves. "You could stay with us for a while," she said. "Think you can find your way to our door?"

"I should be able to get that far," Gretchen Duhamel replied. There was the sharp *chunk* of a car door being slammed shut. "Aren't you the house with those flagstones on your front lawn, kind of like a pathway to your front steps?"

"That's us."

"For a minute there, I couldn't remember if it was the brick house or the Colonial with the flagstones, and I've lived in this neighborhood for over ten years, must have driven past your house a million times. Funny what you can't remember when you can't see anything."

"I know what you mean."

"Keep talking," Gretchen Duhamel said. "All I've got to go on is the sound of your voice."

Lydia tried to think of what to say. "Uh, we moved in about four months back. I've got a job in Findlay, at the downtown branch of the public library."

"The library?" Gretchen Duhamel sounded closer.

"I'm a reference librarian there. My husband runs his own consulting business from home."

"Then I take it he's the guy I've seen mowing your lawn. The tall skinny guy in the Red Sox cap."

"That's Matt."

"I'm retired, but I used to teach introduction to physics at the community college. You know, I've been trying to get National Access on my cellphone the whole way here. Can't get through." The woman sounded really close now.

"Be careful. It's four steps up to the door."

"I'm being careful," Gretchen Duhamel said. Lydia heard footfalls on the steps, and then something brushed against her. "Sorry."

"You're almost there. Just keep coming."

* * * *

By the time Gretchen Duhamel was settled in the easy chair next to the sofa, Lydia had learned that she was a widow and that her late husband had died five years ago. The woman went on to mention a son who lived in Seattle and her two cats, Bartholomew and Percy, whom she had left behind in the fenced-in back yard of her house.

"They're indoor cats," the woman continued, "but I've got one of those kitty doors in the back, so they can get in and out of the house, but they can't get out of the yard." She went on at length about the felines' favorite foods, their luxuriant black and white fur, and the way they loved to chase their favorite toy, a ball of aluminum foil. Normally such a conversation would have bored Lydia mightily, but now she welcomed the distraction, the feeling that things would soon return to normal. The lights would come back on, and Gretchen Duhamel would go home to her cats and toss them their balls of aluminum foil.

"I've lived with those cats for almost four years now," Gretchen went on, "so they're almost like my kids. You don't have any kids, do you?"

"No," Matt replied.

"Not yet," Lydia added.

"People around here aren't having so many kids these days," Gretch-en Duhamel said, "and they're older when they do. It's like they can't count on a stable, normal life any more, doing what they're supposed to do and having things work out. Nothing's that predictable any more. The couple that used to live in your house must have been over forty when they had their first."

"I think that big blond guy across the street has three kids," Matt said.

"Olaf Janssen?" the woman said. "Don't know where you got that idea. He and Vicky just have the one boy, Lars."

"I've seen three kids over there."

"You must be thinking of Josh and Becca, the Bloom kids. They're over there all the time. They and Lars Janssen are as thick as thieves."

Gretchen Duhamel fell silent. Lydia waited for the woman to say something more, anything to distract them from the darkness and the cold.

"Wish I hadn't left my cats," Gretchen murmured.

The power had to be restored soon. The light would restore every-thing to its previous state. Lydia was getting herself worked up over nothing, only imagining that the air was even thicker and colder around her. It was the waiting that got to her, the feeling that there was nothing she could do except wait there in the dark.

The front doorbell rang.

Lydia started. "Who could that be?" Gretchen said.

"Has to be one of our neighbors," Matt said.

"Not necessarily," Gretchen said. "Might be looters or burglars and such. And we can't even call the police."

Matt said, "I'll see who it is." He let out what sounded to Lydia like a forced laugh. "I'll *find out* who it is." She felt him get up from the sofa. The floor creaked slightly as he moved toward the door. "Who's there?" he shouted.

"Olaf," a muffled voice replied, and Lydia heard the door whoosh open.

* * * *

Olaf had found a long length of rope in his garage and had tied one end of it to his front door knob, reasoning that if he got lost crossing the street, he would at least be able to find his way back to his house. As she listened to him, Lydia found herself admiring his resourcefulness and wishing that she had thought of such an idea herself or else that Matt had.

"Good thinking, young man," Gretchen said when Olaf fell silent.

"That you, Miz Duhamel?" Olaf asked.

"Sure is. Anyway, it's good thinking on your part assuming this is just a power failure and not something a whole lot weirder. You know what it's like? It's almost like the light's going out, everything's slowing down, and space is filling up."

Lydia froze. She had been thinking almost exactly the same thing.

"My wife and my boy are still back at our house," Olaf said after a long pause, "but I've been thinking there's no point in just sitting around."

"I tried to drive out," Gretchen said, "but you can't see a blessed thing, not even with the headlights on."

"I thought of driving out myself," Olaf said, "but no way. This just isn't normal, this kind of dark. You know what I saw just before the lights went out? For a second, everything looked kind of like these gray shadowy things in the dark, like I was seeing in the infrared or something. Vicky's face was like this pale blob with black pits instead of eyes." He was silent for a bit. "We could still try to walk out of here."

He outlined his plan. They would tie whatever lengths of rope Matt happened to have in his house to Olaf's rope. They could use the rope like a belay, going on to the next house, picking up more rope, and continuing on that way until...

"Until what?" Matt interrupted.

"Until we get to someplace where we can find out what's going on or until the lights come back on, but if you want my opinion, I don't think they're coming back on any time soon. And if anybody doesn't have any rope, we can use sheets or something else, tie them to the rope. We can just keep going and if anybody changes their mind, they can belay themselves back home."

A giggle escaped Lydia. She clapped a hand over her mouth, but could not stop laughing.

"What's so funny?" Olaf asked.

"You're getting hysterical," Matt said; Lydia felt his breath on her face.

Tears sprang to her eyes. "I'm sorry, I couldn't help it." She cleared her throat. "We'd look awfully silly if everything suddenly went back to normal, standing around out there in a line hanging on to a rope."

"I don't know about you," Olaf said, "but I'd rather do something instead of just sit around waiting for National Access to get its shit together. Anyway, this feels like a whole lot more than just National Access."

"Oh, it's definitely more than that," Gretchen added. "National recess," she muttered.

"Light that doesn't show you anything," Olaf said, "everything so black you can't see a damn thing, and I've never heard it so quiet outside. It's like we're…like we're…" He seemed to be struggling for words.

"It's like we're completely cut off from certain wavelengths of the electromagnetic spectrum," Matt said, "among other things."

"Yeah, like that."

"That's what I've been thinking anyway," Matt said. Lydia heard the fear in his voice as he shifted his weight on the sofa. "Cellphones not working, radios not picking up anything, the cold, the thing with lights—" His voice trailed off. Lydia thought of the match she had struck in the kitchen.

"Whatever it is," Olaf said, "I figure we can go back to my house, get my wife and son, and belay down to the Blooms' house."

"What about your next door neighbors?" Gretchen asked.

"The Murrays? They flew out yesterday to visit his mother in Atlanta. Lucky for them, I guess."

"Unless this is affecting everybody," Matt said. "Everywhere."

Lydia let that sink in. A worldwide catastrophe, she thought. What if they were trapped in this darkness forever? She swallowed hard. They could get out of here with Olaf. If something had really gone wrong, they would be better off in a group, She was pretty sure they had some rope in the garage to tie to Olaf's, and she could throw in a couple of old sheets she had been meaning to tear up for rags.

"Well, what about it?" Olaf said. "I gotta get back to Vicky and Lars. Vicky has a thing about the dark."

"I'll go with you," Gretchen said. "Can't give you more rope, though. There isn't any rope in my car."

"What about you?" Olaf said, and Lydia knew that he was referring to her and Matt.

"Think I've got some rope in the garage," Matt said.

"Think you can find it?" Olaf asked.

"Yeah. Just have to go through our kitchen and the laundry room, and it should be right next to the door." Matt brushed against her as he stood up. "It'll just take a minute."

"Don't get lost," Olaf said.

"Don't worry," Matt replied, his voice farther away. "I'll be back in a sec."

"This blackout," Gretchen said in a low voice. "It's giving me the willies."

"You can say that again," Olaf said, also keeping his voice low. "I gotta tell you, before I came over, Vicky tried to light a candle, just so we could have a little bit of light, and—" Somebody emitted a loud sniff. "It wasn't working."

Lydia said, "The same thing happened to me." She tried to repress the fear uncoiling inside her. "Your wife struck a match, but all she got was a small flame, a bit of light that didn't illuminate anything else. I lit a match earlier, in the kitchen, and it didn't give off any light at all except for this tiny flame."

"Know what I'm thinking?" Gretchen said. "I'm thinking of something Ernst Mach once said."

"Who?" Olaf said.

"He was a physicist," Lydia murmured. "I'm a reference librarian," she continued by way of explanation. "That's how I know things like that."

"Ernst Mach once said that gravity might be our experience of some large motion of the universe as a whole." Gretchen paused. "So in that case, light might be affected if there was any change in that motion."

Lydia said, "Maybe the change is in us."

"What do you mean?" Gretchen asked.

"Paul Valery once speculated that our universe is the plan of a deep symmetry, one that's somehow present in the inner structure of our minds."

"Who the hell is Paul Valery?" Olaf asked.

"He was a French poet and philosopher," Lydia replied. "Wrote that in his *Cahiers*—uh, his notebooks." That was yet another piece of knowledge she had acquired that now had no function except to feed her fears.

Gretchen and Olaf were silent. Lydia strained to hear something in the silence, but the darkness seemed to have muffled sound as effectively as it had doused light. The air seemed thicker, too, as if a fog had formed around her.

Space was not empty. Their human senses deluded them into thinking space was empty when in fact it was full. Space and time were constructs of the human mind, and now their minds were failing them. Everything outside them was as it had always been; it was just that they could no longer impose their mental constructs on it.

She was imagining things again, being too suggestible. She pressed her hands together, trying to warm her fingers against the cold.

"Thought he said he'd be back in a second," Olaf said. The words came from him slowly, and the pitch of his voice was even lower.

Lydia longed to call out to Matt, but restrained herself. She suddenly feared that if she opened her mouth to say anything, she would start screaming. She sat back, struggling to calm herself. Whatever was

happening, there had to be somebody, somewhere, who was already trying to get help to anyone trapped in this darkness.

"Found the rope." She could barely hear Matt's voice. "And a couple
of long cords, too." He had to be talking about the electrical cords he
used with his clippers when he pruned the hedge. "Must be at least thirty
or forty feet in all." He sounded closer now. "But—"

Lydia took a breath. The air had taken on substance; she felt as
though she were inhaling a soft, cool mist.

"But what?" Olaf said, his voice now a bass.

"I'm not…going with…you," Matt replied in a baritone.

Another long silence ensued. "You're not…going with me?"

"We're…staying…here," Matt said.

That was like Matt, speaking for her as well as himself. Lydia wanted
to object, but there was no point in arguing with him, and also no reason
why she could not leave with the others and without him.

"You…sure?" Olaf asked.

Lydia stretched out her arms and hit an obstacle. "Matt?" she said.
"Is that you?"

"Yeah."

She felt around and touched something that felt like coiled cord.
"Give me the rope."

"What?"

"Give me the rope." A long moment passed before the coil was thrust
into her hands. She got up, working hard to stand, struggling with the
weight of the rope. "Olaf?"

"Over here." By the sound of his voice, he was still near the door.
She moved toward him, bumped into the coffee table, stepped back, then
crept toward the entrance. Something suddenly slammed against her
arm. "Sorry," Olaf said.

"Here's the rope." She held out the coil; the invisible man relieved
her of its weight.

"Thanks," Olaf said in an even deeper bass voice. "Now I'm heading outside. Got the end of my rope tied to the railing around your front
steps."

"I'm right behind you," Gretchen's voice, nearly as deep as Olaf's,
was closer. There was the sound of the door opening. Lydia stood still,
uncertain, searching the darkness for some sign of light.

"Lydia," Matt called out.

"Are you coming?" Olaf asked. She hesitated. "Well?"

"I can't leave Matt," she said at last.

"You there, Miz Duhamel?"

"Yeah, I'm here."

"Grab my arm. Okay, I'm gonna take the steps real slow." Lydia heard the dull thud of a foot on the steps; a long time passed before she heard another. For a moment, she thought she glimpsed the shimmering of a soft glow in the sky, and then it was gone.

She backed inside and struggled to push the massive door shut, surprised at how much effort it took.

"Lydia?" Matt said.

She shuffled slowly toward him. The cold air was congealing around her. She struggled across the room, wondering why Matt seemed so far away. "Matt?" The thickened air flowed into her mouth and into her lungs. "Matt?"

"Lydia?" His voice was as deep as Olaf's had been. "Are…you…still here?"

"Yes." She tried to swim toward him, but the air was beginning to jell around her arms and legs. She thought of Olaf and Gretchen and wondered if they were still towing themselves toward Olaf's house along the rope or were already trapped outside on the steps.

"I'm…glad…you…stayed."

She opened her mouth to reply, but was already embedded in the thick, frigid darkness; motion was frozen.

She wanted to say it, but the words escaped her.

"Matt," she whispered, and her voice was as deep as his had been.

Her hand clawed through the solidifying darkness and clutched his as everything stopped.

Afterword to "The True Darkness"

"The True Darkness" was the second story of mine to be inspired by a power failure. The first, "The Old Darkness," was written in the early 1980s by candlelight during a blackout, but this one came after a series of power failures in our neighborhood, caused by a combination of aging infrastructure and unusually severe storms. There's nothing like a power failure, especially one that goes on for a while (hours, days, or even longer than that) to remind those of us who are fortunate enough to live in a technological society of our own fragility and vulnerability.

One of my favorite comments about "The True Darkness" came from an online reviewer who pointed out that the story admirably passes the Bechdel test. In case you're unfamiliar with this notion, the Bechdel test, named after cartoonist Alison Bechdel (who first became known for her comic strip *Dykes To Watch Out For*), asks if a movie or other work of fiction has at least two female characters who talk to each other about something other than a man. I wasn't thinking of the Bechdel test when I wrote the story, but it's surprising how many fictional narratives—movies are the most egregious offenders, but not the only ones—fail the test.

ABOUT PAMELA SARGENT

Pamela Sargent has won the Nebula and Locus Awards, been a finalist for the Hugo Award, Theodore Sturgeon Award, and Sidewise Award, and was honored in 2012 with the Pilgrim Award, given for lifetime achievement in science fiction and fantasy scholarship, by the Science Fiction Research Association.

She is the author of the science fiction novels *Cloned Lives*, *The Sudden Star*, *Watchstar*, *The Golden Space*, *The Alien Upstairs*, *Alien Child*, *The Shore of Women*, and *Venus of Dreams*, as well as the alternative history *Climb the Wind*. *Ruler of the Sky*, her historical novel about Genghis Khan, was a bestseller in Germany and Spain. She also edited the *Women of Wonder* anthologies, the first collections of science fiction by women.

Her young adult novel *Earthseed*, selected as a Best Book for Young Adults by the American Library Association, was followed by *Farseed* and *Seed Seeker*. *Earthseed* is in development by Paramount Pictures, with Melissa Rosenberg, scriptwriter for all five "Twilight" films, set to write and produce through her Tall Girls Productions. Her latest novel is the forthcoming *Season of the Cats* from Wildside Press.

Her short fiction has appeared in magazines and anthologies including *The Magazine of Fantasy & Science Fiction*, *Asimov's SF Magazine*, *New Worlds*, *World Literature Today*, *Amazing Stories*, *Rod Serling's Twilight Zone Magazine*, *Universe*, *Nature*, and *Polyphony*. Her short story "The Shrine" was produced for the syndicated TV anthology series *Tales from the Darkside*, recently re-released on DVD. Her work is available in electronic editions from Open Road Media (www.openroadmedia.com) and Gollancz's SF Gateway (www.sfgateway.com) as well as Wildside Press (www.wildsidepress.com).

Michael Moorcock has said about her writing: "If you have not read Pamela Sargent, then you should make it your business to do so at once. She is in many ways a pioneer, both as a novelist and as a short story writer.... She is one of the best."

Pamela Sargent lives in Albany, New York and her website can be found at www.pamelasargent.com.

ABOUT ELEANOR ARNASON

Eleanor Arnason has published six novels and more than forty works of short fiction, all science fiction or fantasy. She won the James Tiptree, Jr. Award and the Mythopoeic Award for her novel *A Woman of the Iron People*. Her most recent book publication is *Hidden Folk*, a collection of fantasies based on Icelandic literature and folklore.

www.ingramcontent.com/pod-product-compliance
Lightning Source LLC
Chambersburg PA
CBHW061137200626
46817CB00016B/1737